THE CAT'S-EYE

THE CAT'S-EYE

by

Claude Aveline

Translated from the French

by

Peter Green

LONDON : DENNIS DOBSON

First published by Mercure de France, Paris, 1970, under the title
L'Oeil-de-Chat.

Copyright © 1970 by Mercure de France

Translation copyright © 1972 by Dobson Books Ltd

To Henri Jourdan

First published in Great Britain in 1971
by Dobson Books Ltd, 80 Kensington Church Street, London W.8

Printed in Great Britain by
Bristol Typesetting Co Ltd, Bristol
ISBN 0 234 77681 1

CONTENTS

CONTENTS

ONE

Three accents on a pouring wet night

I

O N the evening of Palm Sunday, 1930, a quite unprecedentedly heavy rainstorm took place. From the Place Saint-Germain-des-Prés as far as the Rue du Four, the whole of the Rue Bonaparte had become one roaring torrent. A similar phenomenon could be observed across towards the Seine, since the Boulevard Saint-Germain, which crosses the top of the Rue Bonaparte, commanded the point at which the waters divided. However, the only two people in the vicinity to be immobilized out of doors by this abominable weather were located between the Place Saint-Germain-des-Prés and the Rue du Four: with the rest of the world we are not here concerned. They were, it is true, sheltered to some extent by a tiny festooned glass porch (which also protected the luminous sphere above their heads, inscribed HOTEL DE MAR-SEILLE). The water came cascading down on its well-fitted glass panels, with a high-pitched drumming sound. On the road and pavement beyond, the rain formed a flickering curtain, which reflected the wan street-lights as though through a veil of tears. Every now and then there came a breath-taking lightning-flash, closely followed by a loud peal of thunder. It was not particularly cold.

The two persons standing there were both men: M Bédat, the hotel proprietor, squat and hail-fellow-well-met, but with a very sharp eye beneath his blue beret (it was the kind worn by veterans on a march-past, and he never removed it, except perhaps at night); and his young boarder, Jean-Marc Berger.

The latter wore a winter overcoat, and galoshes over his shoes. A felt hat was pulled down over his eyes, and his mouth was protected by a muffler—though this could not hide the quick, feverish way he breathed, or the sighs—more like tiny groans, in fact—which from time to time escaped his lips. M Bédat kept darting uneasy, anxious glances at him. To keep the boy distracted, he resorted to what fifty years' experience had convinced him was a fool-proof gambit: the monologue.

'Well, you see, M Jean-Marc, it's a bore my having this Niçois accent, I mean, when I try to tell people about tonight they'll sure as death say I'm exaggerating. If provincials get a reputation for anything, it's Parisians who gave it them in the first place. All the same I don't mind telling you, straight— word of honour—I haven't seen rain like this since Verdun. All right, I know, we had more than water falling on us then—shells, bullets, shrapnel—and it was really pitch-black, too, none of these gas-jets! And our issue trench-capes, well, they might be made of tweed and all that, but they still ended up like sodden paper!'

He laughed. No response.

'Want to know why I'm laughing? I was just imagining myself back at Verdun, under a little porch like this one we're standing under now. It'd have been more to the point with a corrugated iron roof over it than all that cathedral glass. I mean, just think of cathedral glass under shell-fire—or even the whole cathedral, come to that.' He was no longer laughing now. 'Remember Rheims? Marvellous building—plastered flat! Well, very badly damaged, anyhow. When I say "remember" like that, I mean, obviously you were too young, and Lyons is nearer Marseilles, isn't it? Still, every good Frenchmen has heard about Rheims's martyrdom, the way those Vandals destroyed it—'

His voice weak with fever, and muffled by the scarf, Jean-Marc said: 'Yes, M Bédat. Of course.'

All the time he was glancing frantically up and down. Just let a taxi appear, he thought. Just one taxi, *empty*. All it needed tonight was a deluge like this, something that would turn Paris into a deserted wildernesss. It's the old Biblical curse, new style.

M Bédat had not so much as drawn breath. 'It's a fine little porch,' he was saying. 'One day, about the same time last year, we had hailstones coming down, as big as that—' He thrust a fist under Jean-Marc's nose, and the young man jumped. 'My old woman said, that lot's going to smash your precious porch. Well, you take a look at it—not a crack, not the tiniest hole anywhere, absolutely perfect! Now it isn't that she'd like to see it busted up, shit no, of course not, it's just that festoon job, doesn't strike her as modern enough. Tell you something else that riles her about it—on rainy days like this people who aren't staying here take shelter underneath it, that's something she just can't stand. Well, you know the way she is as well as I do . . . Anyhow, I haven't the money to pay for a smarter one. Especially since this property belongs to her. I'm just the poor retainer around here . . .'

Suddenly Jean-Marc tore away his muffler with one hand, and began signalling frantically with the other. '*Hep!*' he shouted. But the taxi sped past at full speed, tyres whirring wetly on the macadam. He began to mutter despairingly again.

'I'll miss my train, I'll miss my train. That'd be just too awful—'

'Now don't you go getting upset, M Jean-Marc. The train doesn't leave till eleven-thirty, and we've just heard Saint-Sulpice strike a quarter past ten. Honestly, if I were you I'd walk down to Saint-Germain-des-Prés—it's only a couple of minutes, and you'd stand a far better chance of picking up a taxi there.'

Jean-Marc said, with some irritation: 'What, lugging these two cases? They're not exactly light, you know.'

'You can get your taxi first, and then come back for them. I'll keep an eye on 'em while you're gone. Anyway they'll be perfectly safe behind that door.'

'But I don't want to get really ill. I had a temperature of a hundred when I took it just now. I can't risk getting laid up down *there!*'

'I must say, you don't look too good,' M. Bédat conceded, frowning. 'But what you ought to do is take advantage of your trip down into the silkworm belt—get a bit of rest, come back on top of the world. One good thing, there'll always be a room for you at the Hôtel de Marseille—just shift out an overnight guest, and we'll have you settled right back in again. Mme Bédat's really taken a shine to you, it's extraordinary. You've got a way with people, you have, and not just the young ones, either. Look at the way you handle old folk—asking after their health, running little errands for 'em, making out you're really interested in their boring stories even if you've heard 'em a dozen times before! There's nothing rarer nowadays than a well brought up kid of twenty, believe you me. When you run a low-category hotel in this sort of neighbourhood you don't half get the chance to study real characters. Not guttersnipes, that's too mild a description— proper little brutes, who respect nothing, absolutely nothing! But you're different, you've become like the son of the house. Besides, from what we know of you—'

Jean-Marc began to get agitated again. 'You ought to go inside, M Bédat,' he said. 'Otherwise you'll catch cold, too.'

There was nothing M. Bédat would rather have done. Nevertheless he said: 'I'd feel bad about leaving you there.'

A superb car came gliding down the middle of the road, like some splendid State barge.

'*Hep!*' called Jean-Marc, despite himself.

'Thumb a Rolls-Royce, would you?' said M Bédat, with a certain note of respect in his voice. 'Just suppose it had stopped, and there was a beautiful girl inside! Your being engaged wouldn't make any difference, that sort of thing's always happening to young people in this godless city.' He sighed. 'I got here when I was too old,' he said. 'All right, I'll go in. If my wife's nodded off over the paper, I'll be back again. Otherwise—' He took the limp hand extended to him, and shook it vigorously. 'Have a good trip, and come back soon. If you're still out of luck in ten minutes' time, don't hang around any longer, nip down and catch the Métro from Saint-Germain-des-Prés. You'll have plenty of time, you can take it easy carrying those cases.'

'Goodbye, M Bédat, and thank you again—for the hot grog, for everything.'

'It was nothing. *I* should be thanking *you*, really. I mean, being friendly is part of my job—but there's nothing says the guest needs to reciprocate, is there? You know, despite that ghastly accent of yours, you've convinced me people from Lyons are all right at heart. See you soon!'

2

As Jean-Marc turned his head to watch M Bédat open the plate-glass door, the sound of a car-engine at the far end of the street caught his ear. He stood transfixed. It was a taxi—and pulling up! A good way off, near the Place Saint-Sulpice: but apart from the drumming rain everything was quiet, and the driver should be able to spot him there, under the illuminated sign. He shouted so loud that his vocal cords nearly cracked.

'*Hep! Hep!!*'

The door of the taxi opened. A man and a woman crossed the sidewalk in a flash and vanished into an apartment building. The driver's hand appeared, and turned up the flag.

'*Hep!*' screamed Jean-Marc, '*Hep!!!*' At the same instant a peal of thunder broke overhead. He groaned in desperation: his summons must have gone unheard. The invisible sky overhead seemed to be breaking apart at its very foundations. Nevertheless, the taxi drew steadily nearer—and then turned off down the Rue du Four.

' Oh *no*,' whispered Jean-Marc.

The thunder, like the taxi, now dwindled into the distance, though the downpour redoubled. From the Place Saint-Sulpice the town-hall clock struck twice; in such weather it really did sound like a passing-bell. Yes—ten-thirty. He pulled on the glove he had removed to shake hands with Bédat, and stared disgustedly at his cases through the plate-glass door, on which the words HOTEL ENTRANCE, dimly visible by the weak light of the lobby, were inscribed in a semi-circle. He scanned the street yet again, in every direction. Just one single pedestrian would give him enough courage to make it as far as the Métro. Nobody. Not a soul. Despite this, he opened the door, and lugged out first one case, then the other—which he immediately put down.

'*Hep!*'

No; this was yet another private car, a black saloon, one of the very latest models. Jean-Marc had mistaken it for a taxi because it was cruising along so slowly. He shrugged, and turned back to his cases. Yet he could not stop watching this strange vehicle, which continued to slow down as it approached the point on the pavement opposite which he was standing. Rain was streaming off the windows, so that it was impossible to distinguish anything inside. Then, as the car finally drew up, the driver's window was lowered. Jean-Marc stared in fascination. An unfamiliar face, the face of a complete stranger, appeared through it and said: 'Need help?'

Jean-Marc did not understand. Through his muffler he repeated the last word. 'Help?'

'Yeah,' said the driver, with a thick American accent. 'Didn't you shout "*Help*" just now?' He used the English word, glancing up at Jean-Marc interrogatively as he spoke. His eyes were very black and brilliant, not American at all: Italian rather, perhaps Neapolitan. Terrible, questioning eyes. Jean-Marc plunged into explanations.

'No, monsieur, I don't know what that means—I just shouted "*Hep!*", I mean, I wanted to summon a, I mistook

your car for a taxi, I'm sorry, I've been stuck here so long
now—'

He was almost sobbing as he spoke. The driver burst out
laughing. 'That's good,' he chuckled. 'Oh, that's rich! *"Hep!"*,
indeed! I thought you called *"Help!"*, that's the English word
you use when you want assistance in an emergency, you
see—'

Jean-Marc had had as much as he could stand. 'Yes,
monsieur,' he said, 'I see it all quite clearly now. *"Help!"*—
yes, I agree, it's very, very funny. Well, thank you very much,
and goodbye.'

The driver stopped laughing, and eyed the cases.

'Maybe you're off on a trip?' he suggested. 'Got a train to
catch, eh?'

Jean-Marc's voice regained its urgent note. 'On a trip, if
you want to put it that way, monsieur, but yes, yes indeed, I
most certainly do have a train to catch, I'm leaving Paris—oh,
not for long, just a family visit. And just when I'm sick, too,
with this chest trouble. And I'm stuck with these two cases,
and it's raining, and I haven't even got the strength to lug
them as far as the Métro—'

The American scrutinized him again. His eyes were just as
brilliant and inquisitive as before, but they seemed a little less
frightening. Jean-Marc perceived that there was no one else
in the car.

'Could I give you a lift, maybe? What station are you
making for?'

'Saint-Germain-des-Prés—it's only a couple of minutes
from here—'

'No, no, I mean, which main-line station?'

Like a gambler calling the number on which he has staked
his entire fortune, Jean-Marc said: 'Lyon. Gare de Lyon.
I'm going to Lyons—'

'Fine. I'm going that way myself. *Gare* de Lyon, I mean.
Not Lyons.'

So saying he opened the door, and, without budging from

his seat, stretched out his left hand in the direction of the
cases. Jean-Marc could hardly credit his luck.

'Really, monsieur? You're too kind—'

'Come on, now, none of that nonsense! And stop looking
so worried! Give me those cases of yours, I'll stash them on
the floor in the back.'

'Really?' Jean-Marc repeated. But he was already holding
out the heavier of the two bags. The American, without any
apparent effort, swung it over the back of the seat. He then
repeated this performance with the other one.

'Now,' he said, 'come round the car and get in beside me.'
He shut one door, opened the other. Jean-Marc tumbled in.
The American gave a tiny sigh of satisfaction and said: 'All
set?'

The car shot off, rain drumming on its roof.

3

They slewed round to the right, tyres shrieking, down the
Rue du Four, and almost immediately afterwards repeated
the process as they turned into the Rue de Rennes. The
American drove like a madman. Jean-Marc sat there, hands
clutching the edge of the seat beneath his thighs. At first he
found himself hypnotized by the regular, frenetic movement
of the windscreen-wipers. A twin beam flicked out briefly
from the headlights at each cross-road—but no one could
brake fast enough on such a road-surface. Who *was* this man?
Jean-Marc stole a furtive glance at him, sideways. His face no
longer bore even the trace of a smile. An actor, perhaps: one
of those forty-year-old matinée idols who in their stage roles
are always falling for—and ultimately conquering—very
young girls. But certainly not in the least American to
look at.

The car tore across the Place Saint-Germain-des-Prés without taking any precautions whatsoever. Jean-Marc ventured

a question : 'Wouldn't it have been better to turn right, down the boulevard?'

The stranger started. 'What? Oh.' He gave a laugh. 'The Seine Embankment is so much nicer, even in frightful weather like this!'

The car entered the Rue Bonaparte, and in a matter of seconds emerged on the *quai*.

'Chest trouble, you said,' queried the stranger abruptly. 'Do you mean tuberculosis?'

Jean-Marc, panic-stricken, loosened his scarf and coughed. 'I sincerely hope not,' he said. 'Nothing worse than a dose of bronchitis.'

'Very nasty, all the same,' said the American. 'Like the climate of Lyons.'

Jean-Marc's coughing fit became a violent spasm. Yet before he had fairly got his breath back he managed to gasp : 'Just a flying visit—I'm going to announce my forthcoming marriage to my family—'

His voice choked. The American laughed again : a dry, harsh sound. His manner sounded definitely derisive.

'Oh, *marriage*, eh? Family occasion, right? Good boy, good son, good little bourgeois—and a good Lyonnais accent on top of everything else !'

The car had already reached the Place Saint-Michel. Notre-Dame, behind a curtain of rain, looked like its own ghost. Jean-Marc gradually got his breathing under control. He stole another glance at the profile of the man beside him, and ventured a further remark : 'You know, sir, if it hadn't been for your accent, I'd never have taken you for an American. You look so French ! And this car—'

'Oh, it's a self-drive hired car—very handy for foreigners, you can just pick them up and dump them again when you're through. Every time I come to France that's what I do. An excellent car. And you're right, it's from here—not *here* here, though, from Italy.'

'From Naples?'

'Oh, "see Naples and die!" More or less. From Naples, yes, well, near enough.'

The car was still travelling at the same breakneck speed. Suddenly the engine missed a beat. The American frowned.

'What's the matter?'

The engine coughed twice, three times, and died away. Its noise seemed to have been swallowed up by the rain, which drummed a tattoo on the roof to underline its triumph. The American pulled a horrible face.

'Maybe *not* such an excellent car, for once. Do you know anything about internal combustion engines?'

'Not a thing,' Jean-Marc said. 'Not one damn thing. I'm terribly sorry.'

The American seemed unperturbed.

'That's all right, I'm an expert. Always do my own repairs. And we've chosen a good place to stop, right under a tree. Spring's a dead loss without greenery, don't you think? Oh well, a tree's a tree.'

He took an electric torch from the glove compartment, switched it on and off, and handed it to Jean-Marc.

'Right. Out we go. While I hunt for the fault, you just shine a light for me, and hold up the bonnet to keep the rain off. It's the carburettor, I suppose.'

As they stepped out, a gust of wind came up off the river, driving the rain straight in their faces, whistling, snapping off branches, shaking loose chimney-pots. Jean-Marc shone the torch on his watch; twenty to eleven.

'You coming?' the American called. He had to shout to make himself heard. An adjustable spanner in one hand, he lifted the bonnet and peered inside. Luckily for the engine, the wind was blowing in the opposite direction. Jean-Marc's face was not so fortunate. And since both his hands were otherwise occupied, he had no way of protecting himself.

From somewhere inside the car's entrails the American shouted: 'What time does your train leave?'

'Half past eleven, monsieur—23.30.'

'Good, we've got all the time in the world, then. I only hope you don't catch pneumonia!'

There followed a brief silence on his part, though not on that of the elements.

'There's a screw loose in the carburettor,' he said at length. 'Just hold the bonnet a bit higher, will you? Thanks.'

Jean-Marc heard him breathing heavily.

'I'll see if it starts now. Stay where you are.' The American got back into the driver's seat.

Jean-Marc did not, however, stay where he was. He lowered the hood, wiped off his face, and turned so that only one cheek was exposed to the wind while he looked up and down the *quai*. It was absolutely deserted, as far as the eye could reach. The cars racing past made no difference; they might as well have been aircraft flying six thousand feet overhead.

Meanwhile the American was trying the starter. One quick burst, another rather longer one, then a third, which went on and on. A stupid mechanical noise against the furious din of the elements. Jean-Marc went round to the open door. With some urgency, he said: 'Are you sure you put the points back right?'

No doubt about it, this man's basic reaction to everything was one of derision.

'So you *do* know about cars after all, my dear fellow! What a dark horse you are, to be sure! Yes, of *course* I put the points back right. It must be something else. Plugs, perhaps.'

The whole process began over again. Every few moments Jean-Marc screwed his neck round to get a glimpse of his watch. The American changed one plug, then a second. Still dead. The thunder and lightning were beginning to lose heart. At eleven o'clock Jean-Marc said, in desperation: 'Look, sir, I think I'd better walk from here. I've still got time to make it, even with the cases.'

The voice from beneath the bonnet replied, imperturbably: 'Now, now, take it easy. I'll get it going again, I promise you. I've never yet had a breakdown I couldn't put right in the long run.'

'But if the engine's flooded—'

'What do you think I'm doing? Every part's being wiped dry before it's put back again. Just hold on.'

At eleven-fifteen, his face running with mingled rain and tears, Jean-Marc sobbed: 'I've only got a quarter of an hour left!'

The American's head bobbed up: his expression was one of concerned interest.

'Is that so?' he said. 'I'm just changing the last plug.'

For what seemed the ten thousandth time he returned to the driver's seat. Miraculously, the engine caught at the first touch of the starter. The American shoved his foot down on the accelerator, and raced it till it howled like a banshee.

'Quick!' he shouted. 'Shut that bonnet and get in! Let's go! You'll make it, don't worry!'

As he drove he began to hum the opening bars of *God Save the King,* a curious reaction for an American, even one of Neapolitan origin. Jean-Marc's overcoat smelt like a wet dog.

4

Through the rain and the darkness shone the big illuminated face of the station clock at the Gare de Lyon. Its hands stood at eleven-twenty. The Boulevard Diderot was still crowded with Easter holiday traffic. The American sounded his horn.

'All we need is to get held up now—so near our goal, too!'

Though he was approaching the last stages of exhaustion, Jean-Marc did his best to put a good face on the situation.

'I really am most grateful to you, monsieur. If I can ever be of service to you in any way . . . My name is Jean-Marc Berger, and my parents live at 10 Rue Dumont, in the Croix-Rousse district of Lyons. My own address in Paris is—'

The American interrupted him. 'Croix-Rousse, eh? Like your Lune Rousse!* Thanks a lot. Anyway, I shall cherish a very special memory of you, what with this breakdown and everything.' Then, in a slower, more deliberate voice, he added : 'I hope you'll be able to say as much of me.'

Why the sudden emphasis? Jean-Marc stared at him, and he stared back at Jean-Marc. His eyes glinted as brightly in shadow as they had done under the hotel sign. The moment passed in a flash, but it was highly unpleasant while it lasted.

'Fine,' he said. 'We've just made it. Looks as though the rain's easing off, too.'

Jean-Marc whispered : 'Right to the top of the ramp, straight ahead.'

'Relax,' said the American, as the car raced up the slope. 'I know the main-line departure platforms. When I stop, you nip out, I'll pass you the cases, and off you go. I'll say goodbye now.'

'Goodbye, monsieur, and thanks again.'

No hope of pulling up at the kerb, which was lined with parked cars. Jean-Marc jumped out in the middle of the road. Already the American had one of the cases ready for him.

'There's the first one—and here's the second. Goodbye now!'

The door slammed, the car made a fast U turn and shot off down the ramp like a bullet from a gun. It was at this moment that Jean-Marc began to shout after it, waving one arm in the ineffectual, mildly ridiculous fashion that was so typical of him.

'Monsieur! Monsieur!'

'Here,' said a policeman, huddled under his cape, 'don't stand there, you'll get yourself run over. Want a porter? *Porter!*' he shouted. 'Ah, you're in luck, here's one coming now.'

* The implications of this word-play are quite untranslatable. *Lune rousse* in French can mean both an April moon and a period of domestic strife. Both meanings are clearly envisaged here.—Trs.

'The case,' Jean-Marc muttered weakly, staring at the second one that had been handed to him.

'What about it, then?' asked the porter, seizing the first case and shoving Jean-Marc on to the sidewalk.

'It isn't mine, it's far too small! And it's already twenty-five minutes past eleven! The one you're holding belongs to me, but this one doesn't!'

The porter grabbed it from him and began to run with both of them.

'You want the Marseilles train?' he asked. 'Right, we'd better move fast, it's the end platform. Got your ticket?'

He was a big, fat man, a Parisian edition of M Bédat. And as a runner, something quite out of the ordinary. Jean-Marc, who was finding it hard to keep up with him, panted: 'No, worse luck, I'll have to fix it on the train. But this case of mine—'

'You remember the number of the taxi?'

'It was a private car.'

'That's all right, then—someone you knew—'

'No, that's just it.'

They were at the barrier.

'Come on, mate, open up,' the porter shouted to the ticket collector. 'Gent here for the Marseilles train.'

'Better get your skates on then,' said the ticket-collector. 'She's leaving in one minute from now.'

'We know that,' snapped the porter, and broke into his sprint again, adding for Jean-Marc's benefit: 'I'll shove your bags in the rear carriage, and you can sort yourself out afterwards.'

'Thanks. Thanks a lot.'

They saw *their* platform, with people standing on it in little motionless groups, heads tilted upwards. Against the roar of the rain on the roof came the quack of a loudspeaker: 'The train is about to leave. Please shut all doors.'

They still had the length of a mail-van to run before they reached their goal.

'No, don't shut that door yet!' the porter yelled.

Travellers leaning out of the windows of the rear coach began to get excited. Would he make it? Had he got a chance?

A woman said, sniffily: 'It's ridiculous to arrive like that, at the last minute.'

The train began to move. A man standing in the still-open doorway grabbed the cases as they were tossed up at his feet. Jean-Marc caught hold of the brass safety-grip and swung himself aboard. He saw the porter, already far behind him, waving his arms like a maniac. 'I'll pay him next time,' he muttered, for the man's benefit.

Arms seized and pulled him into the corridor. The door was shut behind him. The train was already gathering speed.

The man said: 'Cut it pretty fine, son, didn't you?'

The corridor and platform were packed. Everyone smelt of mingled dust and dampness. Someone asked Jean-Marc: 'You travelling third?'

'Yes,' he whispered, almost inaudibly.

'Well I don't know, you might just find a corner somewhere, but you haven't a chance in hell of getting a seat. I went right down the train looking for one before we left.'

The train continued to gather speed, and the noise it made grew steadily louder. The first passenger said: 'Try and squeeze in somewhere anyhow. I'll look after your cases for you.'

'Oh lord,' Jean-Marc said, 'that case—'

'What's the matter? Which case?'

'The smaller one. There's been a mistake. The person who drove me to the station. He handed me out a case that wasn't mine. He got them mixed up.'

The two men listened, gaping. The second one, who looked a sharp customer, said: 'Someone you didn't know?'

'That's right. He'd gone out of his way to help me, too.'

The first man said: 'There are good sorts everywhere.'

The second man remarked, thoughtfully: 'It ought to have his name and address on it somewhere.'

He picked up the case and examined it. Considering how cramped they were, this was quite a feat in itself. He turned it over, and back again. The first man, who had taken the cases in—saved them, in a manner of speaking—clearly felt he had some sort of lien on them.

'Here, give me that,' he said.

The second man obeyed without a word. Jean-Marc never took his eyes off the case. The entire platform observed it with him. At last the first man said: 'No. Not a thing.'

TWO

'What Was It I Saw?'

I

SOON after dawn the following morning, crowds of people were gathered on No 1 Platform of Lyons station, waiting for the train that had left Paris at 11.30 the previous night. In addition to numerous prospective travellers, there was a contingent of courageous relatives, cheerfully sustained by the promise of a cloudless day. Jean-Marc's entire family was there to welcome him, except, that is, for Mme Berger senior, to be referred to hereafter as 'Grandmother'—though this (undoubtedly accurate) appellation could scarcely be less appropriate in her case. Joannès Berger was there, with Émilie (his wife), his brother Léonard, and little Marie-Louise, who kept charging about from one intriguing object to another: from a go-cart to a luggage-trolley, from a Senegalese soldier to a basket with a plaintive, invisible dog shut up inside it. This habit of hers drove some member of the Berger family, every few minutes, to shout: 'Come *here*, Marie-Louise!'

She took not the slightest notice of these summonses, right up to the moment when the loudspeaker's all-powerful voice boomed out: 'Attention, please. The Paris express is about to arrive at platform one. Through carriages to Marseilles are at the front of the train. The rear coaches are going no further than Lyons.'

Émilie said timidly: 'He'll be at the back, then. Shall we go down there, Joannès?'

Joannès shook two fingers at her. Though closely united, *they* were not well-matched, either. 'No, Émilie,' he said, gravely. 'There's no reason why he shouldn't have travelled in a Marseilles coach. We're close to the exit, and he's got to come out this way—he can't possibly miss us. We just have to watch out in case people start pushing. Hold Mummy's hand, Marie-Louise.'

Marie-Louise slipped her hand into Uncle Léonard's.

'I want to see him coming,' she said. 'I want to see him coming! Can I sit on your shoulders, Uncle Léonard?'

'No, Marie-Louise,' said Émilie.

'Of course you can, my poppet,' Léonard said. And to the others: 'She's just dying to see her big brother again. He won't recognize her, she's grown so much.'

'I can't imagine where you get such ideas from,' said Joannès, while Marie-Louise, perched on Léonard's shoulders, complained (as usual) that he was so much shorter than Daddy. 'In six months the child can't have grown more than an inch or so.'

'It's been such a long time, though,' said Émilie.

'Oh all *right*,' said Joannès, nettled. 'Suppose he *doesn't* recognize her—'

'Look,' said Émilie, 'we've gone six months without any news, or next to none—and then this telegram suddenly turns up eight days ago! Why not a letter? And no reply to my letter! He must be ill or something, and didn't want to tell us.'

'On the contrary,' Joannès pronounced. 'It's when you are ill that you let everyone know about it.'

'Well, if he caught the train he can't be all that sick,' said Léonard.

'Now there's a sensible remark,' Joannès said. 'Marie-Louise, watch what you're doing with your feet, those white shoes of yours are going to rub off all over Uncle.'

The little girl bounced about on her observation-post. 'I can see the engine,' she shouted. 'I can see the engine!'

'Attention please,' said the loudspeaker. 'The Paris express is now arriving at platform one. Stand back, please.'

Suddenly what had been empty space was filled with the noise and momentum of the moving train. The loudspeaker went on: 'This is Lyons-Perrache. The train will make a ten-minute stop here. Buffet available. Passengers for Avignon, Tarascon and Marseilles only, please.'

A hissing sound from the locomotive, white jets of steam everywhere, people scurrying in all directions, clusters of passengers round every carriage door, getting off and on. Marie-Louise began to cry.

'There's too many people, I can't see Jean-Marc!'

'Well anyway,' Joannès said, 'you can see you might as well have stayed down on the ground.'

'Let's hope he hasn't missed the train,' said Émilie.

Léonard jerked the back of his head into Marie-Louise's stomach.

'Can't see Jean-Marc, eh? Well, who's that coming now, look, *there*, between a couple of policemen?'

'Between a couple of *policemen*?' Joannès repeated, in horror-struck amazement.

Léonard burst out laughing. 'Only through a trick of perspective,' he said.

Amid the general hubbub, Marie-Louise suddenly shouted: 'Jean-Marc! Jean-Marc!'

Behind the two policemen, but between his two cases—one of them somebody else's—his felt hat rendered shapeless by the previous night's downpour, his raincoat all crumpled and pulled tightly about him, Jean-Marc appeared, moving towards them like a sleepwalker. Like a blind man, too: he was wearing dark glasses.

'My God!' Émilie said, clasping her hands together.

Léonard's arms embraced the air in a grand, recuperative gesture. 'This way, Jean-Marc!' he called.

'Quiet Léonard,' said Joannès, 'you'll have people staring at us. There may be some of our customers on the platform.'

Jean-Marc, who had in fact spotted them, now changed

course in their direction. He began by putting down the cases. Then, not certain which of them he ought to kiss first, he said: 'Good morning Papa, good morning, Mama, good morning, Uncle.'

Émilie flung herself round his neck.

'My poor darling! Is it your eyes that are giving you trouble? How pale you are! Oh, let me give you another kiss—'

'We're blocking the exit,' said Joannès.

'Come on, down you get now,' Léonard told Marie-Louise.

She was so impressed by the dark glasses that she did as she was told without a word.

'Am *I* allowed to kiss my own son, too?' Joannès asked Émilie. 'Even if he does look like an out-of-work bum. What's wrong with you, Jean-Marc?'

He hugged the boy to him. They were the same height, but the son was as thin as the father was stocky.

'I must have caught a cold—it's gone down on to my chest. Isn't Grandmother here?'

'No,' Émilie said, reassuringly, 'she isn't.'

Finally he kissed Léonard and Marie-Louise.

'She could have come,' Joannès said, picking up the cases. 'She's always the first up. But this morning she made it quite clear that—'

He broke off at this point, and Jean-Marc did not follow the matter up. Marie-Louise wanted to hold his hand. First of all, however, he had to look through his pockets for his ticket.

'Have you seen a doctor?' Émilie asked him.

'No, Mama, it wasn't worth it. Look, I'd like to send a telegram—'

'Attention, please,' said the loudspeaker. 'The slow train from Grenoble is now approaching platform three—'

'You can send your telegram later,' said Joannès. '*Grand-mother is expecting you.* Léonard, take this little case while I find our platform tickets.'

'Hold on,' Léonard said to Jean-Marc, 'you haven't brought her case back. What have you done with it?'

'I'll tell you about that,' Jean-Marc said. 'It's quite a story.'

Joannès seemed to have heard neither the question nor the reply. 'Four tickets,' he was saying to the ticket-collector. 'Myself, this lady and gentleman, and the child. The young man is my son. He has his own ticket, from Paris.'

2

Joannès reassembled his flock in the station yard.

'I'll go and fight for a taxi,' said Léonard and did so.

'You haven't told us about your illness,' said Émilie, in an agony of anxiety. 'Have you got a temperature?'

'One moment,' said Joannès. 'With a face like that he obviously needs looking after, and he will be looked after. But *first* I'd very much like him to explain why he hasn't got Grandmother's suitcase.'

'Oh for heaven's sake,' said Émilie, 'what's so important about a suitcase?'

'It's not *a* suitcase, Émilie. It is *Grandmother*'s suitcase. We shall be back home in a quarter of an hour. I trust you understand me now?'

'Look, there's Uncle Léonard waving to us!' shouted Marie-Louise, suddenly cheerful again. 'We're going in a taxi, we're going in a taxi!'

'Very well,' said Joannès. 'Anyone would think you do it on purpose. Now: quickly across, and don't watch the right here, just the left.'

While his father and uncle went off to palaver with the taxi-driver, and Marie-Louise did her best to get Émilie's attention by screaming, 'Wanna go in the taxi! I wanna go in the taxi', Jean-Marc gazed wearily down towards the

Place Carnot and the Cours de Verdun, now filled with tar-paulin-swathed merry-go-rounds, fairground stalls (all carefully locked up), and the trucks and caravans of their proprietors. The carnival season* had begun—though at present it was taking a nap. Marie-Louise suddenly stopped screaming.

'Will you take me to the fair, Jean-Marc?' she asked.

'You spent your whole Sunday afternoon there yesterday,' Émilie said. Then she took her son's arm and whispered in his ear: 'Are you really all right, darling?'

Jean-Marc gave her arm a squeeze. 'Yes, Mama,' he said. 'But I really do want to send a telegram—'

'Look,' Joannès was saying to the taxi-driver, 'I know there are a lot of us, but you're only getting us at all because this gentleman is sick. You forget that the No 13 bus would take us straight to our doorstep!'

'*I'm* not stopping you catching it,' said the driver. 'I dunno, this town runs to the stingiest bastards in the world.'

Joannès gave him a searching glance.

'Nothing to stop *you* picking up some other fare, is there?' he said.

'Oh well,' the driver said. 'I guess I've got to lump it, I'm a local myself. Come on, then, in you get, family, invalid, the lot! Just watch the meter and see which of us is stingier, though.'

As soon as they were moving, and without prior consult-ation, Joannès and Léonard both said, simultaneously: 'Well, what about that suitcase?'

Jean-Marc told them everything: his feverish cold, the rain, Bédat, the American, the break-down, the episode at the station. The whole Berger family listened open-mouthed. 'When the American had driven off again,' he concluded, 'I

---

* 'La vogue' is a dialect term employed in certain French *départements* for a patronal festival, associated with the local saint. This is cumber-some to convey in English; I have therefore given a merely approximate rendering.—Trs.

realized he'd handed me out his own case instead of Grandmother's. If I hadn't been in such a flap about missing my
train, I'd have spotted the difference right away.'

'I should think so,' said Joannès, his eye sizing up the
unknown case, which now rested on top of the other one,
beside the driver. 'It's only half the size.'

'Less,' said Léonard.

'I'm not measuring it up like a draper's assistant,' Joannès
said, in a tone that made Léonard start visibly. 'I am merely
giving a rough estimate.'

'But he drove off at such a speed,' Jean-Marc said, by way
of self-justification.

'You must return it to him as soon as possible,' Émilie told
him.

'You'd better drop him a note first,' said Joannès, 'to
organize the exchange.'

'The case hasn't got either his name or his address on it—
not outside, anyway,' said Jean-Marc.

Joannès said : 'That's odd.'

'Not when you're travelling in your own car,' Léonard
put in.

'What do you mean, *own* car?' Joannès said, scathingly.
He definitely had it in for his brother this morning. 'It was
hired! Well, I'll give you *my* opinion, for what it's worth.
Either the label got removed accidentally, or else the name
and address are written *inside* the lid. Other countries, other
ways. The Americans have plenty of faults, but they're the
tops when it comes to organization.'

He cocked a challenging eye at Léonard, but to no effect,
since the latter merely observed : 'I agree. Perhaps the case
is locked, though?'

'No,' Jean-Marc said, 'I sprang the hasps last night. But
there was such a crush in the corridor that I couldn't even get
it half-open.'

Émilie gave a gasp. 'You travelled standing up in the corridor? All night?'

B

'Yes, Mama.'

'What about your own case?' Joannès asked. 'I sincerely hope *that* was locked?'

'Now, Dad,' said Émilie, 'surely you're not going to get suspicious about a gentleman who was so helpful to Jean-Marc?'

Joannès shook his head in a knowing manner.

'One should never trust strangers,' he pronounced.

'Yes, it was locked,' said Jean-Marc. 'Anyway, I had practically nothing in it.'

'But it's *Grandmother*'s case,' Léonard said.

'Don't worry, it's got my name and address on the outside.'

'Your Lyons address?' Joannès asked.

'Yes, of course.'

Léonard relaxed visibly. 'In that case,' he said, 'we shall probably find a telegram waiting for us when we get home. The first Grandmother will hear about the affair is that it's been settled.'

'Let's hope so,' Joannès observed, half to himself.

Up till now Marie-Louise, perched on Léonard's knees, had been exclusively preoccupied with their journey as such —the Rue Auguste-Comte, the Place Bellecour, the Place de la République, all areas that she had never before visited so early in the morning. But at this point she said: 'Jean-Marc, the present you brought me—it wasn't in the other case, was it?'

Her uncle and father both burst out laughing. Jean-Marc looked more disconcerted than ever. 'I didn't bring you anything,' he said. 'I've been desperately busy these last few days, and yesterday was Sunday.'

Marie-Louise began to howl. Émilie said: 'Do you want a smacking?'

All the same, the atmosphere had relaxed a little.

'We are now,' Joannès announced, with pride, 'approaching the St Polycarp Cloth Mills and Silk Factory.' He turned to his son. 'Aren't you going to ask us how business is?'

In a doleful voice enlivened by not the faintest spark of interest Jean-Marc said: 'Yes, of course, Papa.'

'We've just celebrated our centenary—February 1830 to February 1930. It was a most successful occasion, very moving. M Couzon made a really splendid speech, didn't he, Léonard?'

Léonard nodded.

'We toasted the ever-growing future prosperity of the firm in a glass of fine sparkling wine. M Clément, our oldest employee, presented M Couzon with a gift on behalf of the whole staff. In his speech he said: "A hundred years ago today the St Polycarp Cloth Mills and Silk Factory was founded by your father's father. A hundred years hence it will be the occasion of a still more splendid celebration, held by your son's sons!" Mme Couzon was there too, and very properly so, with her children, and wearing a marvellous pearl necklace M Couzon had given her that same morning. Afterwards, well, you might say there was a kind word for everybody. Mme Combe, who's now my assistant in the counting-house, had tears in her eyes.'

'And on the material level?' Jean-Marc demanded. Quite suddenly he looked wide awake and alert. Joannès and Léonard stared at one another in some surprise.

'What do you mean, the material level?'

'Look, if the business is prospering, it's you, the employees, who are responsible. And what has M Couzon offered *you*, apart from a glass of sparkling wine—and a necklace to his wife?'

Léonard said, suspiciously: 'You haven't become a Communist, by any chance, have you?'

Jean-Marc said: 'All I'm saying is that the best way to celebrate a centenary is by giving everyone a pay-rise. It's the least they deserve. Does that make me a Communist?'

Joannès shrugged. '*Everyone*,' he repeated. 'There's today's younger generation for you. *Everyone's* got to get the full treatment, good or bad, loyal or bolshie, it makes no odds. Wait till the end of the year, Jean-Marc, and then take a look at the bonuses. If I may say so, M Couzon will not be niggardly in rewarding those members of his staff who have proved themselves good friends of his.'

'Do you feel hungry, Jean-Marc?' Émilie asked him. 'You could at least tell me that. Have you eaten anything since yesterday evening?'

'No, Mama. And all I want to do now is get a few hours' sleep.'

'You'll have to see your grandmother first. She took it harder than any of us, the way you've been neglecting your family. It's as though you'd forgotten us all.'

'Of course I haven't forgotten you. I'm here, aren't I? That proves I haven't.'

Joannès was telling the driver: 'To get to the Rue Dumont, it's best to turn off at the Place de la Croix-Rousse.'

'The nearer home we get,' Léonard remarked, 'the more I find myself wondering whether there's been a telegram. If there hasn't, we're in for a fine to-do.'

'You never know,' Joannès remarked mildly. 'Sometimes she finds things amusing.'

In the Place de la Croix-Rousse the statue of Jacquard, 'benefactor of silk-workers', to quote from the inscription on his plinth, still served as a handy perch for pigeons.

3

The taxi drew up outside the house.

'Don't wait for me,' Joannès said. 'I've got to settle the fare. I'll bring up the big case. Léonard can carry the mysterious American one.'

The Bergers spread themselves over the pavement. The Rue Dumont was always a peaceful street, and at this early hour absolutely empty.

'Why not the other way round?' said Léonard. 'That way you'll be able to catch up with us quicker.'

Jean-Marc said: 'I can perfectly well take both of them.'

'No, no, no,' said Joannès. 'You're dead-beat, and our fourth-floor apartment is still a hundred and four steps up from the hall. Both of you do as I say.'

The ascent took place in silence. Marie-Louise was hauled up by her brother, who began to shiver more and more as he went.

'Now mind you wipe your feet, children,' said Émilie. 'And ring the bell. Grandmother said we were to ring.'

Marie-Louise reached up and touched the bell-push with the tip of one finger. Then she scampered back and hid behind her mother.

Léonard said: 'You first, Jean-Marc.'

Quick footsteps could be heard behind the door. It opened. Jean-Marc muttered, 'Good morning, Grandmother,' and bent down.

'Ah, there you are, then,' she said. 'Good morning.'

A brief kiss, and then, as the hall was too dark for her to get a good look at the traveller, she led the way to the dining-room. Its two windows looked out on open sky, and a wilderness of roof-tops, behind which rose those pleasant hills known, grandiloquently, as the Golden Mountains. Everyone followed her. Léonard dumped the ill-fated suitcase in the hall.

Grandmother stood and examined Jean-Marc. She was a small, slender woman, who held herself very erect, and was beautifully turned out; she had fine grey hair, and a pair of eyes that never missed a trick.

'Take off those glasses,' she said. 'That's better. Just as I expected. You look like a death's-head.'

'I caught a cold, Grandmother,' Jean-Marc said, humbly. 'It's been awful weather in Paris lately.'

She laughed derisively. 'Yes, I know. Lyons is the place where it's always supposed to be raining. Well, this time it's Lyons that got the sunshine. So you're back at last, are you?

To explain your behaviour, I hope? It seems to me that we are entitled to a certain amount of explanation—'

Jean-Marc was clearly about to blow his top. Léonard quickly cut in before he could say anything.

'He's very tired, Mother, you ought to let him sit down. He's been travelling on his feet all night—'

'All he had to do was travel during the daytime. He's got into Parisian habits, I don't doubt. Get up at five in the afternoon, go to bed at six in the morning. Well, it's not much after six now, and this boy will hear what I have to say to him *now*. Oh, you can flop into a chair; one more discourtesy makes very little odds. But you don't suppose that after playing the artist for six months in the cafés of Montparnasse, which are worse than—Go to the kitchen, Marie-Louise.'

'Yes, Grandmother.' She began to move in the direction of her room.

'I said *the kitchen*. I'm not having you sitting with your ear to the key-hole.'

Marie-Louise went off to the kitchen.

'Wouldn't take much to make her like her brother,' Grandmother observed. 'Ah, there's Joannès. So much the better.'

Joannès came quickly through the hall, and appeared before them, breathless but jovial, clutching the large suitcase in one hand and a pot of cream in the other.

'When it comes down to fares and tips, these taxi-drivers are impossible,' he said. 'No change, indeed! Said it was because he was just beginning work for the day. Can you imagine me opening the cashier's desk every morning with nothing but thousand-franc notes? In the end I had to go and bang on Mme Piochon's shutter. Bought a nice pot of cream off her while I was at it. Go and make us a good cup of coffee, Émilie. I see Mother's laid the table already—that was nice of her.'

Émilie scuttled off. For the first time since the arrival of the train she was smiling. Joannès looked at Léonard and Jean-Marc, who were still on their feet. He put down the suitcase, and, as though addressing no one in particular, said: 'Everything all right, then?'

The cutting voice replied: 'Oh of course, my dear boy; things just couldn't be better. Haven't you seen the prodigal son for yourself? No, don't tell me, I've heard it all already—the weather's been bad, he caught a cold, and so on. Well, it's just not good enough. He can play fast and loose with his mother or his father or his uncle, anyone else he likes, but he's not going to treat me in that way. Because this is my house, and as far as I'm concerned he's not setting foot in it again until he's explained quite a lot of things—by what right he's neglected us in the way he has ever since he left home, what he's been living on—'

Joannès broke in at this point, while the old lady was drawing breath for a further broadside.

'Look, Mother, you're being unfair. Jean-Marc has never asked for a penny more than his monthly allowance—'

'*That* is precisely what astonishes me! Just so; he's never asked for more—and yet the cost of living in Paris goes up almost daily!'

Jean-Marc had come to the end of his tether; his nerves were at breaking-point. 'But look, I've been working,' he exclaimed. 'Quite apart from the School—'

The old lady's answers came like the crack of a whip.

'Ah. That job with Pauguin the art-restorer. Have you still got it?'

Jean-Marc said nothing. Joannès and Léonard stared at him in amazement. Grandmother went on: 'You decide to get engaged without consulting your parents, without any consideration for the promises you had made to Augusta—'

At this point Jean-Marc felt compelled to defend himself. 'I made no promises to Augusta! With a childhood friend a moment always comes when kids get ideas into their heads—'

'Oh of course, what could I have been thinking of? How would you be capable of getting engaged to anyone at all?'

'But look,' Joannès broke in tentatively, 'his fiancée—'

'Yes indeed, let's get back to her! A name and a photograph! And what she looks like I'd rather not say. A Parisienne—'

At this, Jean-Marc could no longer restrain himself.

'Yes, a Parisienne,' he said, 'and I'm going to marry her—soon, very soon. That's what I came to tell you!'

'Isn't that what normally happens when you get engaged?' Grandmother retorted, implacably. 'Was it so uncertain in your case?'

Joannès turned towards the kitchen, the only sanctuary in sight.

'What about that coffee, Émilie?'

'Coming, Dad! Just another couple of minutes.'

That gave Grandmother ample time to return to the attack. But no attack came. She had suddenly fallen silent, staring at something which stood beside Joannès' feet: Jean-Marc's suitcase.

4

'And what about mine?' she said at last, looking up. 'What have you done with mine? Do you mean to say that you left it behind in Paris after depriving me of the use of it for six months?'

Father and uncle both stiffened to attention. The volcanic eruption was beginning right on schedule, and there was no predicting either its effects, or, consequently, its limits. Jean-Marc began his story again.

'The person who drove me to the station made a mistake, and gave me theirs.'

'What person? Your "fiancée"?'

'No! A man, an American. He should have sent me a telegram by now.'

'Why? What American? Where has my suitcase got to?'

'Let me tell this story my own way, Grandmother, I feel so awful.'

'Ah, good,' said Joannès hastily, 'here comes the coffee! Coffee up! Let's sit down, then—sit down, Mother, and you, Jean-Marc, it'll do you good to rest. A good moment to take a look at this unknown suitcase, eh? I'm sure we'll find an address inside it. Where did you put it, Léonard?'

'In the hall. I'll get it.'

Émilie set down the coffee-pot on the table. Marie-Louise clambered on to her high stool.

'Bravo,' said Joannès. 'A nice peaceful breakfast, and then off to the office. The well-balanced man apportions his time between duty and pleasure.'

'There we are, Mother,' Léonard said. 'If we shift the cups a bit, I can put it down close to you.'

'I'm not interested in this thing,' said Grandmother. 'I want *my* suitcase. This is tiny, it's just an overnight bag. However did you come to get them mixed up? And how did this American of yours get involved with you in the first place?'

Joannès said: 'Jean-Marc couldn't get a taxi in the rain, and the American picked him up.'

'I suppose the Métro is only for legless cripples,' Grandmother said sardonically.

'Take care,' said Émilie. 'Push back the tablecloth, but leave the felt underlay, otherwise you may scratch the polish.'

'Nice piece of stuff, this bag,' Léonard said, without touching the hasps. 'Good fibre.'

'It's for air-travel,' Joannès said. 'Americans are always travelling by plane. They like it, it suits their way of life. And you must admit, it's fast. But dangerous. Open the bag, Jean-Marc.'

'I don't like the idea of prying,' Jean-Marc said.

'You've got more scruples with strangers than you have with your own family,' Grandmother snapped. 'Anyway, this rubbishy little case is probably full of old rags, and your

American knew very well what he was at when he made his little mistake!'

'There's no question of prying, Jean-Marc,' said Joannès. 'If we find any letters, we certainly won't open them. All we need is an envelope with the address on it.'

'Come on, Jean-Marc, hurry up!' said Marie-Louise.

With two sharp clicks, the hasps flew up more or less simultaneously. Jean-Marc lifted the lid.

'No label inside?' queried Léonard. 'No.'

The whole family was now crowded round the object—except, that is, for Grandmother, who stayed where she was and poured herself a cup of coffee. She said: 'I don't see why I should let my coffee get cold while you're rummaging around inside there.'

'Oh, what lovely silk,' Émilie said.

Léonard looked at it. 'Despite the Chinese pattern,' he pronounced, 'this silk is from here, from Lyons.'

'*Chinese pattern?*' Jean-Marc repeated. He stared at the yellow and blue silk that covered the contents of the case. A blue dragon against a yellow sky, which the real sky, seen through the windows, rendered almost unbearable. Émilie put her fingers on one of the two webbing straps which held everything in place.

'What is it?' she asked. 'A dress? A dressing-gown?'

'Are you *quite* sure, Jean-Marc,' said Grandmother, buttering a slice of bread, 'that it wasn't a woman who came to your rescue—whether American or Chinese?'

'Take it out, Émilie,' said Joannès impatiently. 'We'll put it back afterwards.'

'Ah, yes, it's a dressing-gown,' said Léonard. 'Will you look at the quality of it!'

Jean-Marc clutched the edge of the table with the thumb and forefinger of either hand. 'It's not possible,' he muttered to himself.

Only Grandmother noticed his gesture: 'It would seem to have memories for you,' she remarked.

He made no reply. He was no longer looking at the dressing-gown, which Émilie had hung over a chair. His eyes were riveted on what still lay inside.

'A towel,' Joannès said. 'It's got something wrapped up inside it.'

'Toilet articles, probably,' Léonard said.

'What's more,' Joannès added, lifting the towel, 'I don't think there's anything else here. Look, there's the bottom. Shall I open it?'

He put the package down on the table.

'I'd be very surprised if you found a name and address inside that,' said Grandmother, through a mouthful of bread and butter.

However, curiosity had by now got the better of Joannès. He unwrapped the towel.

'Why,' said Émilie, 'it's got another towel inside it. And what's that little spot there? Blood?'

'Blood!' said Léonard, in great alarm.

'Oh, come on,' Joannès said, as he began to unfold the second towel, 'haven't you ever nicked yourself while you were shaving?'

'If this was a bearded lady,' put in Grandmother.

Then Émilie screamed, a frightful noise that echoed through the room, to be followed an instant later by a shriek from Marie-Louise, and gasps of horror from Léonard and Joannès. Jean-Marc uttered a faint whimpering sound, and slid to the floor. Grandmother was on her feet in a flash.

'Jean-Marc's fainted!' she observed. She knelt down beside him and shook his head. Émilie's screams continued, interspersed with a spate of hysterical exclamations: 'Oh no, no! I can't bear it, it's too horrible! Get out of here, Marie-Louise! Keep right away! God, what did I see? *What was it I saw?*'

Marie-Louise clung frantically to her dress. 'Mama,' she sobbed, 'I'm frightened!'

Joannès' and Léonard's teeth were chattering gently.

'It's a hand,' Léonard said. 'A woman's hand.'

'It must be artificial,' said Joannès. 'A trick imitation . . .'

'Don't be a damn fool,' said Grandmother. She got up and went to shut the lid of the case. But Émilie, still shrieking, flung across the room and forcibly restrained her. 'Look at it,' she shouted, 'look at it, *that's my ring!* The ring I sent Jean-Marc for Augusta! For Augusta! For Augusta!'

At this point she became completely hysterical, and, like Jean-Marc, collapsed on the floor. By now not only Marie-Louise but even the two men were practically gibbering with fright. Only Grandmother kept completely cool, issuing a series of brisk orders all round. Someone was sent to get water for Émilie. Jean-Marc was taken to his room, Joannès and Léonard were to go straight to the central police station. On the way they were to leave Marie-Louise with Mme Piochon, and summon Dr Guerrier, who was almost sure to be at home still. Meanwhile she announced, as a point of interest: 'This can't possibly be Augusta's hand. Augusta's hands are much bigger. It's the hand of some unknown woman—unknown to us, that is . . .'

Joannès and Léonard were in a state of total shock and bewilderment. Whatever she said they simply answered: 'Yes, Mama.'

'How irritating you two can be,' she told them. 'Both of you go down to the police station, you're only in the way here. And don't forget the case.'

THREE

Advice from a clerk

I

THE two brothers hurried off side by side in the direction of the Croix-Rousse municipal buildings, where police headquarters was located. Literally side by side: they felt the need to keep in physical contact with each other. It was Joannès who carried the case, with its ghastly contents. At first he automatically held it by the handle, like any ordinary suitcase. Grandmother had repacked everything just as it was: the two towels, the dressing-gown, with the dragon in the middle; the webbing straps. Neither of them would have credited how accurately she had observed everything while sitting there over her piece of bread and butter. But as he hurried down the steps, rather faster than usual, Joannès got the impression that *it* was shifting about inside. Oh my God, he thought, and clutched the case to his stomach, with both arms holding the lid. He continued to carry it thus, every now and then emitting a brief and strangled sob. Léonard held him by one elbow, to show affection even if he could not lend him courage. You could only give what you had.

As they emerged from the apartment block Léonard had said: 'Let's hope we don't meet anybody . . .' So they kept their eyes fixed straight ahead, scowling ferociously, both dressed in black suits that bore witness to their involvement in the silk trade, two respectable gentlemen, two model employees of a firm that had just celebrated its centenary. And carrying a severed hand in a bag, a hand that had one of Émilie's rings on it. As Joannès observed, while coming downstairs: 'There are some things that just pass all human understanding.'

Thinking aloud, Léonard ventured an opinion that the police station probably would not be open yet. It was. As they walked in, they heard a clerk on the telephone: 'The Superintendent is never here before nine o'clock. Yes, if you like. Goodbye, monsieur.'

As he hung up, he said to a sergeant standing beside him: 'People are extraordinary. They'd think it quite natural if the Super slept in his office, like Napoleon, just so as he could attend to their piddling little problems in person. You think the character who rang up then would tell *me* what he was on about? Not on your life. Well now, what have we here?'

He turned his attention to the two brothers, noting their harassed appearance.

'Please excuse us, gentlemen,' said Joannès, trembling, 'but it's a frightful business that has brought us here, absolutely frightful! A crime, without any doubt . . . Because of a, a substitution . . . My son . . .'

His voice choked. Léonard tried to take over, but only got as far as 'My nephew' before he too dried up.

'You say your son's been substituted?' asked the clerk. 'What do you mean, substituted?'

'No, no,' said Joannès, 'it's the *case* that was substituted. And it's not my *son* who's been killed but his fiancée, I'm sure it must be his fiancée—'

'Why do you say you're sure? Don't you know?'

Joannès forced the words out. 'It'd be a miracle, with a hand cut clean off—'

'What?' exclaimed the clerk, beginning to get flustered. 'For heaven's sake try to explain yourself more clearly, I can't make head or tail of all this. You mean your son cut off his fiancée's hand?'

'Oh no, monsieur!' Joannès exclaimed. 'Obviously not—I mean, he fainted when the case was opened.'

'The hand was in a case?'

Joannès deposited his burden on the counter. The clerk started back violently in his chair. 'In *this* case?' he said.

Joannès could only give a faint nod. 'Yes,' Léonard whispered.

The sergeant came forward at this point, and the clerk pulled himself together sufficiently to say: 'Open it.'

Joannès sprang the hasps but did not touch the lid. 'We put everything back as it was,' he said.

'I told you to open it!' the clerk repeated. 'We'll have to take fingerprints, don't you understand?'

Joannès began to tremble violently. He looked beseechingly in turn at Léonard and the sergeant, silently imploring their help, but both they and the clerk looked as though they had been turned into statues. He had to do the job alone.

'Ugh,' said the clerk in a strangled voice. 'Horrible! Shut the damn thing up again.'

In the same voice, Joannès asked: 'Shall I wrap it first?'

The clerk cleared his throat and shouted: 'No! Just do what I tell you! Shut the case!' Then, his voice strangling again, he said to the sergeant: 'Get me the Rue Vauban, please.'

By now Joannès had shut the little case again. His face was covered with sweat; so was Léonard's. The clerk was floating in a sea of improbabilities and wondering how to touch bottom again.

'Just now you were talking about substitution. You mean someone switched cases—*this* case, in fact?'

'Yes,' said both brothers, in unison.

'Hallo,' said the sergeant. 'Croix-Rousse police station here. Give me Control Centre. Yes, a crime.'

He held out the receiver to the clerk, whose biliously resentful face was by now a far from pleasant sight.

'Hallo, Control Centre? Maillet here, Croix-Rousse precinct. Someone's brought in a woman's hand in a bag . . . Who? Oh, the family . . . Yes, yes, I agree, quite extraordinary!' He looked up at the two brothers. 'You know who did it?' Vehement denials from both of them. 'They claim not to,' the clerk said into the receiver. He looked up again. 'Where's it come from?' he asked.

'From Paris,' Joannès told him.

'From Paris,' the clerk said over the phone. Then he looked up yet again. 'Whereabouts in Paris?' he enquired.

'We don't know, monsieur.'

'They don't know,' the clerk said. 'Yes, that's right. Thanks.' He hung up. The sergeant had gone out.

'Two inspectors are coming down, gentlemen. You will kindly wait for them here. Meanwhile, I'd better take down your particulars, since we shall have to inform the Public Prosecutor's office as well. I don't want to make any comments on the matter myself, but you might at least have waited till the Superintendent got here!'

'It was because we have to get to the office,' said Léonard, with a glance at the clock on the wall. 'The St Polycarp Cloth Mills and Silk Factory.'

'I'll be surprised if they see you at all this morning,' the clerk said.

Joannès had been mopping his forehead. Now he broke out in a sweat all over again. He seemed not a whit less upset than he had been at the first sight of the hand.

'But we have never, never missed a day, either of us, except in a case of serious illness!' he exclaimed.

'And you think *this* is something less important than an illness?'

'We're not directly concerned in the matter! My son—'

The clerk cut him short. 'That's right, and while we're on the subject, where is this precious son of yours? Why didn't he come down here with you?'

'I told you, monsieur, he fainted, and my poor wife went into screaming hysterics. It was when she recognized the ring, you see. Imagine what she must have felt—'

'That's right,' said the clerk. 'I did notice a ring. Was that how you came to recognize the hand?'

'Not exactly, monsieur. You see, we don't know my son's fiancée. But he must have recognized it.'

'You say "he must have"; is that just a guess?'

'He hadn't come round when we left. We called in at Dr Guerrier's on our way here, and asked him to step round. It was our mother who decided what we ought to do.'

'You mean your mother didn't faint, or anything like that?'

Joannès and Léonard both sighed, and said, as one man: 'Oh no.'

The clerk stared at them, one eyebrow slightly raised. Then he took a sheet of paper, plunged his pen in the inkwell, and shook it over his wastepaper basket. He addressed his questions to Joannès.

'Surname and Christian name, please—just the one you normally use.'

'Berger. Joannès. Born at Saint-Rambert-l'Ile-Barbe in 1882, which makes me forty-eight. Chief cashier at the St Polycarp Cloth Mills and Silk Factory.'

'Address?'

'10, Rue Dumont, fourth floor, the apartment on the left.'

The clerk turned to Léonard. 'What about you?' he asked.

'Berger. Léonard. Same birth-place, same age, same address. I'm a bobbin-winder, sorry, I mean, Chief Assistant Stock-keeper, in the same firm.'

The clerk looked from one to the other of them. Joannès was tall, heavily built, with thick hair and hairy backs to his hands. Léonard was short and slight, with incipient baldness. Even their eyes were a different colour: Joannès' were brown, while Léonard's were grey. With incredulity in his voice, the clerk said: 'Are you two twins?'

'Not identical,' Joannès said.

The clerk quizzed him disapprovingly. 'It sounds like your mother talking,' he said. The brothers exchanged stupefied glances. 'A pretty united family, from the look of it. Married?' he asked Léonard.

Léonard hesitated perceptibly before answering: 'No, monsieur.'

'Why the hesitation?'

'Because you'll accuse me of speaking ill of our mother, whereas in fact we both hold her in great veneration, monsieur, indeed we do.' He drew himself up in an almost heroic stance. 'She didn't want me to marry, that's all there is to it. She wanted us all to live together. She was right.'

'Who is "all"? What do you mean, exactly?'

Joannès said: 'My wife and myself, our two children—this poor boy Jean-Marc, my son, who's twenty-three now, and a daughter of eight, Marie-Louise. My brother.' He paused for a moment. 'And our mother, who's been a widow ever since Léonard and I took our First Communion together. Papa was an officer, he died of a chill.' Joannès added, in a proud voice, and clearly with Léonard's approval: 'She is a dominating woman, monsieur.'

'Right,' said the clerk, after reading through what he had written. 'I suppose I'd better take this bag off your hands, too.'

As he wrote the words he spoke them aloud: ' "Received from M Berger . . . h'm, let's see . . . one small case containing a woman's hand, severed at the wrist, and wearing a ring . . ." What sort of stone? I take it there is a stone?'

'Yes, monsieur,' Joannès said. 'A cat's-eye, sometimes known as a tiger's eye. It's quartz, with fibres of amianthus running through it. It belonged to my wife's family. She sent it to Jean-Marc about four or five months ago, for—'

'You can go into all these details later. What I'm interested in is where that case comes from.'

2

As he recounted the story, Joannès recovered a little of his normal self-assurance and dignity. The clerk sat quite still, chin forward, eyes raised. He had forgotten Léonard, who, indeed, had more or less forgotten himself, being solely concerned with the matter of endorsing every word Joannès uttered. But when the story was finally concluded, he asked a somewhat surprising question.

'You still maintain that we have to deal with an unknown person? An unknown American?'

'Absolutely, *monsieur le secrétaire*.'

'Who mixed up two cases and gave your son another one with his fiancée's hand in it? Not bad, for a total stranger!'

Joannès allowed himself to register a protest at this point. 'Unknown to my son, monsieur. But it's very clear to me now that my son was not unknown to this stranger, isn't that right, Léonard?'

Léonard endorsed this statement vigorously.

'Obviously it was a carefully planned scheme. As far as I'm concerned, there's your criminal, and that's that!'

The clerk shrugged. 'Ah, come on, you can say what you like to *me*. But when you're dealing with the inspectors—'

He clearly saw no point in finishing this sentence. 'With the inspectors?' Joannès repeated, uncomprehendingly.

The clerk, who was quite a young man, now assumed a paternal air. 'Look,' he said, 'I'm going to give you a good piece of advice while there's still time. I know what an ordeal this sort of thing must be for any family, I've got kids of my own. Don't dig your toes in. Try a different cover-story.'

Again, the two brothers reacted almost in unison.

'Cover-story? What cover-story?'

'The one you cooked up to explain the presence of this hand in your son's luggage. It's quite absurd.'

'Monsieur,' said Joannès, laying his right hand on the case, palm downwards, as though on a Bible, 'I give you my word that neither my brother here nor I have worked out any cover-story, as you put it. I have told you the story exactly as I had it from my son.'

'Ah yes,' said the clerk, with an unpleasant grin. 'He told you all this, didn't he?'

'You're surely not insinuating—'

The clerk's mild voice suddenly acquired a sharp cutting edge. ' "Insinuating" isn't a word I like. Let's keep this polite, h'm? What's your son's profession, then?'

'He's a student at the École des Beaux-Arts in Paris. He's a lot of talent, monsieur, his teachers have always told us so. And it was actually our mother who wanted him to study there, she thinks so highly of his work. On top of that, to avoid having to live off us, he's also got—that is, he had till very recently—a job with a restorer of *objets-d'art*, the most distinguished one in Paris, the firm of Pauguin! A fine son, yes indeed, who's gone on as we brought him up, an excellent son!'

'What about his fiancée?' asked the clerk, who sounded terribly unconvinced by all this. 'The one your good lady sent this ring to?'

'It isn't quite like that,' Joannès said, his forehead suddenly wrinkling. 'She didn't actually send it for her—'

'But it was her your son gave it to, right? You just told me he must have recognized her hand. So it follows that his fiancée was the victim. So could you please give me some particulars, about her, that's all.'

'Mlle Sarrazin,' Joannès announced, as if this was something that everyone knew. 'Huguette Sarrazin. As I've already told you, we didn't have the honour of her personal acquaintance. Jean-Marc got engaged in December, and told us about it in January. He sent us her photo. And he was actually here now to announce his forthcoming marriage to us. You can imagine what a shock it's been. Such a very lovely person, oh dear—'

Joannès averted his eyes from the case.

'I suppose you at least know who she is? Her age, profession, address?'

'Who she is? A very respectable person, monsieur, of excellent family, and naturally without a profession. Despite modern fashions, I still maintain that no respectable person of the fair sex should have a profession. As for her age, Jean-

Marc wrote of her as "a young girl". Yes, that's right, "I've met a young girl". When a boy of twenty-three writes that he's met a young girl, that means she's between eighteen and twenty—twenty-one the outside.'

'And her address?'

'Her address?'

'Yes, her address! The address of this young lady, Mlle Sarrazin, Huguette Sarrazin!'

'Ah, her address.' Joannès gave a miserable little laugh. 'I'm afraid I don't know it. What about you, Léonard?'

Despite his pale and perspiring countenance, Léonard now seemed remarkably placid.

'Good heavens, no! It made no difference to us down here which part of Paris she lived in. We never go to Paris. In any case, my nephew knew her, he can give these gentlemen the information they require.'

'Well,' said the clerk, 'at least you won't have to hang around waiting for them.'

A car had just arrived outside the police station, travelling very fast. It pulled up with a loud shriek of brakes. The clerk sighed and said: 'I must ask you to join the sergeant in the next room.'

'The thing is, we're in a great hurry—' Joannès began.

'Take it easy, they'll be in just as much of a rush as you are. Come on now, get moving.'

The two brothers went out through the communicating door, just as another pair of twins, of a different sort, appeared in the entrance.

3

The more important of the two introduced himself as Chief Inspector Senneville. The clerk sprang to his feet.

'How do you do, Chief Inspector. I'm the station clerk here. My name's Maillet.'

Senneville shook hands with him. 'You already know Inspector Delorme, I think.'

'Yes indeed. How are you, Delorme?'

'Morning, Maillet.'

'You alone?' asked Senneville.

'No, Chief Inspector. They're in the other room.'

Senneville looked at the case. 'This it?' he enquired, and flicked open the hasps.

'Oh-ho,' said Delorme. The clerk tried to master his feeling of horror.

'Left hand,' Senneville said, without emotion. 'Cut off with a single blow. You don't need to be Dr Locard to tell it wasn't the work of a surgeon.'

'Feet I've seen,' said Delorme, 'but a hand . . .'

Senneville shut the case again. 'What'll you say when you see a head?' he enquired.

'If it belongs to the character who did that, Chief, I'd say bravo.'

The clerk got his breathing back under control again and said: 'He may not be all that far away. The kid who brought this case down from Paris must surely know more than he's letting on.'

'Is he here?' Senneville asked.

'No, just his father and uncle. He stayed back home—fainted, or so they claim. 10, Rue Dumont, off the Grande-Rue'.

'You sent a man round?'

'No, I was waiting for you.'

Senneville flared up angrily. 'You out of your mind? Delorme, you take that case, we're going round there right away. Get the relatives!'

Somewhat crestfallen, the clerk went and opened the communicating door. 'Will you let me have a receipt for *that*?' he asked.

'We'll send it round.'

Joannès and Léonard stood up, in a great state of anxiety.

'Good morning, gentlemen,' Senneville said. 'The introductions can wait till later. We're going round to your house now, there's not a moment to be lost.'

'Ah, so much the better,' said Léonard 'so much the better.'

Senneville glanced at him in some surprise. Delorme had already gone out with the case. Everyone now followed him. The clerk and the sergeant were left standing there alone, ears pricked, as though a fresh catastrophe might descend on them at any moment. Through the open window they heard someone say : '10 Rue Dumont, that's just round the corner.'

Doors slammed, the engine roared into life, and the car shot off. The two of them sucked all the air they could into their cheeks, mouths closed, and then slowly blew it out.

4

No one had disappeared from the house. Dr Guerrier had come and given injections to Émilie and Jean-Marc. Émilie had never stopped crying since, while Jean-Marc had passed straight from unconsciousness to sleep. Senneville at once recovered that massive imperturbability for which he was famous throughout the region. During the short drive from the police station to the Rue Dumont, he had got a clear enough picture of the Berger brothers to make up his mind, on arrival, that their mother was the only member of the family from whom he could expect any real co-operation. Unfortunately she seemed by no means disposed to give it, simply declaring she knew nothing about the affair, in a tone which discouraged all further enquiries.

The first snag was that the Bergers had no telephone.

'Consequently,' Senneville said, 'it is of the utmost importance that your grandson should give us Mlle Sarrazin's address. My deputy will pass it on straight away—along with that case—to the appropriate department, and have Paris alerted at once—if they haven't already got on to the affair some other way.'

'Here's his room,' Grandmother said. 'Go on in.'

The shutters had been half-closed. Jean-Marc was lying on his back in his shirt-sleeves, looking deathly white. Senneville and Delorme advanced, one on each side of the bed. Grandmother, who had come in behind them, stood at its foot. Joannès and Léonard hovered in the doorway. When Senneville touched the boy's shoulder, Émilie pressed her hands together.

'Oh my God—'

Jean-Marc shot bolt upright. 'No!' he screamed. He blinked in terror at the unknown faces around him. His grandmother's crisp voice helped him to pull himself together.

'These gentlemen are from the police, my boy. They would like you to give them Mlle Sarrazin's address.'

'Yes,' Jean-Marc sobbed, 'yes. It's not possible, it's not possible—' He rubbed his eyes, grappling with the real-life nightmare that had eclipsed the sleeping one. '9A, Rue de la Ferme, Neuilly, near Paris.'

'Telephone?' Senneville asked.

'Maillot 46-79.'

'Right,' said Delorme, after he had noted these details down. 'Shall I be on my way, Chief?'

'Yes. And send me back the car.'

Delorme went out. Senneville said to Jean-Marc: 'Do you think you could get up, or shall we stay here?'

'I can get up.'

Émilie hastened to support him, and Grandmother gave him his coat. Everyone moved through to the broad daylight of the dining-room. Joannès asked, nervously: 'Could my brother or I go down and ring up the office to warn them that we'll be late? It's the St Polycarp Cloth Mills and Silk Factory.'

'Better your brother than you,' said Senneville. 'And don't go laying it on thick about the reasons.'

'No?' said Léonard. 'I mean, it's hard to justify both of us being absent—'

'Tell them you'll explain later. Anyway the papers are bound to do the job for you.'

Both twins went as white as Jean-Marc. 'The papers?'

Senneville shrugged in a resigned way and said to Jean-Marc : 'Right. Talk.'

This time it was very far from plain sailing. To tell a story full of helpfulness and good-will when one knew, now, just what was in that bag called for some courage. When he reached the dramatic dénouement Jean-Marc was on the verge of fainting again. At this point Grandmother, self-possessed as always, picked up the thread of the story. Senneville had not asked a single question.

'This cat's-eye ring,' she told him, 'belonged to my daughter-in-law here. She sent it to her son last December, so that he could give it as a New Year's present to a childhood friend of his, Mlle Augusta Chênelong, who is also a student in Paris.'

The inspector shot abruptly to his feet.

'You mean the daughter of the jeweller in the Place des Célestins? Why couldn't you have said so earlier?'

'You know her?' Joannès asked, apprehensively.

'The reason we didn't mention her,' said Grandmother, acidulously, 'is because she's not the girl involved.' Senneville sat down again. 'We regarded Jean-Marc as being engaged to this young person, and it was entirely on her own initiative that my daughter-in-law sent off this ring. She knew my grandson lacked the means to purchase even so modest a gift; and it also occurred to her that a slightly amusing jewel would perhaps be more appropriate for the only daughter of a jeweller. I take it we are to understand—' here she turned towards Jean-Marc '—that instead of offering it to Augusta, as your mother hoped, you gave it to Mlle Sarrazin?'

Despite the brutal quality of this remark, there was a certain softness in her tone, which became still more noticeable as she added : 'You recognized the hand as that of Mlle Sarrazin,

did you not? Because Augusta's are much bigger. Beautiful,
yes, but clearly bigger.'

Eyes on the ground, Jean-Marc muttered: 'Yes, I gave it
to Huguette, Mlle Sarrazin, that is . . . I wasn't seeing Augusta
any more.' He looked up at Senneville, trying to convince
him. 'There was never anything really serious between us—
childhood friends, you know—'

The Inspector said: 'Did Mlle Chênelong know this cat's-
eye was meant for her?'

'Oh, no!'

Grandmother gave a tiny *tssk!* of vexation and said: 'Yes,
Inspector, she did. A few days later we got New Year greetings from Augusta, as we did every year, but without any
reference to this ring. I told my daughter-in-law to write and
ask her about it. She didn't feel she should, so in the end I
did. I thanked Augusta for her greetings, sent her ours, and
added: "I hope you liked Jean-Marc's ring . . ." '

Jean-Marc turned and stared at his grandmother, flabber-
gasted. Senneville, who was watching him closely, said: 'And
what did the young lady reply?'

'She didn't,' Grandmother said. 'But a fortnight later, when
we got Jean-Marc's letter telling us he was engaged to Mlle
Sarrazin, we understood.'

'Did these two young ladies know one another?' Senneville
asked Jean-Marc.

'No. Not through me, anyhow.'

'Inspector,' Joannès said, in an unsteady voice, 'you don't
suppose that—'

Senneville said: 'I don't suppose anything. I listen—and
learn.' He continued with his interrogation of Jean-Marc.
'When was the last time you saw Mlle Sarrazin?'

'Sunday—yesterday, that is. About four o'clock. And everything was going fine, just fine!'

'Where?'

'At home.'

'At her parents', do you mean?'

Jean-Marc's head went back, and his body tensed as though he were having an epileptic seizure. Joannès exclaimed: 'We'd better call the doctor!'

'I don't think so,' said Senneville, who had risen to his feet, 'the fresh air will do him a world of good.'

Grandmother said, aggressively: 'Surely you aren't going to force the poor boy to go with you?'

'Not force him, madam; merely invite him. He is a key witness. Of course he's upset, I realize that: who wouldn't be in his place? And it's very tiresome to have a chill on top of everything else. But surely he would be the first person to want the affair cleared up with the least possible delay? We may have got a reply from Paris already. It's essential for us to go over any news we may have with him. And unless the murderer has—'

He made a tiny gesture that resembled the sign of the cross, though the allusion had nothing whatsoever to do with pious thoughts. It was Grandmother, however, who finished his sentence for him:—

'—carved up the entire body to get rid of it more easily?'

Émilie gave a little scream. 'Hush, Mama! Don't say such things!'

Joannès was sitting by his son, holding his hand. The seizure had only lasted a moment. Luckily, Jean-Marc seemed to have heard nothing of what was said. Grandmother said, to Joannès rather than Émilie: 'Don't blame me; it's the Inspector's fault. He has just the sort of gestures needed to console a victim's nearest and dearest.' And she imitated the pseudo-sign of the cross.

Senneville said, angrily: 'Don't presume too far on your white hairs, madam. Because you don't seem exactly choked by emotion yourself.' Then, with a return to his usual calm manner, he added: 'Monsieur Jean-Marc Berger; when you're ready.'

His confidence in the human body's natural resources was well justified. Jean-Marc rose to his feet.

'Could I possibly come with you, Chief Inspector?' Joannès asked, beseechingly. 'To take care of my son on the return journey.'

'If you like. There is a spare seat.'

'I'd like to come as well,' Grandmother said.

The Inspector carefully avoided meeting her eye. '*One* spare seat, I said; not two.'

'Oh my precious!' Emilie sobbed, hugging Jean-Marc with all her strength. 'Take your muffler with you, be sure to wrap up well!'

FOUR

In the Rue Vauban

I

THE arrival of a black police car outside the apartment
building—not to mention its departure and subsequent
return—had aroused a good deal of curiosity, some from
passers-by on the sidewalk, and rather more from the neighbours, peering from behind half-raised curtains. Senneville
told Jean-Marc to get in, and sat down beside him. Joannès
went next to the driver. Just as the car was moving off,
Léonard appeared in the doorway of Mme Piochon's dairy,
and waved to them.

Senneville said: 'Your brother doesn't seem in any great
hurry to go back up again.'

Joannès, anxious to defend his twin, said, over his shoulder:
'He probably couldn't get hold of the proper person in the
office right away, Chief Inspector. You must admit that such
matters can't be dealt with by *anybody*, especially on the
telephone.'

'Oh,' Senneville said, 'I admit it.'

The car started off at breakneck speed for the descent to the
Rhône. As they drove past the fresh greenery of Le Gros-
Caillou, only the Inspector seemed to be enjoying the view—
a panoramic sweep of thousands of roof-tops, and glittering
stretches of the Rhône. Joannès was watching the road ahead
as carefully as the driver, Jean-Marc let his tall body jolt
slackly at every bump, and every time the brakes were applied.
Down the steep hill of Saint-Sébastien, across the Place Croix-
Paquet with its hanging gardens, into the Rue du Griffon.

'Look,' Joannès told the driver, his voice faltering, 'there's the Rue Terraille! That's where my brother and I have worked for the last thirty years. In the St Polycarp Cloth Mills and Silk Factory. Thirty years!'

The driver couldn't have cared less. He switched on his siren as they entered the Rue Puits-Gaillot, not slackening speed at all, despite the traffic. In front of them, over the Pont Morand, the morning sun shone in their faces, dazzling them. Another three minutes, and they pulled up outside local Police Judiciaire headquarters in the Rue Vauban, where Superintendent Thévenet, chief of the Crime Squad, was awaiting them with the liveliest possible interest.

2

The phone-call from the Croix-Rousse police-station had immediately provoked another one, from the Rue Vauban to the Quai des Orfèvres. But to the question, 'Have you got a woman's body with the left hand cut off?' Paris returned a negative response. Then Delorme came in, with the 'bloody bag', as it came to be termed—this was at once sent down to the forensic laboratory—and Mlle Sarrazin's address. This time Superintendent Thévenet put through a personal call to his opposite number in Paris, Superintendent Picard, to give him all available information on the case. Picard had a call put through to Maillot 46-79, but got no answer. 'We'll send someone down there,' he told Thévenet. 'I'll call you back as soon as we get on to anything.'

Thévenet said: 'I may call *you* back first. I'm expecting the young man here any moment now.'

That moment, in fact, would have struck then, if the mantelpiece clock (the only decorative object in the office) had been geared to strike every sixty seconds. Instead, it was heralded by a tap on the door.

'Come in!'

Senneville came in, alone.

'They're here, Chief. The fiancé and the father.'

'Paris must be on the scene by now,' Thévenet said. 'What the hell is all this about?'

'Bloody tall story, if you ask me,' Senneville said, and gave Thévenet a brief résumé.

'Right. Have him in.'

'The father too?'

'No.'

Senneville opened the door, and poked his head into the next room. Thévenet stood up and came forward. Jean-Marc appeared, eyes starting out of his head, and Senneville closed the door behind him. Thévenet showed Jean-Marc to an armchair, and introduced himself.

'I'm Superintendent Thévenet, chief of the Crime Squad. My apologies for having to inflict this interview on you, M Berger. I can well imagine how you must be feeling.'

Jean-Marc could hardly summon up the strength to reply: 'Yes, monsieur, it's a frightful business.'

Thévenet returned to his chair, on the far side of the vast table, made a sign to Senneville to be seated, and looked at Jean-Marc.

'Let's not bother, for the moment, about the really extraordinary way in which this case came into your possession. Essentials first. You did recognize this hand as being that of your fiancée, Mlle Huguette Sarrazin, with a ring on it that you had given her?'

'Yes, monsieur.'

'We are going to put a call through to her home number. We tried just now, but there was no reply.'

Jean-Marc's breathing became heavier; it was distinctly audible.

'Would you mind clearing up one point for me? If something's happened to Mlle Sarrazin, it's only to be expected that *she* shouldn't answer the phone. But is it normal for *no one* to do so—no member of her family, not even the maid? And wouldn't you have expected them to have got on to the police themselves by yesterday afternoon or evening at the latest? The crime must have taken place quite a while before this American of yours palmed the case off on you, mustn't it?'

'Mlle Sarrazin lives—lived alone, monsieur. With a maid. But the maid always had Sunday off.'

'Alone?' A curious existence for a young girl, don't you think?'

Jean-Marc began chewing his thumbnail in such a fashion that his elbow was lifted off the arm of the chair.

'Well, the truth is—' he removed his thumb from his mouth. 'I mean, she wasn't all that young. She was about thirty-five, I think. Thirty-five or thirty-six.'

Senneville raised his eyebrows, without lifting his head from the notes he was taking.

Thévenet said: 'What about you?'

'Oh, me. I'm—'

'All right, I see from this report that you're twenty-three. Right. Senneville, would you mind putting a priority call through to Maillot? When we get through, you listen on the other line and take notes.'

Silence fell in the office while the Inspector made the call. Thévenet continued to study Jean-Marc, who sat there with his chin on his chest and his shoulders hunched, as though he were trying to make himself as small as possible, to disappear, even. The operator's voice came through the receivers: 'Maillot 46-79 ringing now, sir.'

Senneville held out one receiver to his chief. A faint voice, unquestionably a man's, said, brusquely, 'Hallo!'

The Paris operator said: 'Is that Maillot 46-79?'

The man's voice repeated this query to someone else close beside him. 'This Maillot 46-79?' A pause. 'Yes, that's right.'

The operator said: 'Go ahead, Lyons.'

'Is that Mlle Huguette Sarrazin's house?' Thévenet asked.

'And who might you be?' said the man, countering one question with another.

'Superintendent Thévenet, of the Lyons Crime Squad.'

The voice changed tone instantly. 'I beg your pardon, Superintendent. Inspector Blondel here. I'll put you on to Chief Inspector Belot.'

'You mean Belot's on this case?' Thévenet exclaimed, with delight. Senneville seemed just as pleased as his chief. Jean-Marc craned his neck forward, as though to say: Who's Belot?

'My dear Belot, good day to you,' Thévenet was saying. 'Thévenet here. A real pleasure to find *you* on this job—'

'If you'll forgive me for saying so, Superintendent,' Belot's voice replied sedately, 'my own pleasure is strictly limited to hearing your voice. For your information, the victim is indeed Mlle Sarrazin, the owner of this house, 9A Rue de la Ferme, Neuilly. She's a nasty sight at the moment, but that's only because of the chopped-off hand.'

'Where is she? In her bedroom?'

'No, on the couch in one of the drawing-rooms—she's got two of them. In her nightdress and dressing-gown, all very respectable.'

'When did it happen?'

'According to Dr Bonnetête, who got here a little while after us, somewhere between three and eight p.m. The hand was done rather later.'

'I sincerely hope so. How was it that no one got on to you before we rang up?'

'The victim lived alone, with a maid. The maid hadn't found out what had happened. She opened the door to us very casually, and only began to look surprised when she heard who we were. She told us she went out yesterday morning, as she did every Sunday, she came back from the cinema, as she did every Sunday, tiptoed up to her room so as not to wake her employer—again, as she did every Sunday. When we got there she was waiting till Mlle Sarrazin rang for her breakfast.'

'Talking about ringing,' Thévenet said, 'when I asked the exchange to call her number a little while back, there was no reply.'

'Mlle Sarrazin had a contact-breaker that she used when she wanted to sleep on without being disturbed. What struck me as rather odd was the fact that her maid had no occasion to go into the drawing-room, or indeed into any room on the ground floor. They were all intercommunicating, and she could easily have seen the victim either from the dining-room or the second drawing-room. What she claims is that she had orders never to start cleaning until her employer was awake—not even to open the shutters. That's quite possible.'

Thévenet, who had been riffling through Senneville's papers as he listened, now cocked a sharp eye at Jean-Marc.

'Look, Belot,' he said, 'would you mind asking this character when was the last time she saw Mlle Sarrazin's fiancé?'

'Hang on.'

Jean-Marc, who was still craning forward, said : 'Monsieur, I'd like to—'

But at that moment Belot came back on the line.

'Yes?' Thévenet said.

'She doesn't know about any fiancé.'

'*She doesn't know about any fiancé?*' Thévenet repeated, with heavy emphasis.

Jean-Marc's tone suddenly changed to one of outraged indignation. 'That's Gisèle, the maid! Ask her if she doesn't know M Jean-Marc Berger!'

Thévenet passed on this message, taking care to repeat the maid's Christian name. There was a confabulation at the Neuilly end of the line. Then Belot said : 'That's right; her name is Gisèle, and she does know M Jean-Marc Berger, very well—as Mlle Sarrazin's, h'm, friend.'

'Friend, eh?' Thévenet repeated. Jean-Marc shrugged. 'My

dear Belot, I get the impression that we're fated to meet again remarkably soon.'

'I'm inclined to agree with you, Superintendent.'

3

They said goodbye to one another, and rang off. Thévenet's expression (which Jean-Marc took at its face value) was now one of cheerful amiability.

'You wanted to say something to me just now?' he enquired.

'Only to put you on your guard, monsieur! This woman Gisèle is an idiot. Mlle Sarrazin never placed any real trust in her. But the way things are today, you have to take servants as they come—when you can find them. Why on earth should we have told *her* our plans? Mlle Sarrazin never needed that sort of confidante—she led a very full social life, and had masses of friends. We loved one another, we were going to get married, I swear we were! I was making this trip to see my family because of that—to discuss the wedding with them. The difference in age between us was no real obstacle. She looked so young anyway, she was so intelligent, so artistic! She loved painting, and I'm a painter—that's the one reason I went to Paris in the first place. We met at a party at the School—we danced together, and arranged to meet again, and—'

Thévenet sounded more understanding than ever as he said : 'I take it you didn't wait for your forthcoming marriage before you, ah—'

He moved all ten fingertips together two or three times without their actually touching. Jean-Marc shrugged his shoulders as though to concede this point. His angry outburst seemed to have brought him back to life. And it was now that Thévenet suddenly turned angry. He did not get into a really towering rage; his was the wrath of a headmaster doing his best to floor some recalcitrant pupil—for the boy's own good, naturally.

'Young man,' he said, 'wouldn't you agree that there's all the difference in the world between fun and games and serious relationships? That the presence of a *mutilated* corpse—'

'Oh no, no,' said Jean-Marc, as though he was going to faint again—but in fact he did not.

'—leaves you, at this moment, in a serious, not to say a tragic, position? If a boy of twenty-three is the lover of a woman of thirty-five or thirty-six, that's their business—both of you were above the age of consent, especially her. But now you come here with a lot of stuff about your future plans together when your unfortunate mistress isn't on hand to contradict you. What sort of proof can you supply?'

With exemplary fairness Senneville said: 'He sent a photo of Mlle Sarrazin to his family around Christmas or the New Year. I have it with my papers, Superintendent.'

'And it's not an old one, either,' said Jean-Marc, who was now trembling uncontrollably. 'Look at it, and you'll see just how lovely she was!'

Thévenet did so, continued to do so, but without vouchsafing any opinion on the matter.

'This is no proof that she meant to marry you,' he said at length.

'I swear that's what she wanted, monsieur.'

'*She* wanted, you said. It was *she* who wanted it—'

'So did I—so did I!'

'Are you quite certain that your main idea wasn't to make a good thing out of her generosity? Here was this woman, twelve or thirteen years older than you, with a private town house—'

'She never gave me a penny, I swear she didn't! Anyway, all you need do is check up on the sort of life I led in Paris. Try the Hôtel de Marseille in the Rue Bonaparte—it's run by a couple named Bédat, M and Mme Bédat.'

'Don't worry,' said Thévenet, 'we will. In that case, why

did you pull a fast one on your relatives with all this talk about a "young girl"? And why didn't you let them know her address?'

'I didn't keep her address from them deliberately. That was just an oversight. Anyway, they never thought of asking me for it. As for the "young girl" business—well, yes, there I did lie, I admit it. But it was the only time I did. My parents were determined to think of me as engaged to a childhood friend—'

'Mlle Augusta Chênelong,' said Senneville, 'the daughter of the jeweller in the Place des Célestins.'

Thévenet nodded to show he knew this already.

'I wrote "young girl" so they wouldn't bring every objection down on my head simultaneously,' Jean-Marc went on. 'That's why I'm here now, why I came down to Lyons, to clear the whole thing up with my family. Oh, I know, I should have written a different sort of letter. My grandmother—'

Senneville gave a little groan. Thévenet glanced at him as he put his next question to Jean-Marc. 'She the one you're most scared of?'

'Yes,' Jean-Marc said. His voice was cracking. He seemed punch-drunk with exhaustion, worry, and plain fright. 'Oh, I'm so tired, so desperately tired—my head's burning, I want to go to bed, please, Superintendent—'

'I'm sorry,' said Thévenet, impassively, 'but we really can't leave the matter there. Paris is going to ask us for every detail of how that mysterious case came into your possession.'

'I've told you everything I know about that already, monsieur, absolutely everything!'

'What do you think, Senneville?'

By way of reply the Inspector turned to Jean-Marc. There was a faint touch of brutality in his manner. 'No,' he said, 'not everything. You say you spotted the substitution of one case for the other at the Gare de Lyon in Paris, when you only just had time to catch your train?'

Jean-Marc nodded agreement.

'You expect us to believe that your American had timed

the whole thing in advance, down to the last second?'

'That's just what he did, Inspector. That's why he faked a breakdown on the *quai*, he could spin out time just as long as he wanted there—it was that *quai* after Notre-Dame, I don't know its name, before the bridge that goes to the Bastille.'

'And no witnesses?' said Senneville (who had heard the entire story in the Rue Dumont without uttering a word). 'Didn't anyone pass by while you were carrying out your repairs?'

'I didn't do any of the repair-work, Inspector, he did it all. I just gave him some light with a torch, a big torch. There were cars going by, but they were travelling fast—none of them slowed down, and it was absolutely pouring with rain. I don't know, there might be just *one* of them that noticed us —we were there from half past ten to quarter past eleven. Maybe if we published an appeal in the papers?'

This got no reaction from either of the police officers. Senneville went on: 'What about outside the Hôtel de Marseille, when he offered to come to your assistance? Nobody around then, either?'

'If he'd only arrived a couple of minutes earlier, there'd have been M Bédat, the proprietor. He'd just gone off to bed —in fact I told him to myself, because of the bad weather. This bastard must have been waiting at the end of the street, hidden in his car. I've never had any enemies, I've never done anyone a bad turn, ask anyone you like—and yet there's somebody who really had it in for me—'

Thévenet broke in again at this point. 'Generally speaking, when a person has it in for someone, it's because of something they've done to him. You know this American, don't you? Come on, you might as well admit it.'

'I swear that's not so, Superintendent! I'd never seen him before in my life! But he must have been jealous of me, there's no doubt about that. Oh, my head's splitting, for God's sake let me go to bed!'

'The victim can sleep for both of you, M Berger. Your story doesn't stand up.'

'But it's true!' Jean-Marc screamed.

With terrible composure Thévenet said: 'No. It's false.'

5

For the first time in his life since joining the St Polycarp Cloth Mills and Silk Factory as a young office-boy, Joannès found himself propped against the counter of a café, in the morning, on a working day. A café in the rue Vauban, small r, so written because Rue Vauban with a capital stood, for its sins, for local *Police Judiciaire* headquarters—whence he had just emerged alone, if one can speak of being alone while caught up in a nightmare with so large a cast of characters. Alone, without Jean-Marc. Not only had the police detained his older child and only son, the heir to his name, on the pretext that he was a key witness—why should *he* be a key witness, we discovered the contents of the case together, didn't we? And in fact it was I, Joannès, who unwrapped the fatal towel—now where was I, yes, not only had the police had the nerve to detain this poor child, but they'd forbidden his father to see him! Was that possible? Was it conceivable? A little more and he would have asked the question out loud, indeed he must actually have articulated some word, 'forbidden' probably, in such a way that it was audible, since the café-owner was staring at him open-mouthed. Begging and pleading had got him nowhere. Better, or rather worse, still, when he had gone down the stairs and was going across the entrance-hall he heard two policemen talking on his left; one was saying to the other: 'They've just got a new tenant for the brig. A nasty business . . .' There couldn't be two 'nasty businesses' that turned up in the same place at the same time. And Joannès knew very well what the 'brig' was: the cell, much like a wild beast's cage, that stood in the corner of every

police-station. Would Jean-Marc be shut up in *that*, like a
dangerous lunatic or zoological specimen? The whole thing
was so appalling that he had to neutralize it, right away, by
doing something more appalling still : stopping for a drink
in a café during the morning of a working day. And now,
although the tiny glass of cognac he was holding did not in
any way prejudice his dignified appearance, the grey gloves
and black suit and hat—anyway he had only just moistened
his lips with it, though he had been at the bar for at least ten
minutes—Joannès realized that by attempting to cancel out
these two appalling happenings he had, in fact, merely piled
one on top of the other, indeed multiplied one by the other
to produce a quite inconceivable catastrophe. The Chief
Cashier of the St Polycarp Cloth Mills and Silk Factory standing solo at a bar at ten o'clock on a Monday morning, and his
son detained by the police, let's not mince our words, under
suspicion, locked up, *arrested*! With all the attendant horrors
of that severed hand, and the case, and the ring. What on
earth could they have discovered? He'd asked them : not a
word. He was the boy's father, and no one would tell him a
thing. And tomorrow, thousands of people in Lyons, *millions*
of people throughout France, would pick up their papers and
read all about it. What's more, either he or Léonard would
have to go and buy a paper too, like everyone else, to learn
as much as they did. And before that, he'd have to go back
home, and face the weeping, hysterical Émilie, and Grandmother's cutting contempt, and find some way of preventing
Marie-Louise being besmirched by this filthy business—but
how? Even Léonard wouldn't be able to console her. Despite
the fact that they were twins, they seldom reacted to anything
in the same way, they weren't identical. Well aware that his
train of thought was verging on the blasphemous, he began
to question the idea of Divine Goodness. He thought : How
can a whole lifetime of hard work and respectability suddenly
be clouded by scandal in such a fashion? He choked with
vexation, put down the glass, said 'How much?', paid, and

went out without finishing his drink. This final oddity was not lost on the regulars, who had been watching him avidly.

As he scooped up the money, the café-owner murmured: 'There goes another one who's just been having a session round the corner.'

FIVE

Touches of local colour

I

In Paris, or rather out at Neuilly, Belot had just hung up after his highly interesting conversation with Thévenet. In order to fix it in his memory, he did not, for the moment, return his gaze to Gisèle, who was standing there in front of him. The location of the white telephone, on a pedestal table —an antique, like all the rest of the furniture, and undoubtedly of considerable value—was responsible for his present position, sunk deep in an easy chair, almost in the middle of the second drawing-room (the second, that is, by way of distinction from the one where the victim still lay, and in which a squad from Criminal Records was at work). From this vantage-point, Belot studied the walls. Van Goghs, nothing but Van Goghs, a whole raft of them. You might not know anything very much about painting, but Van Gogh was something special. There had been one—a reproduction, of course—in the Vicomte de Laeken's room at the Villas Kléber.* It tactfully camouflaged the private safe that was placed in every bedroom for the guests' benefit. *Genuine* Van Goghs were in no need of safes behind them, stuffed with deeds, banknotes or pearls : each one represented a fortune as it stood. How big a fortune? Enormous, surely, when they were all added together : the experts could be left to make a detailed estimate. The setting (an apt term in the circumstances) did nothing to contradict such a supposition. An absolute jewel of a house, Belot reflected, with its freestone blocks, its balustrated rooftop

* See *The Passenger on the U.*

70

terrace, done in Trianon style—Neuilly tended to go in for
Trianon architecture—and far bigger inside than it looked
from the street. Chequered black and white marble flooring in
the lobby. The same motif here, but transposed into heavy
pile carpeting, a pleasure to walk on. Only one servant to
take care of all this? Belot brought his mind back to Gisèle.
Gisèle : the title of a ballet. He'd never seen it, but he remembered the posters, as he remembered everything else he read, it
was a special gift, that was how he came to be regarded as
reasonably civilized, for a policeman. However, there was
nothing of the dancer about *this* Gisèle. She was sturdily built,
stood squarely on her feet, a touch of the farm-girl about her,
though she had well-kept hands and nails. *Titre de ballet,* he
thought, *titre de balai.* The dancer with the broom. Heavens, I
haven't drawn the line at *anything* for quite a while now. It
was true that since that morning he had felt remarkably cheerful. For the first time he had agreed to let his godson, Simon
Rivière, work on a case with him. Simon's father, who had
been killed in action, was one of his two best friends, the other
still being Picard. Simon himself had been attached to the
Crime Squad for a year now; and though, naturally, he had
never allowed himself to pull any strings in that direction, he
had always dreamed of one day working with his godfather.
For this two conditions were essential. They both had to be
available at the same time, and preferably when some rather
unusual case was coming up. This business of the severed hand
had justified his hopes. At the moment Simon was examining
the upper floors, and Blondel the garden. Belot himself sat
watching Gisèle, who didn't bat an eyelid.

'Please sit down, Mlle Gisèle.'

She sat on the edge of a chair.

'After everything that's happened,' she said, '*Monsieur
l'inspecteur* is perfectly at liberty to call me plain Gisèle.'

'By the same token,' Belot replied, 'you don't need to refer
to me in the third person.'

'Very well, Inspector.' She studied her hands, which were

resting on her thighs. 'I'd never have thought that losing an employer could shake me so.'

'You have to admit that you didn't lose this one in exactly a commonplace manner.'

Always alert to the obvious, Gisèle said: 'That's a fact.'

'Have you been with Mlle Sarrazin for a long time?'

'Heavens, no; three or four weeks.'

'No longer than that?'

'That's right, Inspector. And I wasn't counting on staying here for ever, either.'

'Why not, pray?'

'The employment agency warned me.'

'Which one?'

'The Le Bellec Agency, at Les Ternes.'

'I know it. A respectable firm.'

'Thank you, monsieur.'

'And what sort of warning did the Le Bellec Agency give you?'

'They told me, "I shouldn't count on a steady job at Mlle Sarrazin's", that's what they said. "Two months is the most anyone sticks it", they said. "Mlle Sarrazin is *very* temperamental". I'm sorry to be talking about Mademoiselle this way after what's happened, but I'm just repeating what I was told. They even said "She enjoys changing her maid the whole time".'

'And you took the job despite all that?'

Gisèle assumed an air of resignation so ill-suited to her natural appearance that it made her look positively artful.

'When you're out of a job—' She shrugged. 'My old employers had been forced to cut down their expenses. They decided they could only afford a daily woman.'

Belot got out his notebook and a propelling pencil.

'Would you mind telling me their names?'

'Why on earth shouldn't I? I spent five and a half years

with them, they gave me one of those certificates at the end
of it. M and Mme Lecour, 31 Rue de Verneuil.'

'Ah, the chemist's.'

Gisèle's expression brightened. 'Are you from that neighbourhood, then?' she asked.

Belot pulled a self-deprecating face to indicate that he
wasn't, and Gisèle went on: 'I have to admit it, though,
Mademoiselle paid good money. In two months with her
you'd have as much as you would in six with anyone else.'

'And *did* you find her temperamental?'

'On the contrary! No one could have been more straightforward. Once she'd said anything, that was that. And never
a cross word, never even raised her voice.'

'Did she entertain a lot?'

'Never to meals—that's the main thing as far as a maid's
concerned. Anyway, I didn't deal with the top of the house
—Mademoiselle kept the key.'

'Where's your room?'

'On the first floor. A lovely room, too, not the kind you'd
expect anyone to put a servant in.'

They both turned simultaneously in the direction of the
second *salon*, where the bustle and talk had suddenly changed
its tone. Through a vast communicating entrance, originally
designed for a double glass door—another touch of the
Trianon—but now left open, Belot and Gisèle could see the
Criminal Records men packing up their cameras and other
equipment. From the right-hand side of the entry there pro-
truded the end of a chaise-longue, on which lay one tiny foot,
still wearing an elegant Oriental mule.

'That's the lot, Chief,' one of the men said to Belot. 'You
can wheel her away now.'

'Thanks. Tell the ambulance will you?'

Belot got up, saying to Gisèle as he did so: 'You stay where
you are.' He wanted to take one last look at the victim before
she finally vanished, finally lost the pose which the cameras
had frozen in a series of snapshots. One never could tell what

a final scrutiny might reveal. This one, however, merely
served to confirm its predecessors. She must have fallen back-
wards after receiving the blow on her neck, which had hardly
bled at all. Bonnetête's verdict (provisional, until Dampierre
had done the autopsy) was: 'Death instantaneous. Weapon
employed either a knife, dagger, or paper-cutter, not a razor.
An instrument with a sharp point *and* a cutting edge.' Which,
by the bye, had not yet been found, and possibly never would
be, it being far easier to remove a knife than a hatchet. Ah
yes. The hatchet.

'Any finger-prints on the hatchet?' Belot enquired, without
addressing anyone in particular.

Old Nourry, whose job this was, said: 'Not a bloody trace.
Just what you'd expect.'

'Not even Gisèle's?'

The hatchet, or chopper to be more precise, was in the
kitchen. Gisèle had testified that she used it to split kindling.

'Not a trace,' Nourry repeated. 'Cleaned, wiped, polished,
like a bloody fireman's axe!'

A pretty woman's wrist is not very thick. One blow had
sufficed here, too. She had fallen in such a way that the whole
of her forearm—as now—was resting on the ground. All that
was needed was a little strength—and nerve. This was where
the horror came in. Bonnetête had been unable to say exactly
how long after the neck-wound this act of mutilation had
taken place. Had the murderer remained in the house with
the dead woman for company? Or had he had a sudden
brain-wave about the 'friend', the severed hand, and the case,
and come back to carry this delightful scheme out? Yes: she
had been an attractive woman. Very attractive.

'She looks better here,' said Simon, who had come in without Belot noticing, and was now standing at his elbow. 'I
found this photo in her room.'

Belot looked, and saw a ravishing figure in a swimsuit, posed
on some beach. At this moment the white-clad ambulance
men came in, carrying a stretcher.

'All right,' he told them, 'you can remove the body.' He turned back to Simon. 'I'll have a look at that later,' he said. 'Anything interesting upstairs?'

'I don't think so.'

'Right. Just let me finish off here. Oh, go and find Blondel while you're at it; I rather fancy he's got lost somewhere in the garden.'

2

Gisèle had not budged from her chair. Since all the traffic through the other room went by way of the French windows, no one disturbed the peaceful atmosphere still prevailing in this one. Belot slumped back into his easy chair.

'We were discussing Mlle Sarrazin's visitors,' he said.

'That's right, Inspector.'

Her voice was always deliberate, always the same. Masterly self-control or sheer vacuity?

'Did you see any of her family?'

'No. Nobody.'

'Did she have any?'

'I don't know.'

'Well, who did come here?'

'Dealers who came to show her pictures.'

'Van Goghs?'

'You know him?'

'Who doesn't?'

'Mind you, there are others too—put away. Impressionists, she called them. But Van Gogh was her real passion. She told me her collection was envied all over the world!'

'Did she sell any?'

Gisèle could not help smiling: this question clearly struck her as absurd.

'No, why should she, she *bought* them! Those two down the end there—she got them while I was here.'

'What about men-friends? Did Mlle Sarrazin have men-friends?'

Gisèle seemed shocked. 'Really, Inspector! She only had one.'

'I wasn't talking of lovers,' Belot said.

'Oh I see, I'm sorry, I thought you were. If you're thinking of just friends, no, I never saw any here. Ladies, yes; she used to have them in for tea. But the evenings were another matter. Every night by ten o'clock I was in my room. Mademoiselle told me, "Look, Gisèle, if you hear someone ring when you're in your room, don't bother to answer it. If it's someone I'm expecting, I'll let them in myself. If it isn't, they can ring as long as they like, but you won't catch me opening the front door". Neuilly's a rather lonely place, I must say.'

'Did you ever hear anyone ring?'

'Only once.'

'Did Mlle Sarrazin open the door?'

'I'm pretty sure I heard the click of the latch. There's an electric button in the hall, you can open it from there, without going out.'

'Did you see the visitor? Was it a man or a woman?'

'Look, Inspector, I'd have had to get up for that. I'd already gone to bed. No, I said to myself, "that's her boy-friend".'

'All right, then,' said Belot, crossing one leg over the other, 'let's have a word or two about him. This fellow Jean-Marc Berger.'

The expression she had assumed during Belot's phone-call from Lyons now reappeared.

'It doesn't look as though you cared for him particularly,' Belot said.

She at once became stiff and distant again. 'It wasn't my place to like him or not like him,' she said.

'Did he come often?'

'Yes.'

'Did Mlle Sarrazin show a lot of interest in him?'

'What do you mean?'

'Did she love him a lot?'

'I suppose so. She wasn't the sort to chat about her private life to servants.'

'How old is he?'

Gisèle said she didn't know. 'Twenty-two, maybe. Certainly not more than twenty-five.'

Belot whistled softly. 'As young as that? She was at least thirty-five, right?'

'Thirty-six, going on thirty-seven. When you reach that age, these things happen.'

'And how old are you, Gisèle?'

Gisèle looked him straight in the eye. 'Thirty-five,' she said. 'But believe me, Inspector, those things haven't ever happened to *me*.'

'I wasn't asking you anything of the sort.'

She looked away and said, through her teeth : 'Maybe not, but you shouldn't take me for a bigger fool than I am.'

'Relax,' he said, in a voice poised half-way between threat and reassurance. 'What was this boy Berger like? The friendly sort?'

'If you mean did he tip me, the way people do sometimes, no, never. Anyway he had no real call to. But he was always polite.'

'Did they go out together?'

'From here? During the daytime? Never. Still, since Mademoiselle had her little car, and he didn't own one, she might have gone and picked him up sometimes.'

'Very likely. You told me just now that when you heard the click of the latch one night you thought it might be him. Didn't he have a key, then?'

'No, monsieur. Neither he nor anyone else.'

'Who else might have been expected to have one?'

'Why, me, of course. It's the first job I've ever had where I didn't get a key. When I went shopping in the morning, Mademoiselle used to let me in herself.'

'Yet you must have got in by yourself last night. She couldn't have let you in then.'

'That's right, she gave me a key on Sundays. Also any time I went out the same time as she did, and expected to be back earlier.'

Belot was silent for a moment. Then he said : 'What it boils down to is, she didn't mind letting you have a key when she wasn't there. It was when she was in the house that she didn't want you bursting in on her unexpectedly. Not only you, either; even her boy-friend.'

'Except on Sundays.'

'Right. Except on Sundays. She was scared of something or somebody during the week that she wasn't scared of on Sunday. And it was on a Sunday that someone murdered her.'

Gisèle said, under her breath : 'Yes, monsieur.'

'Do you have any suspicions?'

She replied, mildly enough : 'How could I ? I wasn't there.'

Belot ignored this too-facile reply as though he had never heard it.

'One last question for now, Gisèle. Did Mlle Sarrazin always wear her cat's eye ring on her left hand?'

'Her what?'

'Cat's-eye. It's the name of a semi-precious stone. I'm like you : wouldn't know one if I saw it.'

Somewhat contemptuously Gisèle replied : 'Yes, yes, she did always wear it. But sometimes—' her eye shone as she spoke '—sometimes she'd wear a big diamond ring on the other hand, a real whopper. Very beautiful, it was.' She frowned. 'Do you know if they've found that diamond?'

'I've no idea. Thanks, Gisèle. You can go back to your kitchen now.'

Simon and Blondel had been waiting for the past few minutes in the other room, where Belot now joined them.

'Well, lambkins?' He cocked an eye at the divan. 'She who loved colours so much. That red stain on the yellow satin, and the other one on the carpet right in the middle of a white square, I find that terribly sad . . . Come on, let's go into the library.'

3

First, they made their way through the dining-room: glass cases crammed with china and silverware, and still more pictures, still more Van Goghs. The library was undecorated, save for shelf upon shelf of antique books, ranging from floor to ceiling. It certainly went back to Sarrazin *père*, if not to an earlier generation still. They all drew up chairs round one corner of the big empty table which occupied the centre of the room. Simon had a smart handbag and a whole pile of papers, which he dumped in front of him. Belot nodded interrogatively to Blondel.

'Went through the garden with a fine-tooth comb,' the latter said. 'It's one of those rare houses that faces right on the road but has a good bit of ground at the back. Well looked after, too, obviously by a gardener. There's even a statue—look, you can see it from here. Diana, I fancy.'

'Diana, the Huntress,' said Simon.

'The things you know,' said Belot.

'We try to do you proud, Chief,' Blondel said, quite seriously.

'I'd have been better pleased if you'd found the knife or dagger or paper-cutter or whatever the hell it was, the "instrument of the crime", as they say. Preferably with a clear set of finger-prints left on it by some nice co-operative murderer. In Diana's quiver, let's say—why not?'

Blondel said, regretfully: 'The sculptor didn't bother to hollow the damn thing out. Not a thing in the garage, either, except for her little runabout and the usual tools and junk. All so clean, too—not a dirty rag or empty petrol can in sight! This is my first murder case when the victim was a single woman—are they all like that?'

'In Neuilly, yes,' said Belot. 'I wouldn't be so sure about somewhere like Ménilmontant. All right, I'd agree that when someone's that finicky, it gives you a line on their general character. Finished?'

'Sure. That's the lot.'

'Next thing to go into is the lady's financial position. I see you've got her cheque-book there in that pile of stuff—'

'Here,' Simon said. It was a private bank, renowned in the world of business. Belot passed the cheque-book over to Blondel.

'Usual routine,' he said. 'If there are any snags, have a word with Sergeant Gaillardet.' Blondel took himself off.

'Now then, Simon. What about that photograph you showed me?'

Simon picked out a white rectangle from his pile of papers and turned it over.

'It was on her mantelpiece, all by itself.'

'On *her* mantelpiece?' Belot said, his eyes taking in the trim, healthy, muscular body. Almost a sporting type, he thought.

'That's right, in her bedroom. Which she didn't share with anyone, to judge from the width of the bed.'

'Yes, I noticed that. That's what's so unexpected. What do they call it when someone keeps a photograph of themselves— half naked too—where they can always see it?'

'Narcissism.'

'Right. She was a pretty weird character, was Mlle Sarrazin. Now: what about all the mess and disorder? Was the murderer a thief, or what?'

'I'd put it a bit differently. He must have stolen something —but what was he after? Every drawer in the bedroom's been turned upside down, the desk's been rifled, so has the bedside table. There are things scattered all over the floor— jewels, papers, articles of clothing. After the Records boys were through, I had a go myself.'

'Jewels, you said?'

'A casket. Contents scattered all over.'

'You didn't by any chance find a ring with a big diamond, a really big one?'

'Sure, several. And bracelets, and necklaces.'

'You've locked them up again, I hope.'

Simon took a key from his pocket and handed it to Belot, who said: 'We'll leave a man here, anyway. What about the other rooms?'

'Apart from the maid's room they're all unoccupied. Genuinely unoccupied, for years now I should think. That's obvious the moment you look at them. When I think of the people who can't find so much as a dog-kennel—'

'Well, there are compensations. At least no one murders them. What's on the second floor?'

'An attic. Attics. Blondel would say he'd never seen cleaner attics in his life, either. Not one speck of dust. But a whole mass of trunks and suitcases and clobber of that sort, anything that had outlived its usefulness at some stage or other.'

'What about this bag you've got here?'

'Any pretty woman's bits and pieces. Appointments-book— nothing on either Saturday or Sunday. Driving licence, etcetera. A bunch of keys, with tags—all safety-keys. I've checked up on the lot of them: front door, outer door, garage, car. With a St Christopher as insurance against accidents. Obviously it only works when you're on the road.'

He talks like me, Belot thought to himself. His mother was right when she said she didn't want me influencing the boy. After his father died, he'd never have thought of joining the police force if it hadn't been for me. And I didn't *consciously* push him in that direction. Still, now that he's done it, I can't help being very pleased.

4

'Come in, M Belot,' said Picard, from behind his desk. This was Superintendent Picard, head of the Special Branch, also

known as the Crime Squad, and recruited exclusively from
first-class officers. Of these, by common consent, the most
distinguished was the man who now entered Picard's office.
They were both the same age, forty-four, but Belot was the
more sedate of the two.

'Come in,' Picard repeated. 'Sit down. Honour me with
your company. I've just been listening to a panegyric about
you on the phone. For five whole minutes, too—an eternity!'

'From whom?' Belot enquired.

'Ah-ha! Curious, are we? Truflot, let the Chief Inspector
have that transcript of the conversation.'

'Here you are, sir,' Truflot said. He was the perfect clerk,
famous throughout the building for his bald cranium, his
efficiency, and his patience.

'The source,' Picard said, 'is Superintendent Thévenet, of
Lyons.'

'I had him on the phone just now,' Belot said.

'So he informed me,' Picard observed, with emphasis. '*You*
never tell me a single damn thing.'

Belot's patience almost rivalled that of Truflot. 'Has Blondel
showed up yet?' he asked.

'Yes, and so have all the others. Unfortunately, it's always
you I expect to provide enlightenment—although on this
occasion the light seems to have come from down south! Read
that—no no, don't go, I'm not expecting anyone, and we'll
have to face the reporters pretty soon. Just skip the compli-
ments.'

Belot skimmed through the opening part of the conversation, which was, in point of fact, reasonably brief. Then he
began to read seriously. The transcript ran as follows:—

THÉVENET: If Paris has put Belot on to the Sarrazin
affair, you must take it pretty seriously up there in Paris.

PICARD: Don't you take it seriously in Lyons?

THÉVENET: As a murder, yes, of course. But as a mystery
—well, it seems to me we're beginning to see daylight
already.

PICARD: Really?

THÉVENET: This story about the suitcase—it just doesn't stand up, for God's sake. I grilled the boy every which way for half an hour. He just kept repeating the same old patter like an automaton, and without the slightest difficulty: no surprise about that, it's childishly simple. Whereas all his other statements either sound false, bizarre, or too damn cut and dried. His relationship with the victim, the difference in their ages, the difference in background, all these demonstrations of passion—

PICARD: So your conclusion is—

THÉVENET: I was just coming to that. I *believe* that this character Jean-Marc Berger, having murdered his mistress, cut off her hand *himself*, and put it in that case *himself*, together with her Chinese dressing-gown. He could either have bought the case somewhere, or have stolen it from a cloakroom, that isn't important. *I believe* that he quite deliberately made up his mind to open the case in front of his assembled family. All right, it's outrageous. But just *because* it's so outrageous, any other explanation would seem more likely: substitution, vengeance, jealousy, what you will. What it comes down to is this: the kid's line of reasoning was: 'No one will believe me vicious or crazy enough to have pulled off so monstrous a trick.' Well? What d'you think?

PICARD: I find what you have to say extremely interesting. When do you reckon on passing him over to us?

THÉVENET: Unfortunately, I haven't got two inspectors to spare as escort just now. One, at the outside.

PICARD: If I get agreement from the Sûreté, you can have one of mine by tomorrow morning.

THÉVENET: I wouldn't presume to give you a piece of advice, but—

PICARD: —you reckon that if Belot could come down in person, he'd be able to sort things out on the spot, eh?

THÉVENET: Precisely!

Belot ran his eye over the rest of the discussion. It was mostly

concerned with food—local dishes such as *quenelles Nantua*
and *poulardes demi-deuil*.

'Well?' Picard said.

'If you don't mind fixing the papers—'

'Truflot! Are the Chief Inspector's papers ready?'

'I have them here, sir.'

Belot merely grinned at Picard by way of thanks. 'I'll leave
this evening,' he said. 'Would you mind sending someone to
relieve Simon at the Rue de la Ferme?'

'Truflot?'

'Yes, sir. Either Toussaint or Sergeant Malicorne are available.'

'Send Toussaint. Now, talk.'

Late that afternoon, when Belot was once more back in
Picard's office, Dampierre, the lively Director of the Institute
of Forensic Medicine, came round in person to deliver the
results of his autopsy.

'We don't often have the honour, Doctor,' Picard said.

'If it comes to that, you're hardly dropping in on me every
day of the week. But this lot today was a connoisseur's piece.
Oh, I don't mean the severed hand, that was done either in
a furious temper, or by a plain sadistic maniac for the fun of
it. The chopper you picked up was the weapon that did it,
all right. When Bonnetête called me up he expressed surprise
at the amount of blood produced by a post-mortem mutilation.
But if it happens to be made in a hypostatic area, bleeding
can go on for several hours. By that I mean—'

Picard and Belot both stopped him, with a simultaneous
and identical gesture.

'We have been your devoted and enthusiastic readers for
years,' Picard said. 'Your vocabulary no longer holds any
secrets as far as we are concerned.'

Dampierre was not in the habit of tolerating interruptions.

'By that I mean, in the present case, that a dangling arm
provides ideal conditions. In short, nothing of any special

interest. You'll find the necessary details in my report. If it had only been that, I wouldn't have bothered to climb all these flights of stairs. The wound in the nape of the neck, though, that's quite another matter. Death almost instantaneous. Blow placed with exquisite precision. Well, this dredged up from the depths of my memory, or my area of oblivion, take your choice, a perfectly delectable phrase that we learnt as medical students, almost the first time we were put to work on a dissecting-table. Like many others of the sort, it originated with Père Farabeuf. You know Farabeuf?'

'*You* know Farabeuf?' Picard asked Belot. Belot shook his head. 'No, Doctor, we don't know Farabeuf. You never mentioned him in any of your reports.'

'He isn't mentioned in this one either, they'd say I was being flippant. Hence my presence now. Well: the sharp-pointed object the criminal employed—I suspect a paper-knife, you'll see my reasons—penetrated between two vertebrae, the seventh cervical and the first dorsal, at the same time severing two arteries, the vertebral and the transverse cervical. And do you know what Farabeuf christened this minute area? No? *Le carrefour du poignard jaloux*—the spot for the jealous dagger.'

SIX

Augusta

I

BELOT had visited Lyons on three occasions during the
course of his professional career. He found the town itself
admirable, while his Lyonnais colleagues were very much to
his taste : reserved at first, with a coolness that might pass for
hostility, or at least for distrust. Then, when they got to know
one another better, expressions would relax, the conversation
would lighten, and they would work together easily, on a
good and solid footing. There were some, however, who
alleged that this optimistic attitude was merely occasioned
by the personal relationships that Belot developed wherever
he went. To which he would reply : 'That makes it your fault,
then; so much the worse for you.'

He had had dinner in the restaurant-car on the train. It
was already dark, and quite late by the time he arrived. Nevertheless, once he had checked at the Station Hotel to make
sure the room he had reserved was in fact available, he went
round to the Rue Vauban that same evening. He would spend
the following day, Tuesday, making on-the-spot enquiries, but
he did not intend to miss the night train back. By Wednesday
morning at the latest he was determined to be in the Quai
des Orfèvres once more.

Belot had an innate liking for solitude, provided that it was
filled, constantly, by his professional activities. As a result he
always tended to forget, when making his plans, that he might
be expected or met. As he walked through the barrier he was
surprised to see Senneville, one of his opposite numbers

in Lyons, standing there with a broad smile on his face.

'I was the first person on this job this morning,' Senneville told him. 'And three cheers for severed hands if they give me the chance to shake yours.'

'You talk just like a book,' said Belot. 'Actually, I'm delighted to see you again, too. Anything new since our lords and masters were on the phone earlier?'

'The quack gave that young man a going over.'

'Uh-huh. Nervous collapse?'

'We had that after he opened the case! But he was moaning about having caught a nasty chill in Paris.'

'So what was it?'

Senneville shrugged. 'A nasty chill,' he said. 'Which requires neither hospitalization nor treatment in the infirmary.'

He had his own personal car with him. 'I'm not on duty,' he told Belot. 'I was hoping you'd come home and have a bite to eat with us—my kids think you're just terrific, the tops.' He used a piece of Lyons slang, *de première bourre*, to indicate the degree of his sons' admiration; Belot found the phrase somehow unexpected coming from a professional colleague.

On the way between Perrache and the Rue Vauban Senneville gave Belot a run-down on the entire Berger family, including Grandmother, and Jean-Marc himself, whom Superintendent Thévenet—'not without reason', Senneville added—regarded as his number one suspect.

'For the time being, however,' Belot said, 'he's still only a witness in the eyes of the law, so I can go and have a chat with him right away, and no nonsense about infringing a defendant's privileges.'

Jean-Marc was asleep in his cell, mouth open because of his blocked-up nose, breathing heavily and noisily, fully dressed still except for his coat and muffler. The heating was turned on full blast. A policeman opened the cell door, and produced exactly the same reactions as Jean-Marc had evinced in similar circumstances that morning: a cry of 'No!' and a wild, frightened stare. The first person he saw this time was Belot: another stranger.

'Get up and come with us,' Senneville said.

He led the way, and Belot brought up the rear, one eye on the shadowy young figure between them. He thought: Most policemen think they've given you all the facts about a suspect when they haven't breathed one single word about his appearance. This boy's naturally sensitive and elegant. He bears not the faintest resemblance to the Berger family as Senneville just described it to me. Even that air of having been condemned to death, which rousing someone unceremoniously out of their first sleep always seems to induce, can't really eclipse the essential charm and pleasantness of his face. When a student of humble family finds favour with a rich woman much older than he is, there's always that to be reckoned with *at first*. And who gets the most out of it later only time can tell.

When the three of them were seated in an empty office, Belot said: 'I've come to take you back to Paris.'

Jean-Marc seemed both crushed and desperate, like some exhausted animal finally brought to bay. He tried to shout, but scarcely had the strength to whimper: 'You've no right to do that!'

'To do what?' asked Belot, without animosity.

'To keep me shut up like a wild beast! On the contrary, after what's happened to me you should rather—'

'What has happened to you, laddie?'

The tone, no less than the question, took Jean-Marc off his guard. Dumbfounded, he gasped: 'But . . . but . . . the case! that severed hand! My girl's—my girl's—' He burst into sobs. 'You don't understand! Nobody understands!'

'That's exactly why I've come to fetch you,' Belot said. 'The whole of this affair, except for the actual opening of the case, took place in Paris. It is in Paris, and only in Paris, that we have a chance of clearing up this appalling business—with you available to guide us in our enquiries.'

The sobs died away, and Jean-Marc looked at Belot out of the corner of his eye.

'Yes, I see, sir. Then I'm not being treated as a—' He dared not even pronounce the word. 'We're leaving tonight?'

'Tomorrow.'

'Can't I spend the night at home?'

Belot got up; so did Jean-Marc, as though drawn towards him. Senneville watched this double movement in some perplexity.

'Out of the question,' Belot said. 'It's the Press, you see. These journalists won't leave anyone alone, they're absolutely ruthless. You'll be far more peaceful here.'

'The Press,' Jean-Marc repeated thoughtfully. 'Ah yes, I see. Right.' And followed the policeman without another word. The two detectives went back to their car.

'I suppose it's not for me to say,' Senneville remarked, 'but I'll say it just the same. Man, have you got a way with you! Coming round for a drink?'

'I'd rather have a good cup of coffee,' Belot said. 'I can't sleep without a really strong coffee, the stronger the better.'

2

He might not be able to sleep without coffee, but he could always wake up exactly when he wanted. Dawn found him in the Perrache station buffet, dunking a perfect croissant in a liquid which tasted a good deal less pleasant than the one he had been given the night before, and carefully reading the front page of the local dailies, on which the mystery of the severed hand with the cat's-eye ring was given full treatment —as was only to be expected, seeing it was here that the mystery had come to light in the first place. It was Mme Berger senior who had undertaken the task of putting the journalists in the picture. She had told her tale with a cold and detailed lucidity, rather in the style of Mérimée. Mme

Joannès Berger, the young man's mother, had remained in-communicado. Nevertheless they printed her picture—after all, the cat's-eye was hers—but no one mentioned the name of its true intended recipient. There was, of course, a photo of Mlle Sarrazin, taken at a Bagatelle garden-party, and another one, in close-up, of Jean-Marc. This last was about two years old, and very flattering. It made him look every inch the artist, though the expression was neutral. As was to be expected, the police, both in Lyons and in Paris, while furnish-ing all essential information concerning the victim, had not advanced any theories as to the identity of the murderer. The Rue Vauban made it clear that they were not interrogating the principal witness *in situ*, while the Quai des Orfèvres expected him back in Paris, at any time. There was much speculation about revenge, but not a word about the 'brig' where Jean-Marc had been detained. As to the father and uncle, it had proved impossible to get anywhere near them. They had returned, after lunch, to the St Polycarp Cloth Mills and Silk Factory, the centenary of which had recently formed the occasion for a most impressive ceremony. The head of the firm, M Couzon, who always maintained excellent Press relations, had undertaken to receive the reporters in person. 'Gentlemen,' he told them, 'I beg you to spare the feelings of two most excellent men, two model employees. The shattering tragedy which has descended on their heads through the misfortunes of this unhappy boy has not kept them from their daily toil. The mystery will one day he explained—everything in life has an explanation—and when that day comes, as the head of this firm (the watchwords of which are Honour and Loyalty) I give you my solemn word that I will summon you myself, and allow you to communicate with the Berger brothers as freely and for as long as you may desire.'

Well, Belot thought, there's one character I don't need to interview, anyhow. Senneville had told him that the St Poly-carp, etc., etc. started work at eight-thirty. It was therefore about three-quarters of an hour earlier that he rang the door-bell in the Rue Dumont. A quavering male voice said, from behind the door : 'Who's there?'

'I beg your pardon, monsieur, but I've just arrived from Paris. I'm a Chief Inspector from the *Police Judiciaire*.'

The door at once swung wide open, to reveal a small, shadowy figure with a ravaged face : this was Léonard. He stared at Belot as though he were the Messiah.

'You've arrested the murderer?' he asked.

Two more tense faces, those of Émilie and Joannès, now swam forward from the dining-room. The light streaming in through the dining-room door only reached as far as the hall, and in any case lay behind them. The third face to appear, that of the famous grandmother, revealed, first and foremost, an expression of intense curiosity.

'I'm afraid not,' Belot said. He took a step forward. 'May I come in?' he asked.

'But of course,' said the wretched Joannès. 'Please do.'

He had aged ten years since the previous day, though he had not had time to lose the appropriate amount of weight. Émilie had cried herself to a standstill. She looked dazed, and her lower jaw kept trembling incessantly. She was slopping about in an old dressing-gown. Neither of the brothers had put his collar on yet. Only Grandmother was impeccably groomed, even at this early hour.

'From Paris, just think of that!' said Joannès. 'You can stick up for Lyons as much as you like, and other things being equal we wouldn't dream of going anywhere else; but Paris, well, it's still the capital! This way, Inspector—'

'Chief Inspector,' said Léonard. '*Chief* Inspector.'

The table was covered with coffee-cups and other breakfast things. Joannès stretched out an arm towards this intimate domestic scene.

'Just like yesterday,' he murmured, 'exactly like yesterday.'

'But without Jean-Marc,' said Émilie, seemingly indifferent through the force of her distress.

'And without the case,' added Grandmother. 'When you tot

it up, that makes a lot of difference, one way and another. I suppose we should ask you to take a seat?'

'You are too kind, *madame*,' said Belot; and did so.

She stared at him without speaking for a moment, and then said, in the same crisp voice: 'We should introduce ourselves too. I, obviously, am the boy's grandmother. This is his mother. His father. His uncle. My granddaughter has been spending the night with some kind neighbours. As for my grandson, no one has had the common decency to give us any information about him whatsoever.'

At each of these phrases the twins' eyes had their work cut out, first observing their utterance from between Grandmother's thin lips, and then immediately turning to see what effect they had on the Inspector's expression. But Belot merely said: 'Your coffee must be getting cold, *madame*. Please don't let my presence cause any embarrassment to you. Your grandson is going on as well as could be desired. The doctor examined him yesterday evening because of his chill. There is no infection either of the lungs or of the bronchial tubes.

'Thank God for that,' said Émilie.

'Furthermore,' Belot went on, 'he quite understands that we must protect him from, ah, unhealthy public curiosity. I have come down to escort him back to Paris. His presence there is indispensable.'

'Justice takes every possible precaution,' Joannès pronounced. 'A little coffee in return for those kind words, Chief Inspector?'

'Thank you, no,' said Belot. But Grandmother was not so easily satisfied. 'I must have missed something,' she remarked, witheringly. 'What kind words, Joannès? Did this gentleman say that Jean-Marc is going to meet him *here*, so that we could say goodbye to him? Did he suggest that he was acting as escort so that Jean-Marc would not get too bored during his journey?'

Belot said: 'He is the principal witness, and as such—'

'As such, he is entitled to an escort? Is that what you were

going to say? Don't they summon witnesses by letter or telegram any longer? What do they do now? Play nannies with
handcuffs?'

'There is also the possibility, *madame*,' Belot said, quite
unruffled, 'that they might be protecting them against any
possible danger.'

'You mean that the murderer might plan to kill Jean-Marc
too?' said Émilie. Her jaw trembled a little more intensely,
but she showed no other visible reaction.

Joannès had been making an effort to drink some coffee,
despite the fact that his throat had been too tight to swallow
anything for nearly twenty-four hours. He now abandoned
this rash undertaking. Léonard, too, had already drawn his
own conclusions.

'Of course!' he exclaimed. 'Of course—the murder of this
poor girl, the severed hand, the case: it all might imply:
"That was just the first round—your turn next!" '

'Or perhaps,' Belot said, 'the implication might be: "You'll
give us what we want—or else." '

'And just what might that be?' enquired Grandmother,
quite undismayed. 'Has Jean-Marc suggested a possibility?
Has he said anything to you or those two colleagues of yours
who showed up here yesterday morning?'

'No, *madame*, he has told us nothing, for the very good
reason that he perhaps knows nothing as yet himself. His
enemies must have planned to scare him silly as a preliminary
measure, break down his resistance—otherwise they'd have
gone about things in a quite different way.'

'There, you see,' said Léonard, with delighted approval.
'The safest place Jean-Marc could possibly be is in the hands
of the police.'

'Excuse me, Chief Inspector,' Joannès said, after consulting
his watch. 'As perhaps you are aware, my brother and I work
at the St Polycarp Cloth Mills and Silk Factory, and we
must be off there without delay. During the ordeal which my
poor family and I have been subjected to, the understanding

D

and support we have received from our employer, M Couzon, are, if I may so express myself, beyond all praise. We would be showing rank ingratitude if we did not at least express our thanks by strict punctuality.'

'I'm sorry about that,' Belot said. 'I had hoped to have a little talk with you about your son.'

Grandmother said, with a brief snicker : 'Do you know any parents who really know their children, who are capable of discussing them?'

'Yes, *madame*. You.'

For the second time, she remained nonplussed for a moment. Then, for the first time, her expression wavered, and it was almost to herself that she said : 'My own children, perhaps. But Jean-Marc—' Then she recovered her aggressive manner once more. 'For heaven's sake,' she snorted, 'you've got him in your charge, you don't need anyone else's help.'

Belot stood up.

'Just one moment more,' she said. 'My sons are going to work, and my daughter-in-law is going to bed for a little rest. Isn't that right, Émilie?'

'Yes, Mama,' Émilie said. 'Goodbye, monsieur. Please don't let Jean-Marc forget his muffler !'

Joannès and Léonard, both now dressed and ready, exchanged scarified glances and said goodbye to Belot as though he was the person to whom condolences were due. Belot was left standing there face to face with Grandmother. She did not unbend one whit.

'You are very curious, Monsieur— ?'

'Belot. Frédéric Belot.'

'You are very curious, Frédéric.'

'It's a professional characteristic, *madame*.'

'I don't mean in that sense. You could even be dangerous.'

'Never to the innocent, *madame*.'

'Perhaps. But to suspects? I wonder. Not all suspects are guilty : remember that, Frédéric. I leave this child in your care, then. He has a very artistic nature, you know. He's difficult, always prone to believe that people don't understand him—even me. And I can understand that, because we're two of a kind. Or very nearly so.'

3

Odd, Belot thought to himself, as he got into the car that the Rue Vauban had put at his disposal. Not one member of that family mentioned this morning's papers. Didn't any of them feel driven to read them? Never mind the brothers, they could have bought a paper on their way to the office. But what about *her*? She was the one who received the journalists. She told them the whole tragic story, in detail. I'd have credited her with enough vanity to want to read the results.

However, at M Chênelong's jewellery shop in the Place des Célestins—one of the most prosperous establishments in town —things had been very different. Here the papers had had much the same effect as the opening of the case had done on the Bergers. Mme Chênelong had fainted. Her husband rang up the Rue Vauban. Neither of them knew a thing about the story of the cat's-eye. (A *cat's-eye*, indeed! In all its history the Bijouterie Chênelong had never sold such a thing. Why not marble-chip rings while one was at it?) They had always given Augusta complete liberty of movement. From the time she first walked and talked she had obeyed nothing but her own little brain—'an only child, Chief Inspector, one need say no more than that'. Didier Chênelong had been educated at the same monastic school with the Berger brothers, and though they did not keep up a close acquaintance as adults, their children had in turn got to know each other. They went to the same afternoon tea-dances when they were little, and later saw a great deal of each other. Went to films and plays, winter sports and finally Paris. In short, Augusta had made it clear, a year ago, that she was very much attached to Jean-Marc. She had even added: 'We might well get married, it's not such an awful prospect.' He was studying at the École des Beaux-Arts, he was a great artist in the making, and the Chênelong family held artists in very high esteem. Jean-Marc had designed some pieces of jewellery, based on Egyptian and Byzantine motifs, that M Chênelong thought quite remarkable. Yet when offered financial recompense for his pains, he had replied: 'Not for anything in the world!' 'He was so refined and sensitive, Chief Inspector, and he seemed to *adore* Augusta. What on earth can have happened?' The truth was that she had not said one word about him either at Christmas or the New Year, and when her mother asked whether Jean-Marc had come down for the holidays, she had said: 'I haven't the faintest idea, why do you think I should care?'—which offered abundant proof that she *did* care. She had gone back to Paris to resume her literary studies, 'and the few letters we have had from her since then contain no reference whatsoever to her childhood friend'.

Then M Chênelong added: 'I had a long chat with Superintendent Thévenet—he's a good customer of mine. He *assured* me that Augusta had *nothing whatsoever* to do with this disgusting business. Yet now I get a visit from a Chief Inspector, no less, who has come down specially from *Paris* to *Lyons* just to see *me*, or *us*, I should say. It's all very alarming. I'm very upset. Who wouldn't be?'

He was a well-bred little man, rather red in the face (though this could have been merely the result of emotion). He received Belot in his private apartment over the shop. The décor was strikingly like that favoured by Mlle Sarrazin: it revealed impeccable taste, the only difference being that instead of modern canvases M Chênelong opted for antique portraits in period frames.

Belot soothed the anxious father as best he could, giving him the same reason for his own presence in Lyons as he had done to the Bergers. Not a word about the cat's-eye. He was delighted to be shown a photograph of Augusta without having asked to see one. Her address? This, it transpired, was still the same as it had been when Mme Berger senior wrote to the girl saying she hoped Augusta had liked Jean-Marc's ring. Another episode about which the Chênelongs knew nothing.

As soon as he got back to the Rue Vauban, Belot called up Picard, gave him a brief account of the contacts he had made, and said when he hoped to be back in Paris. Then he called in Simon, and told him to pay a visit to Number 80A, in the Rue d'Assas, the home of an attractive girl whose name was Augusta Chênelong.

4

She lived in a charming one-roomed flat—the old 'maid's room'—on the top floor of a fine old Directoire house, with a fine view over the Luxembourg Gardens and the dome of the Panthéon, and a cloudless sky beyond. Simon Rivière did not notice all this immediately, however. First he studied the card that was pinned to the door. It bore the name AUGUSTA, nothing else, in large angular capitals. Just as though she was a fortune-teller, Simon thought. Or something worse. (Why worse, though? he queried. It's just a job—like being a *flic*.) He knocked, and a cheerful voice called out: 'Hi. The key's in the door.'

He went through. She was, indeed, an attractive girl: young, outgoing, innocent of guile. Her straight-cut dress, of some pale material, looked as young and up-to-date as its owner. It had no pockets, which somehow matched her character. A pair of brilliant, merry, inquisitive eyes surveyed him.

'Hey,' she said, 'you're not the person I was expecting. Are you a friend of François? Can't he make it, or did he tell you to meet him here?'

She was standing beside the window. It was at this point that Simon vaguely registered the view. This interview had started badly. It was always better for a witness to be warned right away unless one specifically intended to mislead him. If Augusta had asked 'Who's that?' he would have been compelled to reply: 'Inspector Rivière, of the *Police Judiciaire*. Could I have a brief word with you, miss? Just a matter of simple testimony.' Whereas now, he thought, I'll have to shift her forcibly out of her world—our world, as she supposes— into my world. And that's no joke, because in fact it's not just mine, but hers *too*. Or has been. Unless she's destroyed all evidence. Has she read the papers, I wonder?

Augusta looked him up and down. 'What's the matter with you?' she enquired. 'Cat got your tongue? Is François sick? Look, you can speak freely—I'll be sorry if he isn't well, but he's just a good friend of mine, nothing more.' She smiled again, but this time the smile was for Simon personally. 'You look older than us, but I must say it suits you. You still at the Fac? [Faculté des Lettres]'

She curled herself up on the divan. 'Sit you down,' she said. She was well-built and attractive but there was nothing provocative in her attitude. Simon picked a chair at some little distance from her, and settled himself in it.

'Look, mademoiselle,' he said, 'I'm not at the Fac, neither yours nor any other. And I'm here to see you on behalf of Jean-Marc.'

That phrase 'on behalf of' was an appalling blunder: Simon had carefully chosen it for the purpose. Augusta frowned— she had heavy black eyebrows which contributed not a little to her character—and reacted instantly.

'What does Jean-Marc want with me? He's got no business here, even through a third party. The whole thing's over and done with!'

Simon would not have been surprised to find himself blushing at this point.

'I'm sorry, I expressed myself rather badly. Please forgive

me. I'm not here on his behalf, but rather on a matter concerning him.'

The eyebrows relaxed, but the body, as though against its own inclination, abandoned what now seemed an over-familiar posture, and sat up.

Simon said: 'Haven't you seen the papers this morning?'

Augusta's pretty face went white. 'No. *The* papers, you said—you mean it doesn't matter which one? And you didn't say read, you said seen. That means the front page, doesn't it?' Simon nodded. 'Look, who are you?'

Simon put on his most reassuring smile, and said: 'An Inspector from the *Police Judiciaire*. No, please don't be alarmed. The crime is nasty enough, it's true, but Jean-Marc has suffered from what one might term its after-effects.'

'The crime?' she repeated, horrified.

Simon had no recourse but to tell her the whole story, as succinctly as possible. She listened intently. He dealt with Huguette Sarrazin, and the Neuilly house, and the severed hand. By the time he got to the opening of the case, she was not so much white as green. And when she heard the words 'with a cat's-eye ring on the third finger', one hand flew to her mouth, though too late to stifle the gasp she gave. Yet she did not evince any *surprise*.

'Yes,' Simon said, eager to finish his narrative even at the price of sounding somewhat aggressive, 'the ring that Mme Berger meant you to have, and which she recognized. That's why I'm here, in the hope that you may be able to assist our enquiries. And to help Jean-Marc.'

Augusta, who had been staring straight in front of her like a blind person, now turned her head sharply and said: 'Help Jean-Marc? Why help him?'

'Because,' said Simon, in benevolent, philosophical tones, 'however much resentment you may feel—'

She interrupted him, saying brusquely: 'But that's not the point!' Simon found himself mildly surprised that she hadn't added 'You halfwit'; she had certainly thought it.

'Why on earth should Jean-Marc need help? He's been made the victim of a really nasty revenge job, I see that. But in what way does he need help?'

'Nasty or not,' Simon said, 'a revenge job normally has some motive behind it. Find the motive, and you can often track it back to its author. Such motives may often be taken into account by the judge and jury as extenuating circumstances; but that is not our concern.'

Augusta sat staring at her hands, now resting on each knee: those big, beautiful hands—so much larger than Huguette Sarrazin's—which were trembling, and therefore unquestionably alive. In a low voice she said: 'A revenge job normally has some motive behind it. Yes indeed.'

She was going to talk. She was going to talk to those hands of hers, or so it seemed, since she never took her eyes off them, leaning further and further forward the whole time. Simon's own eyes were fixed on that tumbled mass of hair, which needed no kind of ordering to look absolutely marvellous.

'Last year we were ready to get married—at least I was, and I really thought he felt the same. We'd fixed it so that we could be in Paris together, arranged our courses at the same time. We often slept together—he stayed with me every week-end, I only went out for lectures. Behind that screen we found in the flea-market—' she indicated it with a movement of her forehead, but did not raise her head— 'there's a gas-ring, good enough to fry steak on, anyway. He always used to do the cooking, with a towel round his waist instead of a chef's apron. Life was fun then, everything made us laugh. Or nothing. This is it, I thought. Two people living together. On top of his studies at the Beaux-Arts, he was working for Pauguin's, the famous art-restorers in the Place Vendôme. He was painting, too, his own stuff. We went to museums at least as often as the cinema. We learnt a lot from each other. And then, in December, the beginning of December, before Christmas, he disappeared.'

Augusta lifted her hands, but instead of replacing them on

her knees she crossed her arms tightly above her heart. She was now staring at the little prayer-mat which lay beside the divan during the day-time, and beside her bed at night. She looked as though she were visualizing the scene as she described it.

'It was a Monday morning. He said to me, one Monday morning, "I shan't be round this week. The boss is putting me on a special assignment. Some whim of a millionaire's." That was his expression for a rush job on some very valuable article. Well, he didn't show up that week—or ever again. Not once. He lived in a hotel down the Rue Bonaparte, the Hôtel de Marseille. I called up once or twice, but he was always out, or not back yet, even at times when he *should* have been there. I began to get worried. Not a word from him at Christmas or the New Year. Oh, I kept up my own social life, I saw plenty of friends, in the daytime, in the evening, I'm not the sort of girl to go all solitary and neurotic. But the idea of spending my winter holidays without Jean-Marc! I began to find out how lonely you can be in a crowd. It was as though everything had vanished with him—my parents, the house, all my memories, *everything*. As though I'd become a kind of destitute bum. M Chênelong's daughter, the best bit of jewellery in Lyons! I sent seasonal greetings to the Berger family. Well, of course, I had an ulterior motive. I thought, maybe he's had to go down there. Maybe something happened to a member of the family, his grandmother, for instance. A terrible old lady, that, although she was the one who encouraged him to become a student at the Beaux-Arts. But I knew perfectly well in my heart of hearts that if that had been the case, my parents would have let me know. My mother writes me huge twenty-page letters every week. No, in fact it was the grandmother I heard from.'

Augusta's fingers were digging into the flesh round her elbows. Surely, Simon thought, she must feel those long nails? Perhaps it's her way of making herself go on.

'There was this remark in her letter about hoping I liked

Jean-Marc's ring. I burnt the letter; but you can't burn the phrases which make you burn letters in the first place. I got really hysterical, and swore that the woman who had this ring would pay for what she'd done before I was through with her. I went and waited to catch Jean-Marc coming out of Pauguin's, three days in a row. He never showed up, so it was clear he'd finished with *them*, too. So then I switched to the Hôtel de Marseille. I saw him several times, he walked right past my taxi, I was scared he'd spot me. But the thing was, every time he came back he was alone. That was no use to me. Then, one evening, he went out—picked up a taxi, so I tailed him in mine. He went right out to the far side of Neuilly, number 9A, Rue de la Ferme. It could have been anybody's place. No, that's not true, I was dead certain this was something special. I'd have stayed there all night, if need be, just on the off chance. But the taxi-driver gave me some pretty funny looks, he was a young man too, he'd probably have tried something if I had. So I went back home. I looked up number 9A, Rue de la Ferme, Neuilly, in the street directory. Only one name listed—not surprising, really, for a private house. The name was Sarrazin, a Mlle H. Sarrazin. Telephone Maillot 46-79. I called the number right away. A woman's voice answered, very sharp and clear and decisive. "Hallo," it said. I nearly choked. I said: "Is that Mlle Sarrazin's house?" "Yes. Who's that speaking?" I thought: I'm going to scare you, and I just kept quiet. "Hullo!" she said. "Hullo!" And then, just as she was about to hang up, she turned to someone near her, it must have been Jean-Marc, and said: "What a time to play practical jo—", and then the click of the receiver cut her off. Practical joke? A practical joke, she called it. I went to see her the next day.'

Her labouring breath and tortured voice suddenly made Simon uneasy. He knew, all too well, the hazards involved in making someone relive an unbearable memory to forget which had cost them days, months even, of unremitting effort. He wanted to take Augusta by the chin and tilt her face up to see whether it was still that deathly colour. However, she went on : nothing had interrupted the visual projection of her memories upon the prayer-mat.

'I rang the bell. She opened the door herself—and yet I never dreamed it was her at first. A woman of that age! Oh, very pretty, very elegant, with a pair of ice-blue eyes. I said: "Could I speak to Mlle Sarrazin, please?" and she said : "*I* am Mlle Sarrazin." Hostile, suspicious eyes: really like ice. I couldn't believe my ears. And she said : "Why, does that strike you as so extraordinary?" I said, "*You're* Jean-Marc's lover—", to which she replied, "Yes, and you're the person who rang up last night—I recognize your voice." She wouldn't let me come in, and anyway I'd not the slightest wish to do so. I'd have liked the whole street to hear me. Yet at the same time my voice just wouldn't come. Rather like now. Anyhow, "the whole street", that was a laugh—not a soul in sight. I said, "You stole him from me." She gave a snicker. "That one remark would have been ample reason for him to ditch you," she said. "You're the childhood chum, aren't you, the little provincial miss from Lyons. How on earth could you ever have thought that Jean-Marc would be satisfied with a girl like you, the kind of man *he* is?" So he'd been talking about me to her, and it was pretty clear in what terms, too. I said, "He's a bastard, and you're just a common thief." I thought she was going to hit me then, and all my courage came flooding back. I'd suddenly put two and two together, without needing any proof. "Yes, a thief. Not for taking him from me, you're probably right there. But for accepting a jewel that belonged to me." She said, "What jewel? Oh yes, I'd forgotten, you're a jeweller's daughter, aren't you?" I replied, "That's got nothing to do with it. I mean a ring his mother sent him for me." "The cat's-eye?" she asked. That's how I first found out it *was* a cat's-eye. She was only wearing one ring when I saw her, an enormous diamond, it must have been worth a fortune. She tore it off her finger and thrust it at me. If I hadn't jumped back she'd have left me holding it. She said: "Go on, take it! Keep it! At least that one's worth something, and it's the other one I'll be wearing from now on." Once again, I found myself unable to get a single word out. The diamond glittered at me like a devil's eye, and I was trembling with horror. Her hand moved, ready to slam the door on me. Her left hand, the same one that— And then she said, with quite extraordinary violence, "Go away, get the hell out of here! If anything happens to Jean-Marc now, I'll know who to thank for it!" And then—'

Though she had no particular reason to lose her balance, Augusta now suddenly slid from the divan to the floor, and lay there sprawled over the prayer-mat. Simon picked her up, but just as he was about to lay her out on the divan, she struggled free.

'Leave me alone, that's enough—'

At once Simon resumed his role of impersonal anonymity. Despite her two closing words, which left him with a keen appetite for what might follow, he did not press the matter. Instead, he opened his wallet and took out an official sumons (already filled in) which he placed on the table. Tomorrow, Wednesday, at 4 p.m. precisely, Mlle Augusta Chênelong was requested to present herself at the Préfecture de Police, Police Judiciaire, 36 Quai des Orfèvres, and ask for Superintendent Picard's office (Department of Criminal Investigation).

'Jean-Marc Berger is sure to be there by then,' he said, and took his leave.

SEVEN

Return from Lyons

I

SUPERINTENDENT THÉVENET shook Belot's hand warmly.
They had dined together, extremely well, at a little restaurant on the banks of the Saône.

'So sorry I can't stay with you till the train goes. I know this case is out of our hands now—not that I'm complaining all that much—but keep us informed of the latest developments. And if that American really exists, I swear I'll ask to be pensioned off on the spot! Oh, and send Delorme back here as soon as you arrive—we've got a lot on hand here just now. I'm told you're taking charge of the suitcase and the ring.'

'Have to get something out of my trip,' Belot said. 'Besides your laboratory report, that is, which I may say strikes me as just about perfect—like everything you're responsible for around these parts.'

'You'll have the rest of them hopping jealous if you go on like that,' said Thévenet, hugely delighted. 'I must admit that the photographs of the hand are very good likenesses.'

That afternoon Joannès had been allowed to see his son. Émilie could in fact have come too, but he preferred to leave her in ignorance of such an opportunity. 'There are times,' he told Belot, 'when it is best to spare a mother's feelings.' He had brought a small case full of clean clothes. 'You look a bit shabby, Jean-Marc—after all, a police-station isn't the same as your own home.' Belot had offered to leave them alone together for ten minutes, but this suggestion brought Joannès to the verge of panic.

'It's you who's going to look after my son, Chief Inspector —it's only right that what I have to tell him should be said in your presence.'

His precepts were as solemn as they were ridiculous. Jean-Marc sat and listened, always watching Belot from the corner of one eye. Belot himself sat leafing through the evening paper. Naturally, since that morning the Berger family had had time to read the Press reports, and Joannès brought them for Jean-Marc to look at as well. The story had been accurately reported, without changes. Grandmother had wanted to come too, but the regulation, as Belot had made clear to Joannès, only included the 'immediate direct relatives'.

'Perfectly reasonable', had been Joannès comment. 'A father and a mother, that's just two people. Throw in one set of grandparents, and you double the figure straight off. And just supposing you included all the aunts and uncles —even Leonard,' he added, with a hint of regret in his voice.

Jean-Marc was deathly pale: he looked as though he had spent several nights in a cellar. However, when he had shaved, and put on a collar and tie, and a freshly-pressed suit which had been awaiting him in the Rue Dumont for the past few months, he would not have looked out of place in a first-class compartment—always supposing that those who administered French justice had been so solicitous of their principal witnesses' comfort. They did, on the other hand, provide Jean-Marc not with one ticket only, but with three.

As they emerged from the Rue Vauban, Delorme muttered in Belot's ear: 'Shall I put the darbies on him?'

In an equally discreet voice Belot replied: 'Absolutely not. Out of the question.'

The total number of tickets, it transpired in the end, was not three but eight: the entire compartment, in fact. Delorme drew the curtains on the corridor side, and pulled down the

blind over the big window. 'Because of stopping at stations,'
he said.

Belot watched him, with the ghost of a smile.

'This the first time you've played guardian angel?'

'Yes, Chief.'

'Congratulations.'

It was now Delorme's turn to scrutinize Belot, a trifle
uneasily. Up till now they had attracted no attention, either
when traversing the station or getting aboard the train: were
his precautionary measures a bit overdone?

Belot said to Jean-Marc: 'Stretch yourself out if you like.
We're leaving at eleven and we're not due in till six in the
morning. Why not have a good night's sleep?'

'Thank you, monsieur,' Jean-Marc said, 'but I'm not
sleepy.' He cast a nervous glance at the drawn blinds which
had replaced the bars of his 'cage'.

'If there's anything you want,' Belot told him, 'don't hesitate
to ask. It'll be very surprising if both Inspector Delorme and
myself are asleep at the same time. The one who's awake will
attend to you.'

Delorme gave a satisfied nod. Jean-Marc took immediate
advantage of this offer. He said: 'When we reach the Gare
de Lyon, could you question the porter? He was a witness
to the whole thing, the switching of the cases, I mean. He saw
the car take off, like a rocket.'

'If he's on duty in the evening, he won't be there in the
morning,' Belot said. 'But don't worry, we'll get his testimony
all right.'

'Thank you, monsieur,' Jean-Marc said.

He replied, 'Thank you, monsieur' to almost everything
Belot said. When he had awoken early that morning, he
remembered being interrogated in the middle of the night by
some unknown person to whom Chief Inspector Senneville
showed quite remarkable deference. He made enquiries of his
warder, who told him, with some pride: 'You shouldn't
complain, you're getting the V.I.P. treatment. Chief Inspector

Belot in person, coming all the way from Paris to see you.'
Jean-Marc at once remembered Superintendent Thévenet's
delighted reaction during his phone conversation. 'You mean
Belot's on this case?' 'My dear Belot, good day to you—a real
pleasure to find *you* on this job. We're fated to meet again
remarkably soon.' From now on this was the man in charge
of the enquiry, the master of his, Jean-Marc's, fate. Once
Belot was convinced, the rest, great and small alike, would
fall into line. This was why Jean-Marc said, 'Thank you,
monsieur', for everything: it came quite sincerely, from the
bottom of his heart.

The journey proved an uneventful one. The young suspect
and the young inspector both stayed awake all night. Belot,
on the other hand, slept the sleep of the just, despite not
having had his coffee. When he woke up, he said: 'It must
have been the change of air.'

2

When they reached the Quai des Orfèvres, Belot left
Delorme to watch over Jean-Marc, turned over a parcel containing the case and the various reports to Criminal Records,
and then, despite the early hour, went along to Picard's
office. Truflot was there before him.

'M Picard is furious—' he said.

'Naturally,' said Belot.

'—at not having been there to meet you on arrival,
Monsieur Belot,' Truflot went on, with a hint of polite
reproach in his voice.

He went on to explain what had happened. The Prefect
had summoned the Director-General of the *Police Judiciaire*,
M Malebranche, to an eight o'clock meeting to discuss certain
fairly sharp criticisms—criticisms that he strongly resented—
which had been levelled against his Branch by the municipal
authorities. M Malebranche had asked Picard to prepare a

brief on the questions raised, and to accompany him to the
meeting, since it was a matter of various murders and other
crimes committed in the Paris area during the past six months,
and still unsolved. Picard had spent the night working on this
brief, and would now be spending the morning with the
Prefect. On the other hand, said Truflot, all he could
think about was the Neuilly affair, which had acquired
fresh interest for him since Simon's interview with Mlle
Chênelong.

'So much the better,' Belot said. 'Please tell him I quite
understand. Now: I'd like you to find temporary accom-
modation, of a reasonably non-squalid sort, for young Berger.
I shall have to tell him why Picard can't see him yet. And I
want to talk to Simon.'

Simon, Blondel, and Sergeant Gaillardet were in the general
office, waiting for him.

'First and foremost,' he said, 'what about the visit to
Augusta?'

Simon handed over his report, the product of an excellent,
well-nigh verbatim memory. When he had read it, Belot said:
'Anything to add?'

'Not a thing. I'm anxious for you to talk to her yourself.
She has an appointment for four o'clock this afternoon. She
reacted very badly.'

Out of respect for gradations of rank, Belot now turned to
Gaillardet. Blondel intervened.

'On the question of the victim's bank-account,' he said, 'I
thought it best to put myself in the hands of the sergeant
here.'

Gaillardet took over. 'She had been fantastically rich. She
wasn't *that* rich any more, but most people would do very
nicely on her modest competence. Here's the information I
got from her banker. No specific figures, naturally, until the
estate's been cleared. Oh, he also gave me the address of her
solicitor—Maître Bravais, in the Boulevard Malesherbes, you
remember him? We made his acquaintance over that business

at Les Bruyères-de-Sèvres, you know, the governess, the
trunk—'

'I remember him,' Belot said. 'A very agreeable person,
even though he does seem to be making a speciality of
chopped-up clients. Let's get the financial side finished first,
right? Is there a strong-box?'

'Yes, a big one. It's been sealed.'

'What's the solicitor got to say?'

'No will.'

'Hell.'

'None filed with him, anyway.'

Simon said: 'And I found nothing resembling a will out at
Neuilly.'

'To the best of the solicitor's knowledge,' Gaillardet went
on, 'she has no direct heirs. No children, and her parents are
dead.'

'Was she ever married?'

'No.'

'Where did her capital come from?'

'Mostly from Daddy—and from Mummy's father. Marriages
like that tend to produce more coins than scions.' Everyone
laughed, including Gaillardet himself. 'Chemical industries at
an international level. The banker told me she knew as much
about stocks and shares as she knew about pictures, but added
that "speculation can undo even the cleverest of us"—those
were his exact words. She must have property abroad, too.'

'What's bred in the bone comes out in the flesh,' said Belot.

'Very nice,' Gaillardet said. 'Your own?'

'No.'

'Pity. You paid me a compliment, I'd have liked to return
it. On top of everything else, there's her art-collection.'

'That's where Rivière and I come in,' said Blondel.

'Just let me finish first,' Gaillardet said. 'Anyway, I'm only
passing on what I got from her banker and solicitor. They
both confirm that that's where the bulk of her fortune was
tied up.'

'You may notice,' Blondel said to Gaillardet, to excuse himself for having interrupted him, 'that we're only given confirmation by the experts.'

'And that,' said Belot, 'is by no means negligible. We've all known quite a few collectors who were in grievous error over just what their collections were worth. All right, Blondel, it's all yours.'

Blondel said : 'We interviewed all the leading specialists on modern painting in the art-dealers' world. Rivière did half of them, and I did the rest. Here's a list of their names and addresses. The letter E indicates those that are legally acknow-ledged experts. They were all really shattered by the news in this morning's papers. Not only because of her private collection, which was absolutely alpha plus, especially as regards Van Gogh—they even mentioned certain canvases by name, didn't they, Rivière?'

'Yes.'

'We made a note of them, and it would seem that they include some of the very best known canvases. Where was I? Oh yes. They don't mourn her simply as a client, a potential customer. They regarded her as one of *them*—you see what I mean? There were three of them who said that she knew more about Van Gogh than any other person alive. It seems that no complete catalogue of his works yet exists. No one knows exactly what he painted, and God knows he painted enough! Apparently she was of great service to them in certain lawsuits, too. They kept urging her to undertake the compilation of an exhaustive catalogue. "When I'm an old woman", she would say. Now she'll never do it.'

At this point Simon took over. 'I asked if maybe she didn't go in for a bit of dealing on the side. Sure, they told me, like all collectors, only they don't call it dealing. She'd resell some painting she'd got tired of, in order to buy a better one that she really liked—generally by the same artist. And she *never* resold a Van Gogh. Apparently she used to say, "I've never betrayed my god".'

Belot said : 'According to all these gentlemen—'

'And ladies,' said Simon.

'—and ladies, was she known to have any enemies?'

Both Simon and Blondel said not. On the contrary, she had a great many friends, mostly among other collectors, both men and women, who were in the same class as she was. She would mingle with them at major sales and *vernissages*; and as she was very attractive—'supremely elegant'—she proved a godsend to the Press photographers, posing most obligingly whenever they asked her to. She always arrived alone on such occasions, in her little runabout, and left in the same manner.

'No official escort?'

Never, it appeared; hence the absolute amazement of everyone the two inspectors had interviewed—the same applied to her banker and solicitor, Gaillardet said—on learning from the papers, not only that she had been engaged and to a boy who was so young, unknown, without position when there were celebrities who would have been delighted to marry her!

'Indeed,' Belot said. 'Is that all?'

'I also went round to the Écoles des Beaux-Arts,' Blondel continued. 'Unfortunately it's the middle of the Easter holidays, and I couldn't find anyone there who knew Jean-Marc Berger, except the porter, and he didn't know him well. Oh, he'd read the account in the papers. Yes, he'd known that this student also did a part-time job at Pauguin's, the restorers, but how he came by this information he couldn't rightly remember. But in December he'd thought of asking him to repair a little statuette of Napoleon he had, that'd lost one point of its cocked hat, he planned to give it to an old regimental friend of his whose family—'

'Well, what happened?' said Belot, rather as one might extend a helping hand to someone sunk in wet mud up to their knees.

'Thanks, Chief. Well, Berger took on the job, and in fact did it much quicker than anticipated. When he brought the statuette back he said, "I'm quitting my job, and I'm packing

in Art School, too. Family reasons." He looked on top of the
world, the porter said.'

'Did you go and see the art-restorer?'

'No,' Blondel said. 'I thought you'd rather handle that one
yourself.'

'You were quite right. Thank you, gentlemen. You've done
a good job.'

3

Since the reign of Louis XV, the Pauguins have always been
in the art-restoring business, handing down their professional
skills from father to son (or, on occasion, to a son-in-law; in
such cases the person involved would always assume the
famous family name instead of his own patronymic). The
result is a dynasty more firmly based than that of the Royal
Family, which over the centuries has increased its already
impeccable reputation tenfold. The House of Pauguin has
always mainly specialized in the field of ceramics, but within
this field specialists of every type are called for, in particular
painters and modellers. To restore the missing foot of an
aiguière, or a decorative pattern so worn away that virtually
nothing of it remains calls, as M Louis Pauguin explained to
Belot, for 'real artists'.

'And as far as painting went,' he said, 'Jean-Marc Berger
was just that, without a shadow of doubt. He did some marvellous work for us. Oh, we supplied the designs, but the best
instructions in the world don't suffice to make a master-
craftsman.' Then M Pauguin, rather to Belot's surprise, made
a very down-to-earth comment: 'It's the same in any job
of this sort. I hardly need to tell you that we pay assistants of
that calibre a higher salary than they could get anywhere else.
And if they are still students, as Jean-Marc was well aware,
we make every possible allowance for them. I thought he'd
found a job here for the rest of his life. Some of our workers,

you know, stay on even after retiring age. And then, two or three weeks before last Christmas, he came to see me, and he said—these are his exact words—"Monsieur Pauguin, you've always been kindness itself to me, but I've found a job that I can't give you any details about just at present—except to say that it's so interesting I'm chucking up everything for it, Art School included!" I told him he could do as he pleased, he was of age, but that it didn't seem reasonable for a boy of his age to turn his nose up at diplomas, especially since he was talented enough to obtain them without the slightest real effort. And then what should we learn, after poor Mlle Sarrazin's frightful death, but that the two of them were engaged to be married! Did you by any chance ever meet Mlle Sarrazin during her lifetime?'

'Unfortunately not,' Belot said. 'We more often find ourselves being called in to look at people after their decease.'

It was just as he had feared: not one flicker of a smile from M Pauguin, who said, earnestly: 'I can assure you, Inspector, that if you had met her even once, you would have said, as everyone here did. "Absolutely incredible!".'

'Love is blind,' said Belot, who was beginning to find the atmosphere catching.

M Pauguin lowered his chin till it rested on his overalls: the spotless overalls befitting an artisan established in the Place Vendôme. He said: 'I've been thinking about nothing else since yesterday evening, as you may well imagine. With your permission, I would like to tell you the conclusions I have reached.'

'Please do.'

'What is the obvious bond between two artists? Art, of course: what else?' Belot suddenly began to revise his opinion of M Pauguin. 'If Jean-Marc was, in his way, an artist, so was poor Mlle Sarrazin in hers. Oh I know, at first sight, it's an incredible partnership—the rich, sophisticated Parisian lady and the provincial youth from Lyons, the woman of the world and the naïve young tyro. Absolutely. But wouldn't you agree that two people can fall in love with each other while in front of a picture or an *objet-d'art* simply because it carries the same appeal for both of them?' M Pauguin looked up at this point and added : 'I hold a degree in psychology; as you see, it comes in handy on occasion.'

'Indeed it does,' said Belot. 'So you would admit the possibility that what we have here is an act of revenge on the part of some rejected lover?'

'What other conclusion could one come to? It stands out a mile.'

'I suppose you didn't know any of Mlle Sarrazin's close friends? Or Jean-Marc's, if it comes to that? Most of his fellow-craftsmen here must surely have been older than he was?'

'Yes,' M Pauguin said, 'but he had no friends here. And I didn't know anyone in Mlle Sarrazin's circle. On the subject of Jean-Marc, that reminds me though; we got a letter from his grandmother after he'd left us.'

'Ah. Were you acquainted with the lady?'

'Never met her. She wanted to know whether he was still working for us. I was obliged to inform her that he was not. I must say, I did find it a little odd that he'd said nothing to his family about his new position.'

4

'Come in!' said M Bédat. He was in his little office, busy reading *Le Grand Journal*, and not at all inclined to put himself out for whoever it was had just tapped on the open door. 'Good morning, monsieur. I'm terribly sorry—I can only repeat what it says on the notice outside : we're full up. And you'll find it the same everywhere in this part of town—'

'Monsieur Bédat?'

'That's right,' he said. A familiar card was thrust under

his nose, and he scrambled to his feet. 'You from the police?
You can't be Vice Squad, or I'd know you—'

'No. I'm not. Chief Inspector Belot, Criminal Investigation.'

M Bédat hastily produced a chair.

'Ah, Chief Inspector,' he said, 'I've just had the honour
of reading in the paper that you were taking charge of this
abominable business! Sit down, please! As it happens, I've
been trying to make up my mind this past twenty-four hours
whether I should go along to your office, or whether it'd be
better to see you here, at the scene—I was going to say of the
crime, fortunately not—. But anyway of the principal party—
well, apart from the unfortunate young lady, that is. Oh, and
I did want to express my gratitude to the police, both in
Lyons and here in Paris—no, I mean the other way round,
don't I, order of seniority, ha-ha!—for not breathing a word
to the press, either of them, about the Hôtel de Marseille.
This kind of publicity would be ruinous to any kind of business,
but especially to mine! When I opened my *Grand Journal*,
yesterday morning, you can imagine what a shock I got. He
lived here for a year, that young boy did, and we looked after
him like he was our own son, the wife and I—she can confirm
all I'm telling you when she gets back from her shopping!
About an hour before he left on Sunday night, I made him
a hot toddy. He'd told me he didn't want any dinner, said
the cold he'd got took his appetite away, and anyway
he'd get train-sick if he ate anything. H'm. That cold of
his . . . Have you considered the possibility that—' He
paused.

'What possibility, M Bédat?'

M Bédat thrust the palms of both hands forward and shook
them vigorously in a gesture of negation.

'Nothing, Chief Inspector, nothing at all—you'd begin
to think I was romancing! No, I'm here to answer *your*
questions, frankly and fully, as my conscience dictates, not to
ask questions of my own.'

'If you read yesterday's Press reports—'

'Every last one of them! First *Le Grand Journal*, then all the others.'

'In that case, you will have seen the résumé of the boy's deposition concerning the switching of one of his cases.' M Bédat was now sitting quite still, hands folded across his stomach, fingers interlaced. 'He testified that he spent quite a while with his hotel proprietor, trying to get hold of a taxi in the rain.'

'Quite correct, I have to admit.'

'And that just a few moments after you'd gone in, the car driven by this so-called American pulled up in front of him; that they exchanged a few words; that his cases were loaded into the back; and that it was then, and in this way, that he finally left the hotel.'

'*Exactly*,' said M Bédat, with heavy emphasis. 'And all that was supposed to have been going on outside my front door there without my hearing it? Me, of all people! I've got such a fine, subtle ear that they put me on signal-transmissions at Verdun. When I read that bit in the papers, you could have knocked me down flat. It was as though someone had hit me in the solar plexus—'

'But if the door was shut?' Belot persisted. 'We can't hear anything now.'

'*You* may not be able to, Chief Inspector, but *I* can.'

'But it was pouring with rain,' said Belot, sticking to his point. 'You've got a glass porch out there. The rain must have been drumming on it?'

M Bédat said, magnanimously: 'Of course you're right to insist in a case like this. The innocent must not pay the penalty for the guilty. But at the same time you mustn't treat an ear like mine as though it was half deaf—' He exclaimed aloud, as though struck by some sudden revelation. 'Wait, I can prove to you that he lied! I'll show you how the idea of such a lie came into his head. When we were standing outside, he was so jumpy, so nervous about missing his train, that he'd try and flag down any sort of car—he even waved to a Rolls-

Royce! And I told him, as a joke, that he wouldn't half have been embarrassed if it had stopped. Well, obviously, when the Lyons police interrogated him, he remembered my idea. He must have thought, *that bloody old fool Bédat—why not, eh*?'

Belot scratched the scar on his neck, a nasty souvenir from another case. 'That is an extremely serious accusation, M Bédat,' he said.

'I'm not accusing anyone of anything,' Bédat protested, in the same vigorous tones. 'I'm just saying what I think. When someone makes, h'm, mistakes, I say so, that's all.'

'And did he make other—mistakes?'

Bédat narrowed his eyes to the merest slits. 'More a case of omissions, like,' he said. 'He seemed to talk freely with us about everything—his art-school, his work, his family—and *his fiancée*. But when we read who this fiancée of his was— well, I ask you! Twelve years older than he was! Another five, and she'd have been the same age as my missus! Still, I must admit, there's nothing like a good stack of banknotes in the mattress for making wrinkles vanish—does the trick quicker than raw steak, any road. It's all one hell of a mystery, though. Glad I'm not in your shoes, and that's a fact—'

'How did he spend that last Sunday?'

'That's the trouble, *I haven't a clue*. We don't serve meals here, the place isn't organized for that sort of thing, and any-way so long as we don't we can keep on good terms with the local restaurants. The only ones we have to worry about are those that get sick and take to their beds, and we can always fix them with some oxo or some camomile tea. That's what he should have done, under *normal* conditions, before making a long journey in the pouring rain—rest up in bed for a bit.'

'What time did he go out?'

M Bédat pointed his forefinger at Belot, then at once with-drew it, to avoid any accusation of insolence.

'Now there, Chief Inspector, you touch on a delicate point. We more or less live in this little office, the wife and I, doing the accounts, or reading, or whatever. The door's always left open, and the key-rack's right outside—you can see it from where you're sitting. When the footsteps are those of a stranger, or a new arrival, we look up instantly—we keep our ears and our eyes open, keep a sharp eye on them, you might say. But if it's a regular, your ear gets accustomed to 'em, you don't take any notice after a while. They've all got their own way of unhooking their keys, too. Sometimes you'll say, ah, there's No 5, or 14, or 9. But sometimes you don't react at all, you don't even hear the noise, it's become so regular a part of your life. The long and the short of the matter is, I never noticed him come in.'

'Well, what time did you see him that Sunday?'

'Not before the late afternoon. He was in No 5—the number I was on about just now—and the door of his room was ajar. He was busy packing. Actually, I offered to lend him a hand. Must say, he looked pretty off-colour—I put it all down to his cold, at the time. He smelt of drink, too, slightly.'

'Did he tipple a bit, then?'

M Bédat pulled a contemptuous face. 'Never. A proper little prude, that one, I'm telling you!'

'Did he have any visitors?'

'Never. But there are plenty of *bistrots* in the Latin Quarter or Montparnasse where you can keep doubtful company, even if you don't drink! Those are the places the police ought to investigate, instead of poking their noses into hotels like ours every so often—I'm not talking about your visit here today, that's different, I mean those routine check-ups by the Vice Squad—'

'They do investigate them, M Bédat, they do.'

'Not thoroughly enough, Chief Inspector! This business, now, it's as fishy a story as I ever heard—twelve years older than him, and as rich as they come. I ask you—'

'When did he decide to make this trip to Lyons?'

'Over a week before. He told us that if he didn't go, his grandmother was quite capable of coming up to Paris and fetching him—tough old bird, it seems. And that was something that really scared him, no doubt about it. He wanted to make it clear to her that this affair was serious, on the level, that the wedding was going to take place any day. But if that was true, why couldn't he have seen his grandmother here, and introduced her to his fiancée?'

'Did you raise this point with him personally?'

'Chief Inspector, when the boss puts up a specious argument, it's not for any underling to point out its weaknesses. A hotel proprietor is always at his guests' service. But that doesn't stop him thinking!'

'Did he leave any of his possessions in your care when he took off?'

'Some of his own paintings. They weren't up to much.'

'I'd like to see them, please. And after that—' Belot rose to his feet '—after that, we're going to arrange a little meeting.'

M Bédat, who had also risen—without bothering to conceal his relief—now stiffened like a pointer.

'A meeting?'

'Your evidence is crucial as far as the cases are concerned.'

'I don't see why, Chief Inspector.'

'You told Jean-Marc Berger you would look after them while he went down to Saint-Germain-des-Prés in search of a taxi.'

'Out of kindness—purely out of kindness.'

'I don't doubt it. Do you recall what they looked like?'

M Bédat allowed himself a smile. 'Well, now! A couple of cases—that shouldn't be so difficult!'

'Just so. I would like you to come round to the Quai des Orfèvres this evening. There you will be shown the case—'

M Bédat's smile vanished. 'The blood-stained case?'

'That's right. If you can identify it as one of the two cases you originally saw, you will have proved that the story about the American was a complete fabrication. But if you think it was a larger, or smaller, case than the one in front of you—'

Belot left it at that. M Bédat kept his eyes fixed on the toes of his carpet-slippers.

'Now that,' he said, 'is another thing again. If it's a matter of hearing, I'll stake my opinion against anyone's. But on visual accuracy, you might say, I'm not so hot. The thing is, Chief Inspector, he carried those bags down himself, *and* dumped them behind the entrance-door. I didn't actually handle them at any point, or *really* take a good look at them, either. I'm sorry, but with the best will in the world—'

EIGHT

In which a voice is silenced, and a wall talks

I

IT was four o'clock.

A moment or so earlier, Belot had taken out his notebook, scribbled some words on a blank page, and held it out to Truflot. Truflot had come over, read the message, shaken his head, and gone back to his seat. Picard was interrogating Jean-Marc, who had been on the point of answering a question, but now stopped dead. Belot could not risk the slightest movement without Jean-Marc taking fright, and convincing himself that he was lost, abandoned. There was something very dog-like about the boy's attitude. Picard did not, on the whole, care for dogs, though he made exceptions in favour of the genuine article, especially his daughter Ginette's wire-haired fox-terrier, Hector, who barked too much but was at least open-hearted—in sharp contrast to the devious, mumbling creature he had had in front of him for the past quarter of an hour, concerning whom his mind was already made up.

He banged his fist on the table, and Jean-Marc jumped. Belot slipped his notebook back in his pocket. The sentence he had scribbled in it, which provoked a negative response from Truflot, was: *Has Mlle Chênelong arrived yet?*

'Don't make me repeat all my questions, Monsieur Berger! And don't suppose that playing for time in this way will work to your advantage!'

'Monsieur Berger' pulled himself together. In fact, despite his anxious expression and a still-noticeable shortness of breath, he did so quite effectively, and what he had to say was very much to the point.

'I don't understand, monsieur. You're taking exactly the same line as they did in Lyons. Why? Why are you picking on *me* like this, why are you grilling me about *my* activities, instead of asking me things that might help you to track down the murderer? Isn't that the main object of your investigation? You accuse me of having kept my departure from Pauguin's a secret from my family, or of explaining it differently to different people. Do you know any young people who haven't kept things hidden from their families—especially with a grandmother like mine? Or who haven't ever told people white lies when stretching the truth a bit would make life easier for them?'

' "A Bit", you call it,' Picard exclaimed angrily. 'You stretched the truth a bit, you say! In December, you informed the porter at the École des Beaux-Arts that you were going back to Lyons. You told your employer that you'd found a "sensational" job. Well, you did not return to Lyons in December; and when I ask you for details of this so-called "job", you appear incapable of answering.'

'I can give you an answer, all right, Superintendent. Not about the "job", it's true—there wasn't any job, any more than I had the slightest intention of going back to Lyons in December. I just said the first thing that came into my head. I told the porter at the School the sort of thing that would sound reasonable coming from a provincial student. I told M Pauguin a story that flattered me on the professional level. I mean, I could hardly tell either of them that Mlle Sarrazin and I had fallen madly in love with each other, let alone that she'd said to me: "I don't want you to work any more! I want to have you around whenever I like, all day long if I feel like it!" '

Picard said: 'And was it because she didn't feel like it any longer that you decided to take off for Lyons on Sunday?'

Jean-Marc denied this with some heat. 'Far from it,' he said. 'On the contrary, in fact. I've been telling you all this for two days now! I was going back home to explain about our engagement. To tell the family we seriously intended to get married.' He got excited, and his voice rose. 'That must have been what started it all! Someone didn't *want* us to get married!'

In an even louder voice, Picard shouted: '*Who?*'

'I haven't the faintest idea, how should I have? Or rather, yes, I *do* know who, but I'm in the dark as to his true identity! The driver, of course, that fake American, fake Neapolitan, whatever the hell he is, the bastard, the shit—'

'Ah yes,' said Picard, suddenly crafty, helping himself to a cigarette from the box in front of him, 'the famous American and his black car. With *your* big cases and *his* little one, lurking in the stormy primaeval darkness, right, the angel who came to your rescue, the demon who encompassed your destruction! You didn't know him, of course. If you had known him, he could hardly have woven his web round you like the true shilling-shocker spider he was, eh? Still, you did talk to Mlle Sarrazin sometimes about people she knew, didn't you? You keep on complaining that we don't bother to ask for your collaboration in this affair. Well, the moment has come. Go ahead, collaborate! I'm all ears.'

Jean-Marc hunched himself together in his chair. A tremendous effort to clarify his own mind? Or, rather, the sort of sudden collapse induced by total helplessness? The latter, surely. Picard gave Belot a faint wink, as though to say, 'I told you so'. Truflot, who was making a transcript of the interrogation, took advantage of this momentary silence to look up, in some curiosity.

At last Jean-Marc replied, 'Oh yes, we talked. Obviously we talked. About dealers, and her relations with them. About anyone who had the slightest connection with painting.'

'Fine, fine,' Picard said, very amiably now. 'Let's look for possible candidates among these people. A dealer, h'm? Why not?'

'Mlle Sarrazin took no personal interest in anybody—'

'Except you. But never mind about her taking an interest in other men, didn't she ever complain that they were getting too interested in her? She was attractive and well-off, surely she must have had some aspiring suitors? Didn't she ever come back home some day when you were there already, and say something like, "Oh I can't stand So-and-So or Such-and-Such, he just bores the hell out of me every time we run into each other"? And what about those fireside chats in the evening? You certainly discussed Mlle Chênelong with her—'

'Me?' Jean-Marc abruptly snapped into focus. 'That's completely untrue! I gave Mlle Sarrazin the ring that was meant for her, that I admit, but I never said a word about her—'

'Oh dear,' Picard said, clasping his hands in a disappointed fashion, 'there you go, holding out on us again . . . Truflot, show Mlle Chênelong in, will you?'

The door was behind Jean-Marc. He hunched his head into his shoulders, as though he hoped that when Augusta first saw him from behind, he would look so different that she would fail to recognize him. Truflot glanced at Belot, hesitated, and then said: 'Yes, sir.'

But hardly were the words out of his mouth, before the phone began to ring. 'Hallo?' he said. He listened for a moment, then said: 'I'll put you on to M Belot.'

Belot came across and took the receiver from him. Picard picked up his own, flicking on the intercommunication switch as he did so. Simon's voice came over the line.

'I'm at Mlle Chênelong's flat,' he said. 'I had to break the door down to get in. She's taken poison. A tube of some stuff, I don't know. I've just been getting an ambulance.'

'What sort of state's she in?' Belot asked.

'Looks like a coma. She left a note on the table. I'd better

E

read it to you: "Forgive me, Jean-Marc. Forgive me for everything".'

2

Picard and Belot reached the Cochin Hospital at the same time as the ambulance. It passed through the main entrance just ahead of them, with Simon sitting beside the driver. He saw them, and shook his head slowly, from right to left and then back again.

'What's that mean?' Picard asked Belot. 'That she's had it?'

'Let's hope so,' was Belot's response.

Picard flashed a quick glance at him. 'Yes, I get you. But if it's what you think, that would prove two things: first, that young Berger isn't the murderer, and second, that the case is closed.'

'Let's hope that too,' Belot said.

A white-uniformed attendant showed them into a waiting-room. Every minute or so Picard would glance at his watch. Belot remained absolutely motionless. After twelve minutes Simon appeared. He said: 'She's dead. I showed the intern the tube. According to him she took exactly enough to kill her. They're going to do an autopsy.' He took a piece of paper from his wallet and gave it to Picard. 'That's the note she left.'

'Sure it's her handwriting?'

'Yes. I checked it.'

He looked very unhappy. Picard stood up and said to Belot, who had not moved a muscle: 'If you're agreeable, we might as well all three go back. There's nothing more for Simon to do here. We ought to study the situation together, I think.'

Belot got to his feet. 'Have you locked up at her place?' he asked Simon.

'Of course.'

In the car Belot asked another question. 'Why did you go down there again, anyway?'

Simon, who was in the front seat, shrugged his shoulders. Without turning round he said: 'Just a nagging instinct. Ever since last night I've been telling myself that I shouldn't have left her like that in the afternoon. I was afraid I might have really upset her by being too brutal.'

'Oh for God's sake,' said Picard. 'We don't want to bother about our little psychological problems, it's other people's that concern us in this game. And a little plain speaking can sometimes produce very positive results.'

'We have proof of that,' Belot said, in a completely neutral voice.

Picard glanced at him again: profile this time, rather than full face. Simon went on: 'I thought maybe she'd get in such a panic that she wouldn't come, that I might be able to encourage her. If I'd got there and found her gone, that would have reassured me—'

Picard said: 'Thévenet will have to go and break the news to her parents in person. He'd better give them the text of her note, too—otherwise they're capable of refusing to believe it was suicide. On the other hand, we need say nothing to the Press—about the note, I mean. Not for the time being, at any rate.'

As soon as they were back in his office he said to Truflot: 'She's dead.'

'Really,' said Truflot, politely.

'After taking the blame for everything.' Truflot's eye lit up. 'Get me Superintendent Thévenet. Priority call.'

'Right away, sir.' Truflot turned to Belot, and said: 'Inspector Blondel wants to see you as soon as possible. Found something sensational, it seems.'

'Where?' Belot asked.

'Here.'

'What? The discovery?'

'No, him.'

Picard sank back into his armchair, and waved Belot and Simon to the two visitors' chairs. But Belot did not sit down. He said: 'Would you mind if I just went and found out what this was all about?'

Picard picked up his solid ruler and absent-mindedly tried to bend it. Then he burst out: 'Look, before you vanish, tell me one thing: Is it her or isn't it?'

Simon stared at him in blank puzzlement. 'Her? What do you mean, sir?' he asked.

'*Her!* "Forgive me for everything"—isn't that a general admission of guilt?'

Belot turned a thoughtful eye on Simon, who continued, in the same dazed manner: 'You mean—the murder of Mlle Sarrazin?'

'I'd like to know what the hell else I could have meant,' Picard snarled.

Though the respect he felt for Picard was no less profound, if less filial, than that he felt for Belot, Simon nevertheless replied at once, without circumspection: 'But that's impossible! *Impossible!*'

'Right,' said Belot. 'I'll leave Simon to rationalize his conviction—which, I may say, strikes me as a useful pointer. Back later.'

As he went out he heard Truflot say to Picard: 'Superintendent Thévenet on the line, sir.'

3

He found Blondel in the Crime Squad general office, hunched over a table and scribbling away furiously. At the sight of Belot he sprang up from his chair.

'Ah, there you are, Chief! I was just starting my report. Looks as though I may have started one of those hares—'

'Come on, sit down and tell all.'

'About an hour ago, Toussaint called up from Neuilly—
he's splitting the guard-duty there with Sergeant Malicorne.
Asked if I'd mind coming over. Off I went, and found him
outside in the street, staring at one corner of the house. If you
looked right, you'd got the front façade, and to the left you
had one of the sides looking out on the garden. He pointed
up at the roof on this side, and just said: "The skylight". I
looked at the skylight, seemed perfectly ordinary to me. Then
he explained. "Look," he said to me, "when you went through
the attics, you saw *three* skylights—and there they are, to the
right, along the front façade. But what about this fourth one?
What's it doing there? Where's the attic that corresponds to
it, eh? Well, just let me show you something!" So up we
went, two flights of stairs, same old mess of junk as before—
trunks, suitcases, boxes, and, sure enough, *three* skylights. But
there was a pile of boxes that Toussaint had shifted away
from the wall—no problem there, they were all empty
—and believe it or not, *he'd found a door*. Locked. No
key.'

'Easy to open?'

'Absolutely impossible. Safety lock.' Blondel had so proud
an expression on his face as he recounted all this to Belot that
he was positively blushing, like a virgin at the sight of her
first naked man.*

'But—?' Belot enquired, in confident anticipation.

'I don't know what put it into my head—I mean, I had no
logical reason to think of Mlle Sarrazin's key-ring, since
Rivière had already checked on all four keys: outer door,
front door, garage, car. Still, I thought I'd try them just the
same. The car-key fitted.'

'Remarkable,' Belot said, appreciatively.

Still blushing, Blondel resumed his Diligent Schoolboy
expression.

'We didn't go in, though,' he said.

---

* *Note by Belot*: This particular virgin has had quite a lot of experience
since 1930.

'Why not?'

'Oh, we opened the door, sure, but we didn't set foot inside. No, the investigation's your pigeon, Chief. And Criminal Records, and that lot.'

'Can you at least tell me what you saw?'

'That's what I came back here for. Struck me that if you were too taken up with your bit of luggage, you might not be able to come out right away. Well, it's a bit of all right. Really nice, it is.'

'You don't say.'

'Surprised us no end, just like it did you. Anyone who fits up a room like that under the eaves, *and* camouflages its door, must really want to hide something—or somebody. Proper little *salon* they've got there—chairs, divan, wall-to-wall carpeting, even a tapestry—antique piece too, by the look of it—and low bookshelves right the way round. Like I said, really nice.'

'Just like the two lower floors, by the sound of it.'

Blondel collected his thoughts, hesitated. 'Well, it is and it isn't. You'll see just what I mean the minute you look at it. Actually, what I liked best was the way the light filtered down from the skylight, through a little silk curtain—'

'Right,' Belot said. 'Order a car and wait for me downstairs. Alert Criminal Records, too, but tell them not to touch anything if they get there before we do. I'm going back to have a word with the boss.'

When he entered the office, he happened to have hit a moment when no one was talking. Simon was still sitting in the same chair, and Truflot was busy with his papers. Picard scarcely glanced up, but spoke at once. His voice was calm; he neither felt nor pretended any vexatious contrariness.

'I'm not convinced,' he said. 'Unlike you, or him—' he jerked a thumb at Simon—'I'm never convinced by merely sentimental arguments. I will admit I'm a bit shaken, though —because Thévenet takes the same line as you do. He knows the Chênelong family, he knew Augusta, she wouldn't have been capable of killing a fly. The trouble is that everyone is capable of just that. When you're too sensitive to do it yourself, you use sticky paper strips, or sugar-traps, or insecticides. This girl's last words—and Simon admits he recalled them even before I had to remind him of them—were, of all things, "And then—". What happened between her call on La Sarrazin early in the year and last Sunday? Somebody's got to clear up that "And then" for me.'

This was an order. Simon stood up, and Belot said to him: 'Of course. And since you're the only one of us actually to have met her, you're going to tackle the job. Begin with the concierge. Try and find this François the girl was waiting for when you turned up at her flat. He may have come after you left.'

'I had that in mind,' Simon said.

'And the very best of luck to you,' said Picard.

'Just a moment, before he goes,' Belot said to Picard. 'I want him to hear what I've just been told by Blondel—something that makes me extremely impatient to get out to Neuilly.'

The news of Toussaint's discovery caused great excitement. Picard, who really had it in for Simon that evening, observed during Belot's recital: 'All this fine-tooth comb stuff. Could have done with it in the attics a bit earlier, right?'

Simon admitted it. When Belot had finished, Picard said: 'I was going to have another session with young Jean-Marc —start from the girl's suicide. But if you'd rather go out there first, you've probably got a point. We can begin the interrogation again after you get back.'

'Thought I might as well make a slight diversion to the Gare de Lyon on my way back, too,' Belot said. 'Have a look at that porter while I'm at it. That should give us ammunition and to spare for Jean-Marc.'

4

Out in the courtyard the official driver started up his engine the moment Blondel, who was standing by the car door, waved his arm. Belot hurried across and got in. Blondel followed suit. When they reached the Rue de la Ferme, Toussaint was waiting for them in the doorway.

'Congratulations, son,' Belot said. 'Records not here yet?'

'No, Chief.'

'And what about our Gisèle?'

'Still here. Said she'd been paid in advance.'

Gisèle must have been listening at the keyhole. When Belot called her name, she did not even trouble to wait for the amount of time it would have taken her to come from the kitchen or the pantry, but appeared at once.

'Good morning, Inspector,' she said. Same expression and bearing as always.

'Good morning, Gisèle. I haven't had the pleasure of seeing you since Monday.'

'Nor I you, monsieur.'

'I hope you're not too bored.'

'I've got a wireless in the pantry. And I'm a great reader.'

'These gentlemen giving you any trouble?'

Quite seriously she replied : 'Oh no. We don't have much to do with each other, it stands to reason.'

Belot said : 'Our colleagues from Criminal Records will be here any minute now. Ask them to hold on until I call them. We'll be upstairs, all three of us.'

'Where abouts upstairs?' she asked, with a faint hint of uneasiness in her voice.

'Second floor.'

She relaxed. 'Right,' she said.

They went up the stairs in silence, very fast, Belot leading and the two younger men behind. It was as though they were all three animated by a single mechanism. When they reached the second-floor landing, Toussaint went ahead of Belot: his was the privilege of acting as guide. As they made their way through the attics, he explained why they were encumbered with more junk than previously.

'After Blondel left,' he said, 'I moved out all the trunks and boxes that were still stacked against the walls. But I didn't find another door.'

'Disappointed, eh?'

'Well, yes, rather.'

His laugh sounded oddly under that low roof, boxed in by multiple surfaces of wood and fibre and leather. Night was falling; everything not directly along the line of the three skylights had already been swallowed up in darkness. Toussaint produced the key-ring from his pocket and showed them the famous key before inserting it into the lock. He opened the door, then stood aside. Belot took a good look before going in. Blondel watched his expression to see what effect the mysterious room had on him.

'You're right,' Belot said. 'It is very nice. And all brand-new.' He took a step forward. 'Traces of mud and colouring on the carpet—they'll need analysis. Hey, you never told me about the easel.'

'You think that's what struck me as odd?' Blondel asked.

Toussaint completed the question: 'Because there's nothing on it?'

Belot put on his reassuring expression. 'No, there's no reason why one shouldn't have an empty easel available to put a favourite picture on when one feels like it. A picture, or drawings, maybe. There's a big portfolio of drawings over there under the skylight, on a support or a tripod or whatever the right name is for it. And a couple of empty frames—'

He suddenly gripped Blondel by the arm. '*I'll* tell you what makes this room different from all the others. It's not just the easel that's got no picture on it. *Look at the walls!* Mlle Sarrazin has never hung a damn thing on them. Turn the light on, will you, Toussaint?'

It was bright indirect lighting, without any shadows. Noses glued to the pale beige wallpaper, the three detectives went over every surface in meticulous detail, using the palms of their hands as well.

'Not a sign of a nail anywhere,' Belot said. 'Not even a thumb-tack. Let's take a look at this portfolio, shall we?'

Here they met with a fresh surprise. There were no drawings, nothing but colour reproductions of paintings, on paper, with large numbers of pencilled notes in the margins. Reproductions of Van Gogh, naturally. Belot bent over them—he did not need to bend far, the tripod was very conveniently placed—and began to decipher the notes, which were written in what he had recognized as Mlle Sarrazin's handwriting. Names of countries, names of collections, dimensions, dates, references, numbers, initials. Sometimes, indeed, a line would lead from one of these notes across the picture itself, and ring some particular detail in it.

While he was making this examination Belot said: 'I can see why the dealers begged her to compile a catalogue! All these notes could well have been made with just such a task in view. But why wrap up the whole process in such an atmosphere of secrecy and suspicion?' He turned to Blondel and added: 'What about the books, then?'

Blondel, who had settled himself on a pouf before one of the low bookcases, read off the titles from the spines. Nearly all the books were large ones. 'Renoir. Monet. Manet. Picasso. Braque. More Picasso. Ah, here's our friend Van Gogh. Van Gogh. Van Gogh. Van Gogh. Nothing from here on but Van Gogh.'

'In that case,' said Belot, closing the portfolio again, 'what in God's name is a Gobelins-style tapestry doing in a room like this? It's got about as much in common with Van Gogh and the rest of them as the Château at Versailles has with the Samaritaine!'

'It looks as though it's been stretched on a frame,' Toussaint said.

'It's been stretched, all right—over a door! You wanted another door—well, now you've got it. Look on the left-hand side here—you can see the hinges.'

'But no door-knob,' Blondel said. 'Second door, second hiding-place.'

'Maybe. Still, if you insert your fingers here, on the right, behind the edge of the frame, and pull towards you—'

Belot suited the action to the word, and the door yielded. In fact it was as flimsy as the partition itself, one of those temporary affairs rigged up to make two rooms out of one. The tapestry might, quite simply, be there because Mlle Sarrazin had liked the look of it; but Belot had no time to fall back on this eminently reasonable conclusion, or, indeed, to ask himself on what part of the roof this new skylight—the fifth—was located. The three men were too preoccupied by the scene of wreckage and destruction which lay before them. Gradually, with many exclamations of astonishment, they began to take it in.

'All those tubes of paint squashed and broken on the floor—'

'And the palette—someone's stamped on it and broken it in two—'

'It's disgusting!' (This from Toussaint.)

'Extraordinary!' (This was Blondel, who loved paints.)

'And that canvas, it's got a hole kicked right through it—'

'*Those* canvases, you mean. There are several stacked against each other.'

Belot began to count them.

'The amazing thing is that there's nothing at all on the first one. Why smash up a blank canvas?'

'Nor on the second, nor on the third,' Belot said. He finished counting the pile: there were nine canvases in all. 'Whoever took a kick at this lot only got through as far as the fourth—but they're *all* blank! He must have been practically out of his mind. Ruining canvases, stamping on tubes and brushes! With mud all over his shoes, too—must have happened on Sunday, like everything else. Even so, he shut the two doors as he went out—'

Blondel said: 'He might have shoved this one to automatically, without thinking, and pulled the other one shut behind him.'

'Wasn't it locked when you found it?'

'It didn't need a key—it locks automatically when you shut it. You only need a key to open it.'

'The boxes were all back in place outside, though.'

'It needn't have been the same person who moved them,' Blondel said.

'Very true. Toussaint, nip down and see if the Records boys are here yet, will you?'

'Right, Chief.' He was half-way across the first room when he suddenly changed direction. 'Well, well, *well*,' he said. Belot and Blondel came through and joined him. 'The stove,' he explained. 'Just look at the guard—someone gave that a kick too, the mud from his shoes tarnished the copper.'

Blondel took out a handkerchief, wrapped it around his fingers, and lifted out the grate.

'Will you look at that, now, *mes enfants*?' Belot said, with greedy anticipation. 'Must have burnt tons of stuff to make such a pile of cinders. And not all of it is burnt, either—I can see some bits of canvas sticking out—'

Toussaint was down on his stomach in a flash. 'Hey!' he exclaimed, 'there's painting on them, too! Someone's been trying to destroy a real picture—'

'Treasure-trove,' Belot said. 'Better lock it up. Such beautiful findings demand priority.'

Criminal Records (who had arrived ten minutes earlier) now took over the two rooms. Nourry was in charge. Belot went back downstairs to the kitchen, where Gisèle was busy knitting, and listening to Marlene Dietrich sing *Ich bin von Kopf zu Fuss*. The moment he came in, she switched off the radio and stood up. This time Belot made no polite small-talk; he had his suspicious look about him, something no one found at all comfortable.

'You knew what's up there in the attic, didn't you?'

'Trunks and boxes, you mean?' Instinctively she imitated the heavy frown Belot was wearing: it seemed to have a hypnotic effect on her. 'Mademoiselle never let me go up to the second floor alone.'

'Really? Now you just listen to me, Gisèle. I'm quite ready to believe you're perfection itself, that you've never disobeyed a living soul. But you're not going to pretend that after nearly a month here you've noticed nothing peculiar about this house? Even before it came to the very nasty crime we're investigating, there were some pretty odd goings-on, weren't there? Don't try and kid me you didn't realize there were three furnished rooms up there behind those boxes—'

'Three?' Gisèle interjected.

Belot smiled, and his smile was even more alarming than his air of suspicion.

'Ah,' he said, 'it's the *number* of rooms that surprises you, is it? Not the fact of their existence, but how many of them there are.'

She made an attempt to retrieve her slip. 'Well, I mean, three hidden rooms—that's an awful lot of space—'

'Come off it. You made it one too many, and you were right. Toussaint!' Toussaint came hurrying down. 'I've got to be on my way, but I'll leave Blondel here with you. The two of you might try and get this paragon to explain why, if she didn't know there were any concealed rooms in the house, she was so surprised at the idea of there being three, especially since there aren't three. From now on Mademoiselle is to be treated as a suspect. Oh, and you'd better search her room and her belongings.'

Gisèle's lip trembled. 'You haven't the right—' she began.
'Oh, you know that too, do you? We policemen are a weak-
minded lot, that's our trouble, we're always following bad
examples. You hadn't the right to lie to us. See?'

NINE

'For everything' is not for everything

I

FOR the past thirty-six hours, ever since yesterday morning's papers had devoted a good deal of their front-page space to 'the mystery of the bloody case', Lucien Girouard, porter, forty-two years old, a native of Paron near Sens, married and the father of four children, could have become the uncrowned king of the Gare de Lyon. Yes, he'd picked up this case, he'd run down the platform clutching it in one hand, he'd chucked it into a carriage doorway like he might have done with any other last-minute traveller's luggage—and it with a severed hand inside it! He hadn't slept a wink since, couldn't eat a thing. Funny, when you thought back to the war, and you saw bits and pieces of your best chums strewn through the tree-tops. But the whole difference between war and peace was that in ordinary times trees didn't have that kind of thing in them any more, just leaves and birds; and what was more, in war-time your mate's leg or arm or whatever didn't make the front page of every newspaper, there was just this communiqué saying 'Nothing to report from the rest of the front'. His mates here in the station understood all that—one thing you had to admit, the lot you worked with were a real team, just like *that* (fingertips pressed together). When the first journalist turned up yesterday and asked for the porter who carried that bag, he, Girouard, was actually there, it wasn't his duty shift, but after reading a bit of news like that you don't feel like staying home, even with your family, and they were all having a good chin-wag together about it, well,

he made a sign to the rest of them like he wasn't there, and
Bespetro, the sharpest one of the lot, put on his oh-what-a-pity
face and said, 'There, just fancy, it was only this morning he
went off to attend a First Communion, down in the Landes
somewhere, he'll be sorry he missed you!' And for the rest of
that afternoon, and all the next day, one or other of them
would reel off the same line of patter to any journalist who
approached them. When they asked what his name was, or
where he lived in Paris, they were supplied with a name and
address that would never find him in a thousand years—

Girouard and Belot laughed over this story together, clink-
ing their *petits blancs*.

'Your good health.'

'*Santé.*'

They were in a quiet café, the one nearest to the station.
When Belot had said, 'Why don't we go and have a drink?',
Girouard had replied, 'Never mind about the drink, let's get
the weight off our feet'.

He went on with his story. As he watched the rear-light of
the Marseilles train vanishing down that long platform, he'd
said to himself: One good turn like that at every main-line
departure, and I'll soon have to put my kids on Assistance.
Afterwards, though, he'd felt bad about this thought of his.
Maybe he'd see the young man again; travellers were coming
and going the whole time, some even got to have one special
porter, wouldn't entrust their baggage to anyone else, preferred
to carry it themselves if they couldn't get 'their' man. But this
was the first passenger he'd had news of through the papers
—the first suitcase, too, if it came to that. Once three detectives
from the Narcotics Squad had stopped his trolley: two of
them had taken charge of the bags, while the third latched
on to their owner, who was walking beside them. But drugs,
well, that was like banknotes, forged or genuine made no
odds, it didn't really hit you where you felt it. A *hand*, though,
that was something else again. In the end he'd hung about
near the entrance till midnight, most of the cars had gone by

then, but he told himself that this fellow's friend, the driver, was bound to come back when he found out the mistake he'd made, and then he, Girouard, could put him in the picture, that was always worth something. Not all that much, though, he hadn't got much information to pass on, after all—

Girouard pulled himself up, and apologized. Unless he shut up altogether, he explained, he ended by having so much to get off his chest that no one could stop him, he couldn't stop himself when he wanted to. This was something Belot could very well understand. But as for what he had seen, Girouard was really sorry he couldn't help more (genuinely so, not in the way Bédat had been). He sketched the scene : how the policeman called for a porter, and he'd come up through the parked cars, in the rain, to see the young man standing there, looking a proper nit in his sodden raincoat, one case on the ground and the other—*that* one—in his hand, while he just stared at it, muttering 'The case—the case!' Girouard gave a vivid description of the marathon that followed—when it came to a run for it, Jean-Marc had been lucky to get him, forty-two years old or not, with anyone else he'd have missed his train—and also what they had said to each other; everything, in fact, that Belot had already heard twice over, from his colleagues and from Jean-Marc in person. What he wanted was some personal, first-hand recollection of the car itself, and that—

'Hold on,' Girouard said, suddenly. 'What about the policeman, the one who called me over—'

'You know him?'

'I should think so ! It was Raoul. Actually, he ought to be on duty today. Unless something special turned up, he was supposed to do a full week from Sunday. The others were only on because of it being a public holiday—'

They went back into the station.

'There he is, I can see him from here.'

Larrouy, Raoul, officer no 425, from the XIIth *arrondissement*, aged twenty-eight, thought he had seen the back of the car in question. Mark you, he wouldn't care to go on oath as to what it was like, it went off at a tremendous lick, and the lights weren't up to much because of the rain pouring down. On the other hand, what he certainly could testify was that the young gentleman was waving after it and shouting 'Monsieur! Monsieur!' as though he could have made himself heard.

And without any risk of *being* heard, Belot thought, as he walked back to the Préfecture car. He was still convinced that the episode had really happened: but conviction has no legal value, and often lacks even the power of persuasion.

2

Picard, Truflot and Belot had a beer-and-sandwich supper, topped off with coffee. This had been Picard's idea, early though it still was. Better not to resume Jean-Marc's interrogation until the lab reports were through—at least those dealing with the fingerprints, and the ashes, in the hidden studio. In any case, the policeman's First Commandment was supposed to be:

> Thou shalt ignore thy stomach
> For the benefit of all thy clients.

The author of this distich was one Chicambaut, a massive character who ate non-stop from morning till night; a habit which induced one of his colleagues to produce this variant on the original couplet:

> Thou shalt ignore thy stomach.
> Provided it is permanently full.

Thus while the three of them ate and drank, Belot was busy on his report, Truflot was taking notes to help him, and Picard was sitting and listening—having announced (a) that Augusta's autopsy confirmed death by straightforward poisoning, (b)

that M Chênelong, her father, was arriving in Paris the following morning, and expected to be met at the station; and (c)
that M Malebranche, their boss, wanted a situation report
that same evening, no matter how late.

There was a knock at the door, and Cavaglioli came in,
better known as Cava: taciturn, gloomy Cava, with the
keenest eye and sharpest brain in the whole of Criminal
Records. He plunked down a paper in front of Picard and
said: 'First results.'

Picard had got into the habit of copying his laconic man-
nerisms when talking to him.

'Fingerprints?' he queried.

'Mlle Sarrazin's. Jean-Marc Berger's.'

'Any unidentified ones?'

'None.'

'Ashes?'

'Painted canvas and stretcher.'

'What about the canvas itself? A Van Gogh?'

'Either genuine or fake. We're not experts. Signed, anyway.'

'Signed?' Picard ejaculated.

Belot laughed: it was the 'genuine or fake' that had tickled
him. 'You think anyone'd burn a genuine Van Gogh?' he
asked. 'In the pundit's house, too!'

Cavaglioli made a gesture which indicated: 'You're outside my field, that's not any business of mine.' Picard, addressing Belot, actually managed to enunciate a complete sentence
again: 'All the same, we'll have to call in an expert tomorrow
morning, just to cover ourselves. Thanks, Cava. Can go
now!'

'Bring rest later,' Cava said, and vanished.

Picard, now well away, turned to Truflot and said: 'Can—'
he picked himself up immediately '—you can bring in the
witness now.'

He said 'the witness' in spite of the burnt painting.

3

Belot was fond of making bets with himself. He made one
now. 'The moment he's brought in, I bet his eye will stray
round all the seats in the room, with the absolute conviction
that he'll find Augusta sitting on one of them.' Picard had
never been able to understand this kind of wager. 'Bet with
me,' he used to say, 'bet with anyone else you like—but not
with yourself! You're the winner every time, whichever way
it goes!' Logically speaking, this was quite true; nothing, in
actual fact, could have been more mistaken. Belot identified
himself exclusively with the better, and was very put out when
he lost. Nor did he ever lay odds on material facts, where the
margin of certainty presented too great a hazard for comfort.

The moment the door opened, he won his bet. Then Jean-
Marc lowered his eyes, and made his way to the chair in
which he had sat at four o'clock.

'Sit down, Berger,' Picard said. His tone was more polite,
but had lost none of its cutting edge. 'I have a piece of news
which is bound to come as a shock to you. On the other hand
I must tell you that it does not prejudice your position. Quite
the reverse, in fact.'

Jean-Marc's face brightened: 'You mean you've found the
American?'

'No. Mlle Augusta Chênelong committed suicide this afternoon.'

Jean-Marc's immediate reaction was a furtive glance at
Belot: as always, the dog looking to its master for a lead.
When he drew blank there, he turned back to Picard, mouth
agape, and waited for the rest of the story. Nothing happened.
Both Belot and Picard were waiting too. There were, interest-
ingly, only two possible reactions, distress or surprise. Then
Jean-Marc said: 'How—how did she do it?'

His finger on a paper that lay before him, Picard said: 'She
took poison.'

Nevertheless, surprise can assume unexpected forms, and run deeper than one might guess at first glance. Jean-Marc went into a sudden daze, muttering, in a vague, incredulous tone: 'Augusta—'

Picard's finger tapped three times on the paper. 'And she left this message,' he added.

'Ah-ha, that made the animal sit up and take notice! Quite a different reaction. Jean-Marc thrust his head and shoulders as far forward as possible, as though he had some hope of reading the paper upside down. Picard himself had no need to read it. Eyes fixed on the taut figure in front of him, he quoted from memory: *'Forgive me, Jean-Marc. Forgive me for everything.'*

The silence that followed was so intense that the sound of traffic on the *quai* outside assumed, momentarily, an importance of which long familiarity had robbed it. With even greater incredulity, and in the same tone as he had uttered Augusta's name, Jean-Marc finally said: *'For everything?'*

Picard held out the paper without actually giving it to him. 'You recognize her handwriting?' he asked.

'Yes,' Jean-Marc said, in a low voice.

Picard said: 'What had she done—what had she done, above all, to *you*—that could justify such a prayer, and, even more, such an action?'

Jean-Marc still sat hunched forward. His eyes were fixed on Picard, yet did not see him. Clearly, some sort of 'idea' was germinating in his head. Then his eye brightened, and he exclaimed: 'He was her lover!'

Now it was the other side's turn to show surprise. Both Belot and Picard leaned forward, as the latter said: 'Who?'

Jean-Marc seemed caught up in a kind of feverish excitement. 'Why, the American, the fake American, of course! Don't you see? It's all as clear as daylight now! When she found out about the cat's eye—she went to see Mlle Sarrazin, you know—she felt wounded and humiliated. Huguette told me she, Augusta that is, was in such a violent state that she wouldn't even let her inside the door! Augusta said, then, that she wanted to do her a mischief, though Mlle Sarrazin didn't believe her at the time, Superintendent, and with good reason, Augusta wouldn't have been capable of such a thing. But he, that man, *he* would! He obviously had the same relationship with Huguette as I did with Augusta. He must have got Augusta into his toils—oh, he's a good-looking man, he could have charmed her all right! Augusta obviously fell for it all, and then he roped her into his scheme, his plot. Maybe it wasn't too hard a job, either—jealousy's an emotion you can't control, especially if you're a girl, it just dominates you! Oh, I'm not saying she was an accessory to the murder, I don't know a thing about that, and anyway she's dead now, and she's asked for forgiveness. But what she did want was to get her own back on me, to see me accused, made a target for calumny, under arrest!'

Picard remarked, very calmly, as though they were having a normal conversation: 'You don't kill yourself when a wish that's been tormenting you is fulfilled.'

'It depends in what way, Superintendent,' Jean-Marc went on, in the same feverish tones. 'Obviously he wouldn't have warned her what he was up to, the trap he had in mind. A severed hand in a case, for God's sake! No, she learnt about it from the papers, that must have given her a horrible shock, and small wonder. Had you summoned her to appear here, Superintendent?' He did not leave Picard time to reply, even supposing the latter had intended to do so. 'Or else she may have called you up, because of a sudden revulsion against this monster she had taken into her confidence? But the nearer the time came for her appointment with you, the bigger panic she got into. She went out and bought some drug—she never touched pills in the ordinary way, Superintendent, she was a healthy, down-to-earth girl! If she hadn't been, I'd never have broken off with her without taking precautions on her behalf. Anyway, Superintendent, we both left each other absolutely free—we cared for each other, we got on fine, but there was never any hint of a *grand amour*, absolutely not. She was perfectly well aware of the fact, she must have known she'd let herself be eaten up with jealousy without ever having experienced the passion from which it sprang! Especially since—' ideas were now crowding into the boy's brain thick and fast '—the man must have disappeared after switching cases like that at the station. He must have worked out that I was bound to tell the whole story, that no one had any reason to disbelieve or distrust me. Even though he knew that I knew nothing, he thought it was better to stack the odds in his favour as far as possible. So he didn't see her again, and she didn't know where he was, or how long he'd be gone for. Not only had she discovered that he was a despicable, abominable creature, but she felt utterly alone—deserted, abandoned! Unless—' and here Jean-Marc swallowed with some difficulty, '—unless—'

For once the spate of words had run up against an obstacle.

'Truflot,' Picard said, 'give Monsieur a glass of water.'

Jean-Marc took the merest sip from the glass. Then he tried to calm himself by breathing very slowly and loudly through his mouth, in the way that people do when the doctor is going over them with a stethoscope.

'Unless—?' Picard said, encouragingly.

Jean-Marc squeezed his eyelids tight shut, so that he could see nothing as he said the words. 'Unless he *forced* her to take poison? And to write that note accusing herself—'

Picard allowed another moment of silence to hang heavy in the room. Then he turned to Belot and said: 'Any further questions?'

'No,' said Belot.

His eyes still shut, and his features relaxed, Jean-Marc looked like someone who had recovered from a normally fatal illness. But a sudden change of front at once recalled him to reality. Picard burst out laughing. He leaned back in his chair, clapped both hands together, and began to laugh uncontrollably, a sort of dry, quiet giggle, that Jean-Marc found

completely baffling. Then he said, in the tone of one announc-
ing a special treat : 'Right, that's that. And now, we're going
to have a little chat about *painting*.'

4

'Painting?' Jean-Marc repeated, one eye on Belot.

Belot did not look quite so amused as Picard, but even he
was smiling a little. 'Yes,' he said. 'Painting.'

'You are completely familiar with Mlle Sarrazin's house, I
take it,' Picard said. His euphoric manner suggested relief
at having got the difficult side of this interview out of the way,
at least for the time being. 'You know the attics, don't you?
Well, speak up!'

'Y-yes,' Jean-Marc said, looking very confused. Picard was
quite sure he would give anything to get back to Augusta's
tragedy, and have a long discussion about his theory, or rather
theories, concerning it. 'Yes, I know them.'

'The upstairs rooms?'

'Yes. Them too.'

'That was where you lived in Mlle Sarrazin's house?'

'Certainly not, Superintendent.'

'I'm not talking about where you slept. Obviously you didn't
need a separate bedroom—'

Jean-Marc broke in at this point. 'But I never spent a night
over there, not one single night, I swear to you—'

'Would you also be prepared to swear that you never spent
a single day in the upstairs rooms?'

'Oh no, Superintendent, of course I did.'

'Were they specially fitted up for you?'

'No, indeed not.'

'Indeed they were,' Belot put in. 'The work's less than six
months old.'

'The thing was, Mlle Sarrazin wanted me to work at my
painting—'

'Ah-ha,' said Picard. 'Now we're getting to it.'

'She used to tell me, "You're wasting your time on other people's work. Why be no more than a craftsman when you've got it in you to be an artist, a great artist? The thing is, though, painting is a professional craft, like any other, and it has to be learnt. I'll set you up in some corner of the house—" You see, Superintendent, this house was going to be ours, and that was one more reason why I should want to make a lot more money than I was doing—I mean, I didn't want to be financially dependent on my wife, and I could never hope to make a big enough income at Pauguin's—but as a painter I very well might. Especially with all Huguette's connections. She told me, "That's every collector's ultimate ambition. Not just to deal in accepted masters, whether old or modern, because after all that only calls for unlimited cash. But to discover just *one* great painter of their own day and age! That's what Dr Gachet did for Van Gogh, and that's what I want to do for you!" '

'Yes, yes, yes, yes,' said Picard. 'Precisely. Van Gogh. Am I not right in saying, Chief Inspector, that the books and other material in those rooms deal exclusively with Van Gogh?'

'No,' Belot said, in initially conciliatory tones, 'plenty of the books bear the names of other artists. But there is indeed a large portfolio which contains nothing but Van Gogh reproductions. With liberal annotations. Would M Berger care to explain the reason for this?'

Jean-Marc imitated Picard's dry little laugh. 'Oh, I never bothered my head about that,' he said. 'The fact that the rooms had been converted for my use didn't prevent Mlle Sarrazin from using them as she thought fit. She must have stored her research material there. She was always complaining she hadn't enough room.'

'With attics on that scale,' Belot said, 'she could have made six rooms instead of only two.'

'She loved being up there with me, Chief Inspector. Sometimes she'd watch me working, sometimes she'd be busy going through her books and annotating her reproductions.'

'And what did your "work" consist of?' Picard enquired. 'How does a would-be artist go about acquiring professional expertise?'

Jean-Marc had gradually recovered during this conversation, and was now ready to hold forth. Suddenly the dominant element in his nature seemed to be immaturity, a kind of childish pretentiousness.

'I don't mean to condemn present-day painting, Superintendent. The thing is, it doesn't call for hard work any more. Young people of my age think genius is enough by itself. But if you want to be a serious artist—Mlle Sarrazin explained this to me very clearly—you've got to spend time on scales and exercises, just like musicians do. Among painters this is known as copying. All great artists began by copying masterpieces, every one of them! In the end people exhibit their copies alongside their original compositions, because it's so interesting to see how they developed, and at what point they broke away and formed their own style. That's all there is to it, Superintendent.'

'I think not,' Picard said. 'So you started copying, eh? Copying what?'

'Why, Van Gogh, of course,' Jean-Marc said, as though this was the most obvious thing in the world. 'It gave her so much pleasure—'

'Superintendent, could I just make a point?' Belot asked. Picard did not so much as bother to nod in acquiescence. 'M Berger has provided us with some very interesting details concerning the apprenticeship of an artist. On the other hand—' here he turned and spoke directly to Jean-Marc '—don't you find it surprising, in retrospect, that Mlle Sarrazin thought it necessary to put you through that kind of thing? You, of all people—a sensational copyist, a top-flight specialist, the pride of the House of Pauguin? Shouldn't she have done just the opposite, in fact—encouraged you to seek, and discover, your own true bent by giving you a completely free hand?'

Jean-Marc raised his head with a challenging air. 'But she did, Chief Inspector! I painted my own pictures too—what I liked, and how I liked. And if she chose Van Gogh for me as a model, she had a great deal more in mind than her own personal enjoyment. She wanted to *counteract* my obsession with technique, my—my passion for finicky detail! You must realize that a painter can come to learn the meaning of freedom through Van Gogh!'

'In that case,' Belot said, 'it seems you still had a lot to learn. Because your passion for finicky detail, as you call it, drove you to make absolutely exact copies, even down to the signature.'

'Well, yes—you see, it was an exercise, Chief Inspector.'

Belot inclined his head. 'Thanks for the information,' he said.

Jean-Marc said, not understanding: 'Information?'

'You have just confirmed that your copies bore Van Gogh's signature.'

'At which point,' Picard added, taking over again, 'they ceased to be copies, and became fakes.'

Jean-Marc found himself losing all the ground he thought he had gained.

'But Superintendent,' he said, 'that made no difference, surely? I mean, you see, I burnt them afterwards—you must have found some ashes in the fireplace?'

'Now there,' said Picard, 'you're telling the truth—for once.'

'You burnt them *all*?' Belot demanded.

'Yes, I swear I did!'

'*Why?* Why didn't you preserve the best ones? You've just been telling us about exhibitions where they hang copies and original works side by side. Didn't you even consider the possibility of doing the same, at some future date, when you'd become famous?'

'It was Mlle Sarrazin who told me to burn them—I always followed her advice.'

But Belot pressed home the attack, scarcely giving him time to draw breath. 'What about your own paintings? Did you burn them, too?'

Jean-Marc suddenly went bright red, as though in anger. 'Oh no! I took them back to my hotel—'

'Yes, I saw the ones you left with M Bédat, he showed them to me.'

Just look at the dog waiting for its piece of sugar, Picard thought. But it was Belot who answered the unspoken prayer: 'I'm not going to give you my opinion on them, I don't know anything about art, but I will say I found them pleasant to look at. What did Mlle Sarrazin think of them?'

Jean-Marc tried to regain his earlier excitement as he said: 'She liked them enormously, Chief Inspector! She'd never have done all she did for me if she hadn't liked them! "You'll see!" she told me, "you'll see!"'

'If that was so, why didn't she have a *single* one of them hung up *anywhere* in her house?'

Jean-Marc's teeth nibbled at the back of his left hand. But his reply came promptly enough: 'You've seen her walls, haven't you? The place is just stuffed with masterpieces, didn't you realize? She wasn't going to move out a Sisley or a Renoir to hang my stuff!'

'It would have been a fine way of encouraging you, and a really splendid mark of confidence. What about your room upstairs, though? Not a thing on the walls there. Couldn't she have hung her favourites? Or even stood the latest one on the easel?'

'She never did,' Jean-Marc said, in a low voice.

'Not even on the easel, eh? I was pretty sure about the walls, but the easel was just a guess. Not even on the easel. Well, well.'

Jean-Marc said nothing.

'And couldn't you have left some of them propped against

the walls, at floor level, with their faces to the wall if need be—or even in some spare corner of the attics? I mean, if only to avoid cluttering up space *chez* Bédat? When I saw them, the old boy had got them all shoved away in a closet, and he was still complaining about them taking up too much room.'

Jean-Marc put a hand—the left hand, the one he had bitten—to his forehead. He was about to become the frightened, moaning victim once more. Belot nodded to Picard, who rapped on the table and raised his voice as he said: 'From all of which, Monsieur Jean-Marc Berger, we are forced to conclude that the only "work" you were doing in those hidden rooms was the production of artistic forgeries! That your own paintings were no more than an excuse, an alibi, the purest eyewash! And don't keep up this pretence that you burnt them all, you're an appallingly bad liar. What did you do with them? Where are they? Will you kindly get it into your stupid head that tomorrow morning the most distinguished art-experts in Paris are coming out to Neuilly to examine the Sarrazin collection in the light of our suspicions —and if none of the pictures are found to be fakes, we shall simply assume that the fakes are elsewhere. *Where?* Are you going to tell us or not? In any case you're going to be charged with forgery. That'll do till we can nail you for selling the stuff you forged. And it won't just be the experts who get out to Neuilly tomorrow. The world press will be turning up in force. So wherever you've put your fakes into circulation, there's sure to be *someone* who'll spot them!'

Jean-Marc snivelled: 'When I didn't burn them, it was because Mlle Sarrazin said to me, "Leave it alone, you can go now, I'll take care of it—"'

Picard picked up his unbreakable ruler. 'What about the destruction, the wreckage?' he exclaimed. 'The crushed paint-tubes, those torn canvases, that smashed-up palette? Weren't you responsible for all that?'

'No! That I'll swear I wasn't, Superintendent—'

Picard glanced at Belot, who shrugged his shoulders, and said to Truflot: 'Keep this young man within easy reach, we'll be having another chat with him soon.' To Jean-Marc he snapped: ' "Forgive me for everything" doesn't mean for *everything*!'

TEN

Two remarkable women

I

THE moment Jean-Marc had been led away, Picard went into action. 'Truflot,' he said—all the time he was talking he was busy sorting and collecting the documents of the case, now scattered over his desk—'get on the blower to a few journalists, will you? Not now, I don't know anything about it officially.' He was still standing as he worked. 'We've got to get this forgery story on to the front page of every first edition tomorrow morning. I'm going to have a word with the boss.'

There was a connecting door between his office and that of M Malebranche. Belot took himself off to the Crime Squad general office; he had to see Simon as soon as possible about the Augusta affair, and either Blondel or Toussaint, or both, about Gisèle. He found all three of them there, since Sergeant Malicorne had relieved Toussaint out at the Rue de la Ferme. All three had an air of anticipation about them, though Simon, to judge from his expression, was expecting a far from sunny interview. In the circumstances Belot decided to begin with the other two—quite apart from the fact that in Simon's case the subject-matter under discussion would be rather more delicate.

He said: 'You two look as though you found nothing when you did find something. Or do I deceive myself?'

'Never, Chief, never!' Blondel exclaimed.

'Idiot,' Belot said, amicably.

'You don't deceive yourself, but that Gisèle didn't deceive

us, either, even though we drew blank on our search. She had a way of following our every gesture with those great globular eyes of hers, looking as though she couldn't care less what we were up to, she thought—and then, the longer we went on, and still found nothing, she began to look so relieved that we both reached the same conclusion, didn't we, Toussaint? Oh, she'd got rid of something she didn't want us to find, all right, hidden it somewhere else—but she must have been wondering whether maybe she'd forgotten some item or other, which suggests that she did a pretty quick removal job last Monday. We asked her whether she didn't have a place of her own. Oh no, she told us, said she'd always lived on the job. As though that stopped anyone having a little place of their own for fun and games, or retirement! Go on, Toussaint, you tell him the rest.'

Toussaint said : 'I made a slight detour on the way back, and called in at the Le Bellec agency in Les Ternes. The secretary looked up her register, and told us quite a different story. "Oh yes," she said, "Mlle Gisèle Charpentier lives at No 37, Rue Fondary, in the XVth *arrondissement*." Well, by then it was too late for us to call round, but if you're in favour of the idea, Chief, Blondel and I could get there by crack of dawn tomorrow morning.'

'Good idea,' Belot said. 'She's immobilized at Neuilly, is she?'

'Sergeant Malicorne keeps her locked in her room and sleeps by the phone.'

'All right, go and get your warrant fixed up for tomorrow. And until then, sleep well, and happy dreams!'

Alone with Simon, he said : 'Well, what about you?'

Simon, clearly, had not yet got over the double shock which Augusta's death—and the manner in which it was caused—had given him. However, he did his best to appear unconcerned.

'The concierge is a very civilized, nice young girl,' he said. 'Absolutely shaken rigid by what's happened. She was responsible for cleaning the studio, so she had, as you might say, a front-row seat for the drama—if she'd bothered to use it. That's just where we're out of luck. Augusta left letters and papers scattered all over the place—and this girl never once so much as glanced at them! That's what she says, and I'm absolutely certain she's telling the truth. Augusta paid her well, spoilt her in fact—always giving her things, a blouse here, a scarf there. They often chatted together, though never about personal matters. The girl knew young Berger, though not to speak to—she knew his name, that is, because Augusta would say, "M Berger will be back before me this evening", or even "He's staying for the week-end"—straight out, just like that, not confidences, just plain information. The girl said she saw her crying a lot round Christmas and the New Year, about the time the boy vanished. After that things seem to have settled down, Augusta became her old self again, and other young men began visiting her—though no one else ever "moved in", or was even "going steady" with her. There was one of them who came past the concierge's cubby-hole pretty regularly, though, a tall brown-haired boy who always said hullo to her, very politely; but she couldn't say whether or not his first name was François. I asked her if she'd seen him yesterday, after my visit. She began by apologizing for not having seen *me* come or go, but yes, she said, she'd certainly seen him; the two of them went out together about dinner-time. She didn't see Augusta come back, either. This morning she went up to do the cleaning, as usual, and Augusta wasn't there. If it hadn't been for these bloody Easter holidays, I'd have gone round tomorrow and made enquiries in her Faculty. Maybe her father knows this character François?'

'I'd be very much surprised if he did,' Belot said. 'Best to rely on the Press.'

Then Simon muttered what he had been turning over in his mind for hours. 'It's all so inexplicable. What has Berger got to say about it? Does he know?'

'Yes, he knows. And *he's* got an explanation.'

F

Belot quickly summarized the early part of the interrogation. Simon managed to control his temper, because in the Police Judiciaire one never interrupts a superior officer; but his feelings were all too clear when he got a chance to express them.

'Why, the little bastard!' he burst out. 'When I think that he was lucky enough to sleep with that girl, that he could have spent his life with her if he'd chosen to do so—and the only explanation he can find for her last message and her suicide is that she must have been the murderer's accomplice, and his mistress into the bargain! You must have thrown him a line, that "and then" gag, I bet he grabbed it—'

'Take it easy, will you? I did *not* throw him that particular line—or any line, if you really want to know. For the sake of that poor girl, I'm touched by your disgust and anger. But if you want to refute an argument, *of whatever description*, you must either demonstrate its falsity, or else produce a more convincing one of your own. We've got a near-blank page here, Simon: "and then" at the top of it, "forgive me for everything" at the bottom, nothing in between. Until we fill in that gap, we can't afford to discard *any* hypothesis out of hand; I don't care if it makes your hair stand on end, I don't care if the person who dreams it up isn't exactly a little plaster saint, do you understand?'

'I'm sorry,' Simon said.

Belot relaxed. 'As far as that side of it goes,' he said, 'I've got some good news for you. He spent his time up in Mlle Sarrazin's attic painting copies of Van Gogh—and signing them with Van Gogh's name, too.'

The phone rang while Belot was still speaking. Simon picked up the receiver and then passed it to Belot. 'Truflot,' he said.

'Monsieur Belot? M Picard wants you in M Malebranche's office. Immediately.'

When Picard asked for someone 'immediately', this did not mean 'right away' or 'as soon as possible' or 'as early as you make it'. It meant there and then, that second, stop-watch in hand.

2

'Morning, Belot,' Malebranche said.

'Good morning, Commissioner.'

Malebranche and Picard both seemed equally delighted at the surprise they had in store for him. Malebranche pushed over to Belot one of those official forms on which international cables are translated.

'Sit you down,' he said. 'It's the best position when you've got something really interesting to read.'

'FROM: F.B.I. CRIMINAL SECTION WASHINGTON D.C. TO: DIRECTION POLICE JUDICIAIRE PRÉFECTURE DE POLICE QUAI DES ORFEVRES PARIS FRANCE.

'Worried by articles describing murder in Neuilly famous specialist Van Gogh paintings Mlle Huguette Sarrazin rich industrialist but tyro collector Springfield Illinois got expert to check painting this artist bought early in year from French gentleman in exile (?) supposedly last vast collection but forced sell SOLE (capitals) piece saved from disaster (?) stop Expert refuses authentication certifies picture as remarkable forgery stop concurrently same worry affects second collector same category ear nose and throat specialist Richmond Virginia same artist same source same verdict though different expert stop subjects these two paintings variants on famous pictures in museums Amsterdam Netherlands and Paris France sending photographs stop victims claim purchases made all good faith this office convinced their sincerity stop both bringing suit against BARON RAYMOND DE LUZARCHE name on visiting-cards French type printing no address or phone-number stop agreed description height about 1 m. 85

weight 80 kilos age 40-43 sporting appearance black hair very black eyes straight nose swarthy complexion European-type elegance Commander Legion of Honour stop no matching entry records passport control etcetera stop request you inform us whether any connection certain presumed or possible exists between this affair and Sarrazin murder stop your reply urgently needed prior to publication details necessary for encouragement other possible complaints.'

Belot passed the cable back to Malebranche. 'The news seems to be getting back to us before we send it out,' he said. 'That's my main reaction to all this. Obviously no one's going to find any trace of Luzarche, either here or in the States. This baron—his real name's probably Dupont, or some such —entered the U.S.A., and left there, on his *real* passport. Maybe he only used a false one internally—or were those visiting-cards enough?'

Malebranche said: 'He had to have one in the various hotels he stayed at during his trip, in case his prospective victims needed to call him up or make an appointment to see him.'

'All this stuff about genuine and fake passports is beside the point,' Picard muttered. 'Even the one you refer to as his "real" passport might equally well be a fake, too. Unless you extend the "real" category to genuinely anthropometric photographs, I mean those taken according to the principles we apply, in our own studios, I defy anyone to catch up with a character who's changed his appearance a bit simply by asking to see his passport! First you have to find the fellow. When you've done that, fine, you can fingerprint him and all the rest of it—but until then—!'

'And how do we know that there is another passport, anyway?' said Malebranche. 'How do we know this Frenchman isn't really an American? If his clients are no better judges of an accent than they are of a painting—'

'The chaps who sent this cable aren't much to write home

about, either,' Picard said. 'They go on about a Legion of Honour rosette as though you could only get it with a court order, and once it was in your buttonhole it was there for life. They might just as well have told us what colour socks he was wearing at the time. And what's all this about "European-type elegance?" What does *that* mean for a non-European?'

Malebranche studied the cable again. 'In any case, our first reply should be: Certain connections between the murder and the forgeries.'

Picard rose to his feet, and Belot followed him.

'One moment, Commissioner,' he said. 'We're just about to grill this boy Jean-Marc again. It might be a good thing to let them have some idea how many of these pictures are in circulation. In the United States or elsewhere, obviously.'

'Agreed,' Malebranche said. 'And in the meantime I'll have all the records gone through, usual routine check-up job—though frankly I don't think anything will come of it; there I agree with you, Belot. *Luzarche*, indeed! And pass the description on to all branches.'

3

'How many fake Van Goghs did you paint?'

'How long did each one take?'

'What were their dimensions?'

'What models were they based on?'

'Who selected them?'

'Where are the originals?'

'How much are they worth?'

'Who decided on the "variations"?'

'How much did you sell them for?'

'Apart from the two canvases we've already tracked down in America, at Springfield and Richmond, which other countries did you sell them to?'

'In which towns?'

'On what dates?'

'Names and addresses of purchasers?'

'Apart from the French accomplice who pulled off the two American operations, how many of you were there in on the game?'

'What nationalities?'

'Names, addresses?'

'Where did you meet?'

'How much did you get, personally?'

'Who fixed the percentages?'

'Did Mlle Sarrazin have a partner?'

'Or partners?'

'How much did you get, personally?'

'Where did you stash your loot away?'

'What was it made your little scheme begin to come unstuck?'

'What produced the final break?'

'Was the murder a direct or indirect result of it?'

'Did Augusta know you were a forger?'

'Had you begun your forgeries when you were still her lover?'

'Did she threaten to turn you in?'

'Did you panic when she threatened you?'

A non-stop barrage of questions, one on top of the other, sometimes contradictory: whether they emanated from Belot or Picard made little difference. The two voices struck an identical note, they were the same voice, urgent, aggressive, provocative, never letting up for a second, never giving Jean-Marc the chance to think or to pull himself together. Once, when he was five years old, Jean-Marc had set a little paper boat afloat in the gutter, and it had gone bobbing down a steep slope somewhere in the Croix-Rousse district, too fast for him to keep up with it. He felt like that boat now; another moment and he, too, would capsize and go under, just as it had done. He swore he'd told them all he knew, he swore that when he didn't give them an answer it was because he didn't know the answer, he wanted to pray and weep and grovel—but every time he fell silent the awful verbal hammering began again.

'And we'll keep this game up all night if we have to, my lad! We can rest whenever we like, there's always someone else to take our place—but you'll still be here, without any rest or food or drink or sleep. We've enough people in this place to keep you on the go for days and weeks at a time if need be. Think a miserable little squirt like you is going to stand in the way of truth and justice?'

This kind of violent interjection, much akin to a cloud-burst, was Picard's speciality. Belot's line rather resembled a steady, relentless downpour—the sort of rain that had been rattling on the glass porch of M Bédat's hotel that fatal Friday night.

'Well, how many?'

'I must have painted a dozen at the most, nine maybe, yes, nine, each one took me about a week.'

Dimensions?

Large. Mlle Sarrazin picked large models, since paintings were sold by size, so many thousand francs for so big an area of canvas.

The models?

He listed them, while Picard counted on his fingers. 'That only makes six, and you said nine. Come on, let's have the seventh!'

As for the variations, Mlle Sarrazin decided on these by herself, though sometimes he had an idea and she would adopt it, because it was a genuine painter's idea, she told him—

Skip that, we want the rest of the facts—how much were they sold for? In what countries? To whom? By whom? On what dates? What connection had all this with the murder?

'How do you expect me to know all this? I swear I never knew anyone involved, never even saw anyone—'

Augusta?

No, she'd nothing to do with this business at all, and he'd never said a word to her about it.

The emoluments, then, the pay-off?

He snickered at this last word. 'Huguette never cut me in on a penny!' he said. 'Oh, she helped me pay my hotel bill, and she gave me a bit of pocket-money, but how could I save anything on that?'

'You were working at Pauguin's, too. They gave you a good salary.'

'I spent it all, I swear I spent it all—'

Belot cut in and brought him up short. 'She never *cut you in* on a penny? *Cut you in*, eh? Talking like a proper little accomplice, aren't you?'

But at this point Jean-Marc made one of those unexpected recoveries that he had already done more than once during earlier interrogations. Suddenly conceding the facts he had hitherto denied, he now assumed the role of the worm that turned.

'Am I? I don't know anything about these usages, I'm afraid, Chief Inspector. The truth of the matter is that Mlle Sarrazin never agreed to pay me for my work! I swear I had no idea where my copies were going—I never heard the United States mentioned in that connection until this evening. All the same, I had a pretty shrewd notion they must be going somewhere. I said to her, "Look, you're making a packet out of them—what for?" And she replied, "So I don't have to sell the ones I've got." She sold forgeries as a means of hanging on to the genuine stuff. And that, do you see, I could understand. But what became of me in all that?'

'Her husband,' interjected Picard.

Jean-Marc was not in the least put out by this comment. 'Yes indeed, Chief Inspector,' he said. 'She told me that when we were married everything would be different. She said, "You're absolutely right, I want to drop the whole thing. It's shameful to think of a boy with your talents being dragged into doing such work. Please forgive me. From now on, it's over and done with. No more copying—we're going to change our whole way of life. And for a start, we're going to get married, and we'll go on a trip—to Holland, I'm dying to show you Holland—'

Picard said: 'Funny how women are always asking you to forgive them. And just when did she tell you all this?'

'Just over a week ago, the Sunday before last. When I cabled my parents.'

'And during the time since then there were no new developments, no change of attitude on her part?'

Jean-Marc replied instantly: 'None! None whatsoever, I swear it!'

'You swear too often,' said Belot. 'It's the sure mark of a liar. Just when do you suppose anyone can really believe you?'

'Chief Inspector, I'm not lying, I sw—' Jean-Marc broke off short, and then whispered: 'I'm scared, scared of everything. Someone's trying to destroy me.'

Belot turned to Picard and said: 'Don't you think, Superintendent, it might be a good idea to acquaint Berger with the description of the gang's agent in the U.S.A.? Even if he didn't know anyone?'

Picard picked up the cable and began to read at 'height about 1 m. 85, weight 80 kilos'. When he got to 'very black eyes straight nose swarthy complexion', Jean-Marc started up in his chair and exclaimed, just as Belot was waiting for him to do: 'The American!'

4

Scarcely had the door closed behind Jean-Marc and his guard when Belot, quite exceptionally irritated, declared: 'Tomorrow morning I'm going to have the whole Sarrazin house turned inside out, from cellar to roof. It's simply inconceivable that an organization like that hasn't got some sort of records tucked away somewhere—papers, notebooks, lists of names, I don't know—'

'I agree,' Picard said.

But neither of them had a chance to follow up their provisional conclusions, since at that moment the orderly appeared, holding an interview card.

'I didn't like to interrupt you during an interrogation, Superintendent,' he said. 'Anyway this person told me it wasn't urgent.'

Picard scanned the card. '*Name*,' he read, 'François Boucheny. *Object of visit*: Death of Mlle Chênelong.' He rubbed his hands briskly. 'Ah-ha,' he said, 'the elusive François! Show him in.'

His features were drawn and haggard, despite a rather terrifying smile, caused by a scar which ran from one corner of his mouth to the middle of his cheek. Apart from this he was a good-looking boy, though without any inclination to play the *beau garçon*. Same height and age as Jean-Marc. He spoke in a careful, studied manner, but with great distress in his voice.

'I'm not certain whether you're the person I need to see, sir. Downstairs they assured me you were. Besides, it's very late. I could come back at some other time more convenient to you.'

'We don't keep set hours, Monsieur Boucheny. And since you're here about the death of Mlle Chênelong, you're in luck: this is Chief Inspector Belot, who is investigating the case with which her death is connected.'

The young visitor inclined his head. Belot just managed not to acknowledge it with a parody of Boucheny's own lopsided smile.

'Gentlemen, I feel I am to blame for this girl's death,' the boy said. 'It was my responsibility. But it never occurred to me for one moment that with her in the state she was, I was crazy to suggest she took a couple of my sleeping-pills. In any case I should never have left her the whole tube—nearly full, too! She would still be alive now if I hadn't—'

'Or else she'd have thrown herself out of the window,' Picard said, soothingly. 'But it's not your degree of culpability which concerns us, or indeed even her death, much though we, like you, regret it. We are primarily interested in what happened before. Tell us, to begin with, how you learnt what had happened.'

Despite his tone, François's distress remained just as noticeable as his smile. 'I was round there only a little while ago,' he said. 'I wanted to know how she'd got on at her interview with you, and I planned to take her out to dinner, just like yesterday evening. I saw a policeman outside the house, but it never occurred to me why he was there until I found the seals on the door. I saw the concierge, who told me about Augusta being taken to Cochin—she'd found out which hospital from one of the ambulance men. I've just got back from there. My uncle's a surgeon, you see, same hospital, and one of his interns who's a friend of mine was on duty, and went to find out what was happening. She'd done it with my pills, he said. I felt I had to come round right away and explain, make it clear it was my responsibility—'

'You hadn't seen her today, then?'

'No. I should have done, it's all my fault—'

'It would help us more,' Picard said, 'if you began at the beginning, and took things in their proper order.'

'I'm sorry—it's just that I'm so upset—'

Like Simon, Belot reflected.

'I was very much in love with Mlle Chênelong. She accepted me as a friend, but didn't reciprocate my feelings. Still, I hadn't lost all hope, I felt she might come round to it little by little. Until yesterday I thought this scar of mine, due to a fall when I was a child, might be the trouble—it's perfectly natural, people just can't help a physical reaction of that sort. But yesterday I found out it was something quite different. I shall never regret our relationship—it was marvellous even to be her best friend. She always had such a positive attitude to people or ideas or events. Style, too. Really tremendous style —and a sense of humour. I met her in the Faculty, not all that long ago, two months maybe. She came and spoke to me after a paper I read. We went to a café together and had a marvellous discussion. There was such passion in her arguments—the moment I saw that light in her eye I knew that—that I—'

He broke off, and gnawed the inside of his cheek, the one with the scar on it. This hardly improved his appearance, but seemed to help him control himself.

'Yesterday morning I skimmed through a paper, as I generally do, but without noticing anything about the Neuilly murder—I'm afraid crime stories don't really interest me very much.' This last was said in apologetic tones. 'Anyway I had *never* heard Mlle Chênelong mention this fellow Jean-Marc. Is he the one who came out just as I was coming in, the one I saw the guard put handcuffs on outside the door?'

'Yes,' said Picard.

'But why? He's innocent—I have proof of his innocence.'

'He's just been arrested for painting fakes.'

This unexpected announcement shook François Boucheny out of his private drama for a moment.

'I was talking about the murder,' he said.

'Yes, we realized that. Go on.'

'Well, I was supposed to meet her yesterday afternoon. I got there a bit later than the time we'd arranged. Your inspector had just left. She was quite unrecognizable. Dead white, looked like a corpse—and at the same time somehow detached and remote. When I came in she was hunched up on one corner of the divan. She said, "Oh, it's you, François", in the way one registers the presence of some natural, familiar object that can't be of any help to one in one's present state. She got up and began to pace up and down the room, hugging her arms round herself. Then she began to talk. She went on and on. She wasn't talking to me, or to herself. She wasn't addressing anyone in particular, she was just talking, period. I even found myself wondering if it wasn't possible to die of pouring out all those words, it was like a haemorrhage. When she said, "He dared to pretend that he was here on behalf of Jean-Marc Berger—Jean-Marc, indeed!" I didn't understand for a moment whom she was attacking. It turned out to be your inspector. What she went on about was her interview with him—she repeated it word for word. You'll know about it already, of course.'

'No matter,' Picard said. 'We would be very interested to hear Mlle Chênelong's version of it, too.'

François Boucheny's memory was no less accurate than Simon Rivière's. Picard and Belot had proof both of the accuracy of the report which they already knew by heart and of the girl's honesty, despite her vehemence. The present narrator made only one comment on his own. 'I learnt about everything at the same time,' he said. 'The murder, the severed hand, the business with the case—and Augusta's liaison with this person Jean-Marc. She still loved him, too—she didn't say so, but it was obvious . . .'

He then resumed his story. Augusta got the letter from his grandmother. She followed Jean-Marc. She telephoned Huguette Sarrazin. She rang her door-bell. They confronted one another. At this point both Picard's and Belot's attention wandered : their minds were darting ahead to the climax of the scene, ready to pounce on certain all-important words as one might pounce on people from an ambush. Huguette delivered her final threat to Augusta : *Go away, get the hell out of here! If anything happens to Jean-Marc now, I'll know who to thank for it!* Picard and Belot had to exercise great self-restraint to avoid saying, in chorus : *And then*—For Christ's sake, they thought, he's got to the right point, why can't he get on and say it? But no.

'Augusta had paused in front of me. She uncrossed her arms, and placed them on my shoulders. Then she looked me straight in the eyes, though she still didn't really see me, and

left a moment's silence to emphasize that something important
was coming. Then she said, "Naturally I couldn't imagine why
anything should happen to Jean-Marc, the hatred and violence
were directed against me—there was something really quite
extraordinary about that violence of hers. And then—" '

Picard and Belot both felt the same keen stab of delight, at
precisely the same moment. At last they were going to know
all. François, wholly unaware of the effect he had produced,
went on with his story.

' "—I realized just how much she loved him, and I saw
she really *could* help him in a way a little provincial miss never
would be able to, for lack of means and important connections.
I wasn't even sure whether I now found Jean-Marc's behaviour
disgusting or not. What I *did* know was that I was getting out
of his life for good and all." '

Was that all? Both Picard and Belot, without looking at
one another, now listened with dutiful attention to the rest
of the narrative, though without the slightest hope of hearing
any new or unexpected detail. So indeed it turned out.
Augusta, it seemed, had now let her feelings out in a really
alarming manner. ' "I should have made it quite clear to them
that they'd never see or hear from me again—that they were
free to live in peace and happiness just as they pleased!
Instead of that they questioned each other, and discussed the
situation—in the hearing of some former lover of this woman's,
who'd been betrayed as I was betrayed, but hadn't resigned
himself to his fate as I had. He must have planned the whole
thing. Even down to the hand. The hand, my God! And now
Jean-Marc must surely feel that I'm responsible for the whole
thing!" '

François paused, then went on: 'How on earth was I to
calm her? I tried to make her sit down, and I wrapped her
coat round her shoulders. But I couldn't think of one single
thing. Even down to the hand. The hand, my God! And now
saying, over and over again, teeth chattering, "They're going
to confront us with one another, that's what's going to happen

tomorrow afternoon. He'll accuse me, he'll accuse me, and *he'll be right!*" She was really out of her mind. Then I made the gesture for which I can never forgive myself. I got out my tube of sleeping pills—I was going to make her take one there and then. She calmed down a bit, and said, "No, leave them with me, I'll take them when I go to bed." I invited her out to dinner, and she accepted—she even said she'd go and change and make up. In the restaurant she really seemed back to normal again, honestly she did, even though she ate almost nothing. But she was chattering away about everything in her usual way. It's true that she wanted to get home as early as possible. Outside her door she said, "Thanks, François. I really want to thank you—" Then I said I'd come along with her here today. She said, "No, that won't be necessary." I left her feeling proud and happy, I thought I'd brought off a miracle. Oh, it's a frightful business—'

Picard said : 'She betrayed your trust.'

'No, monsieur, that's not so. You can only betray those you love. Anyway, the most important question now is something quite different. Did she have any reason to regard herself as responsible?'

'None whatsoever,' said Picard. 'Any questions?' he added, with a glance at Belot.

'No.'

François stood up like an automaton, without waiting to find out if the interview was over. He looked even more distressed than he had done on arrival. Picard nodded in Truflot's direction and said : 'Would you mind just giving this gentleman a few personal particulars that he'll ask you for? We may possibly have further need of your testimony. Many thanks for coming along to see us off your own bat.'

Alone with Belot again, Picard intertwined all ten fingers and cracked them zestfully.

'There's an Italian counterpart of mine I often used to meet at international conferences,' he said. 'Every time some really ridiculous person was mentioned in his presence—

criminal, victim or cop, it made no odds—he used to say, "Any stupider than that, you die, baby." Well, poor Augusta went the limit, all right. When I think I was ready to move heaven and earth to find out what her "And then" signified! And how I practically acquitted Jean-Marc just because of that "Forgive me for everything" stuff! Wasting all that time on a busy day like this—'

'I don't think it was entirely wasted,' Belot said. 'I'm highly impressed by the kind of devotion that this boy inspired in both dead women. He's weak, egotistical, and a chronic liar, agreed. But I'm now inclined to believe in his sincerity. They were all right, those women were—'

'Come off it,' Picard said. 'I mean, just look at Mlle Sarrazin —the moving spirit behind a series of artistic forgeries, a top-flight crook, in fact! Which reminds me, the Press'll be here any moment now.'

'My reply to you can take a leaf from poor young François's book,' Belot told him. 'I was talking about the murder, and got on to the suicide as well. Whatever may have been Huguette Sarrazin's original motive for contracting this liaison, I'm certain Jean-Marc is telling the truth when he says she didn't want him to paint any more forgeries. And it was because of that she died.'

Picard bowed his head with exaggerated deference.

'Everyone in the trade admires you for your flashes of intuition,' he said. 'But there are occasions when just a little bit of tangible proof would suit my book better.'

Belot said, half to himself: 'Two quite remarkable women.' He paused, then added: 'Not counting that grandmother.'

ELEVEN

Lyons comes to Paris; Paris goes to Montmartre

I

AND not counting a certain Mme B., who was
· · · much preoccupying the thoughts of that same
grandmother in the train to Paris: the same train which
Jean-Marc and his two guardian angels had caught the
previous night. She was feigning sleep at this moment, to
avoid the fixed, staring, and decidedly disconcerting gaze of
M Chênelong, who sat there opposite her, under the sinister
blue light of the night-lamp. In her mind's eye she saw him
as he had been a few hours earlier, when the bell rang in the
Rue Dumont, and the door opened to reveal him standing
there, hatless and coatless, like some wild animal, crying:
'Madame Berger, Madame Berger—it's Augusta! She's the
person who killed that woman at Neuilly, and now she's committed suicide!' Behind him, motionless on the threshold,
there stood that same Superintendent Thévenet who had
refused to let her communicate with her grandson, but who
now had no option but to bring this bereaved father round
to see her. And Thévenet had told him: 'Don't say such
things, M Chênelong! That note the poor child left doesn't
mean what you suppose—tell him so, *madame*, see if you can
convince him!' Behind her closed eyelids she could see
them so clearly, and recollected the scene in such clear-cut
phrases, that she found it hard to believe no one could hear
her.

Well of course, she thought, Augusta's no criminal, that's
out of the question. The worst that could have happened is

that she was guilty of imprudent actions which had extremely
unfortunate results for her. But this wasn't the kind of thing
he wanted me to say. What *did* he hope to hear from me?
That it just *couldn't* have been her, because of—well, *what?*
Those ill-bred louts of provincial policemen were dead against
Jean-Marc, from the word go. And as for the hypocritical
attentiveness of that Parisian colleague of theirs—! Belot.
Frédéric Belot. They use every weapon. Even their charm,
even on an old woman like me. Poor Chênelong. The state a
man can get into. What a fall *that* was—such a successful,
important person, yet there he stood, biting his nails, and not
taking in a word anyone said. 'The shock'll kill my wife,' he
said. Well, lucky she's got a brother who's a doctor. It's
frightful to think so, but I really do think all this may have
done Émilie some good. Oh, I know she was never affected
for one moment by the outrageous theory the police have got
about Jean-Marc, but this must have cheered her up all the
same. No one likes to feel they've got a monopoly on this
world's misfortunes when they're being shared out. She can
cry as much as she likes over Augusta's death, it's another
family she's weeping for, and one that's suffered more than
we have. The Bergers aren't even in mourning for a daughter-
in-law; somebody obviously couldn't wait.

   Grandmother opened her eyes just a crack, enough to see
that her travelling-companion's face still maintained the same
tragic immobility, and quickly shut them again, plunged back
into her reverie. 'Madame Berger,' he had begged her,
'Madame Berger, don't let me go to Paris all by myself!
After all, it was Jean-Marc she asked to forgive her. Come
with me, let's go and see him together!' Would he be at the
station? No reason for him not to be. But supposing this
Frédéric character's guess had been correct, and the murderer (or murderers) now were anxious to get rid of him, too?
What sort of bad company had he wandered into? What was
the meaning of these accounts, that notebook? On Monday,
in the Rue Vauban, they'd undoubtedly made him empty

out his pockets. He must have noticed that the notebook was missing. Would he think he'd lost it? Or rather that one of the family had been through his coat pockets while he was unconscious. His grandmother, for instance. She thought to herself: Would I have come to Paris if I hadn't found it? I must show it to Frédéric. I must. 'Entrusted to Mme B.' Who is this Mme B.? Why not Mlle S.? Because this money came to him through her? Was he in fact living off her? With a good-looking boy of his age, any thirty-five-year-old Parisienne worth millions would think it perfectly natural to make him some sort of modest allowance. In that case, Mme B. might have been the confidante, the go-between, the Queen of Hearts, maybe? No, not after he'd come to tell us of his impending marriage. Could Mme B. possibly be a Bank? He's a liar, she reflected, but he's not really crooked. He lies to protect himself. And there's nothing which makes him protect himself from us, he despises us too much.

The train rattled on. Chênelong was so still he might have been dead. She wondered how he would react if she got up and closed his eyelids. Then she sank back into her thoughts once more. The obsessive quality of these last few hours. She escaped from them sometimes, as during these last few minutes, but she would never be able to exorcise them completely, never, unless somebody in the know (Frédéric?) assured her to the contrary. Her letter. Her letter to Augusta. Which Chênelong surely knew nothing about—otherwise he would hardly have come round begging her to travel with him. Her letter about the cat's-eye. 'I hope you like Jean-Marc's ring . . .' At that point there might not yet have been anything serious between the Sarrazin woman and Jean-Marc—merely a whim, a passing adventure, which would not have stopped the boy going back to Augusta. Perhaps he had not even bothered to break off the relationship at all. Young people nowadays don't bother about scruples of that sort, she thought. If it comes to that, the older generation didn't either, they just pretended to. Had the letter upset everything, or precipitated everything? She hated the thought, she did not want to believe it. *But she wondered.*

Jean-Marc despises us all. Even me. But I scare him, because I treat him rough—like the others. And because, again like them, he's a coward. Only he's a rebellious coward, while the others are cheerful, submissive cowards. Oh, they're brave enough when confronted with an officially approved enemy, they proved that at the front. But with their mother, or their employer, or their firm, it's another matter. M Couzon and the St Polycarp Cloth Mills and Silk Factory. They enjoy their condition of servitude, they roll on their backs when anyone gives them a lump of sugar. And Jean-Marc despises me, because he thinks that the reason they're like that is that I've done nothing to make them any different. He's wrong, in fact; I did what I could. But I didn't create them single-handed, after all. With my grandchildren hope returned to me. Marie-Louise looks like meeting my standards, she's an independent little cuss; anyway, it's always easier for a girl. Jean-Marc's always been different. He wants sugar-lumps too, but without needing to say thank you for them, because he feels he's just as entitled to the things as those with too many. I treat him rough, but *not* in the same way as the others. I want to make him defend himself, fight back a bit. He has the right to; he's got a gift. Maybe he even earned all this money by perfectly legitimate means? Paintings can sell at high prices once you've broken through. And the Sarrazin woman had just the set-up necessary to support him. I like his work. He'd never have gone up to Paris in the first place if it hadn't been for me.

About two o'clock in the morning, she said to Chênelong in a kindly voice, low enough for him to pretend not to have heard it if he chose to refuse her offer: 'Would you care for a sandwich? I've got either ham or anchovy.'

His immobility seemed to have had the same effect on his lungs as a hard race does on a runner's. He breathed in several times, slowly and deeply. His expression gave not the slightest indication that he had re-established contact with here-and-now reality. When he had got his breathing under control again, he said : 'I'd rather have something sweet.'

Poor man, she thought. That makes two of them. She got down the new bag that she had just bought to replace the ill-fated case, and put it on her knees. From it she produced several slices of the gingerbread which Émilie had made for Jean-Marc the day before.

2

At first crack of dawn the following day, Thursday, Blondel and Toussaint went down to the Rue de la Ferme in a police car, to take Gisèle into charge. In return, they gave Sergeant Malicorne a briefing on his morning, which looked like being a busy one. At nine o'clock M Malebranche would receive the experts in person, with Belot to assist him. At half past nine, Malicorne would put the demolition team to work. Unlike their opposite numbers in the building trade, these specialists left nothing standing but the stones. Gisèle, who had been warned of their arrival by phone, was ready, but in a peevish mood.

'You might have let me sleep a bit longer, anyway,' she said, in the car.

'You too,' Blondel said.

'And where are you supposed to be taking me now?'

'Home, darling.'

'What, all the way to Coulommiers?'

'No, your Fondary flat. If you haven't the key with you, we'll manage.'

Without the slightest change of tone, she said : 'Luckily I have got it. Know everything, you lot, don't you?'

'Little bird told us.'

'I wasn't hiding the fact, mind you. But where I lived wasn't anyone's business but my own. You won't find anything there, either. You'd be better employed catching Mademoiselle's murderer than pestering an innocent girl like me.'

'Maybe he's holed up at your place?'

She flushed bright red. 'That's a disgusting suggestion.' She hunched herself away in her corner, obviously determined not to say another word. Not that anyone wanted her to: Blondel, Toussaint and their colleague Lacroix, who was driving, were busy swopping tips about the races next Sunday —Easter Sunday—at Auteuil. The apartment block in the Rue Fondary was an old one, and the concierge's curtain still drawn across her window. The staircase was very clean. Gisèle's flat was on the third floor. They switched on the light. Two rooms and a kitchen (looking out on the court-yard), all spotless, with furniture as solid as its owner, bought on H.P. and guaranteed for years. There was a smell of encaustic soda about the place, and a high-quality deodorant in the W.C. It all hinted at first-class positions and flattering references. A few books on a whatnot, and numerous odds and ends on pierced lace mats. The general impression was of a very much lived-in place.

'Very nice,' Blondel said. 'Now we'll get to work.'

'What for?' asked Gisèle. 'You won't find your murderer hidden here.'

Blondel opened the door of the biggest cupboard. Toussaint saw Gisèle's protuberant eyes take on exactly the same expression as they had betrayed the previous evening, at the beginning of their visit to her room at Neuilly. And almost immediately, in fact, up on the left-hand side of a shelf that ran about face-level, between two bath-towels which did not even attempt to conceal them, Blondel spotted a small square jewel-box, a pair of almost new grey suede gloves, and a musical-box, rather like the sort that children are given, except that it was silvered, and made in the shape of a miniature champagne bucket.

Gisèle slumped into a chair. 'Oh God,' she said.

Blondel was sorting through his treasure-trove. 'Sure,' he said. 'It's a right laugh when it comes out of the blue like that.'

He put down the gloves and the musical-box on the table, and opened the jewel-box. From its shape and size, it could only be for a ring. The ring itself might conceivably have been a modest one; but what appeared now was anything but modest. Though the light from the ceiling was fairly dim, the diamond gave a dazzling demonstration of its powers.

Toussaint said : 'When they're that size, Madam Gisèle, aren't they known as solitaires?'

She raised her eyebrows, and the corners of her mouth went down. 'It's nothing compared to the one Mademoiselle often used to wear . . .' she said. Then she added : 'Me, of all people—I've never stolen a thing from anybody—'

'Never too late to begin, dear,' Blondel said, shutting the jewel-box and slipping it into his pocket. 'You would admit that these three—' he paused, unable to find a common term for such disparate objects '—come from Mlle Sarrazin's house?'

'They couldn't come from anywhere else,' said Gisèle. 'I must have been in such a state of shock that I brought them back without noticing it—I mean, look at those gloves, they're six and a half at the outside, and I take an eight. Fat lot of good they'd be to me!'

'I don't know about the gloves,' Blondel said, 'but that ring is going to earn you a good long spell out of circulation, fare paid and all.'

Toussaint, on the point of picking up the musical-box, said to Blondel : 'Maybe it's got some fingerprints?'

'Sure. So many that we might as well add ours to the rest.'

'Here, there's an inscription, too,' Toussaint said. 'The *Seau Grenu*, written as two words. What a horrible pun!'*

* The pun, unfortunately, is quite unreproduceable in English. The French adjective *saugrenu* means preposterous, ridiculous, absurd; *seau* is a bucket, *grenu* means grained or grainy, as of wood or leather. The logical connection between these verbal tricks is fairly scanty.—Trs.

He turned the handle slowly, and a little three-note tune timidly emerged. He increased the speed, and it became more lively. Slow again, and it was timid and melancholy once more. Gisèle at this point broke down and began to sob noisily.

'All those jewels, just lying about on the floor with the rest! I went up soon after the arrival of M Belot and these gentlemen last Monday, while they were all examining poor Mademoiselle. I wanted to find out if there had been any ructions on the first floor—I even came back down to tell them what sort of state the room was in, do you see. I must have picked it up then, along with the gloves.'

'What?' Blondel enquired. 'The musical-box?'

'No, the jewel-box. Oh, I was wrong to do it—the dead are sacrosanct. Maybe I just wanted a souvenir?' She glanced beseechingly at the Inspector. 'Perhaps I'd have given it back?'

'You can ask our bosses that question. You must have whole stacks of souvenirs by now, from this situation and all the other ones you've been in. Especially with that trick you've got of ferreting about everywhere—we'll go into all that later.'

'I swear I never touched a thing!' Gisèle exclaimed. 'Just a few table-napkins, maybe—'

Blondel had sat down, and was now studying the musical-box in his turn.

'Later, I said. First I want to know a bit more about this instrument. Was it among the stuff emptied out of the drawers?'

Toussaint bent over his shoulder, and they examined it together. It was made of imitation repoussé silver, with tiny deckles raised on a plain base, and stamped in the middle with an escutcheon which bore the words *Le Seau Grenu* in copperplate.

'All good publicity,' Toussaint said.

It was Blondel who asked the questions.

'Was Mlle Sarrazin keeping this thing as a souvenir? A very new one, by the look of it.'

'No, Inspector,' said Gisèle, who by now was ready to do anything to aid the course of justice. 'I found it somewhere else, and at a different time. It was Sunday morning, when I took Mademoiselle's breakfast up to her. Generally she used to wake up on the dot, and the first thing she'd do would be to look at her watch, I've never seen anyone so precise in their habits. But this Sunday she just couldn't wake up.'

'Was she unwell?'

'Oh no, she must have come home very late, that's all—I didn't even hear her, I was asleep. She went out after dinner on Saturday, wearing one of her most décolleté dresses. And when she got back home she must have undressed any old how, she'd just scattered her clothes all round the room, dress, stockings, slip, the lot. I even found one shoe under the chest of drawers. And normally she was so neat! There was a bunch of dance souvenirs, too—a bag of multi-coloured balls, a paper streamer. Fun and games, you might say.'

'Had she told you where she was going?'

'No, but then she never did.'

'She left alone?'

'That's right, Inspector. In her little car.'

'She was alone when she came back?'

'All I can say is, she was alone in the morning, like any other morning.'

'What happened to these dance souvenirs?'

'She told me to burn them.'

'Where?'

'In my kitchen stove, where else?'

'Did you?'

'Yes, of course. Except for the little music-box. I found that later, after she'd got up. Under the chest of drawers, like the shoe. It wouldn't have burnt, and anyway it was a nice toy.'

'Night-club publicity,' Toussaint said.

Blondel cheerfully spun the handle, *allegro con brio*. 'You've got highly eclectic tastes, Gisèle,' he told her. She stared at the floor, not understanding. 'In this particular case, I fancy you may well be entitled to some congratulations.'

3

When the three of them reached the Quai des Orfèvres, there should, on the face of it, have been a second (revised and augmented) edition of this interrogation. But although Belot, Picard and Malebranche were already there, nothing of the sort happened. Belot was simply not interested in Gisèle, despite his two juniors' conviction that this was by no means her first theft—even if on previous occasions she had never aimed as high as valuable jewellery. On the other hand he was absolutely fascinated both by the musical-box itself, and the Saturday evening excursion with which it was associated. He put a call through to the Vice Squad. A quarter of an hour later Vavasseur appeared. Sergeant Vavasseur had for some while now been on the Vice Squad's most fashionable beat. Not for nothing, one thought, looking at him, was the Squad popularly known as the *Brigade mondaine*. People tended to take him for a diplomat, and his nickname was The Cigar.

'So you want some information about the *Seau Grenu*, do you, Chief? Well, that's not too hard a problem—I was there on opening night. Oh, not on duty! The proprietor of this *boîte*—really, a four-star evening restaurant would be a more appropriate description—sent a couple of free invitations round to the Squad. Quite an expensive gesture on his part, when you saw the price of supper. We drew lots to see who went. I took a girl who adores places of that sort when they've got real chic. She was tremendously impressed. It's up the top end of the Rue des Martyrs, where it joins the Rue Condorcet.'

'What is there about this particular nightclub that might

qualify for the epithet *saugrenu*? Who's it specially cater for? Men? Women? Drug-addicts? What was going on when you were there?'

'A first-class floor-show. Getting Gina Hermann at the top of the bill is quite something—my wife has got all her records—'

But not a decent enough evening dress, Belot thought.

'From one o'clock in the morning,' Vavasseur went on, 'we were presented with flowers, and gifts, and dance souvenirs. The music was provided by a London jazz combo. Lots of atmosphere, the real thing, too.'

'What about the proprietor?'

'The place is owned by a company, which is lucky enough to have found a manager called Mercier, who's very well thought of in the business. He's run quite a few other establishments before this one—always very luxurious and very pricey, nothing at all *saugrenu* about that side of it. On Saturday he invited a representative selection of fashionable Paris—actresses, people in smart society, some artists, a couple of Academicians.'

'What sort of artists? Painters?'

'Don't writers count as artists? I recognized one of them.'

Belot produced the photograph of Huguette Sarrazin in her bathing-costume. 'Did you see *her* there?' he enquired.

Vavasseur scrutinized the picture appreciatively. 'I must say, that's quite a bright idea, showing someone a girl in a swimsuit in order to find out whether they've seen her in the flesh. Not half bad—oh, excuse me, Chief Inspector! Sure I saw her there. I don't know who she is, but I saw her all right. Care to enlighten me?'

'Huguette Sarrazin, murdered next day, Sunday, in her house out at Neuilly.'

'No kidding,' Vavasseur said, in real surprise. 'The hand in the suitcase, eh? The pictures in the papers didn't give any real idea of her. She turned up just after us, unescorted.

She was shown to a reserved table, laid for one only; unusual enough to excite comment. My girl-friend thought she was terrific. Various people said hullo or waved to her. Later, she went over and joined a party at a bigger table. Mercier had welcomed her with effusive politeness, but then he was the same with everybody. She started drinking pretty heavily, and got a bit excited and jumpy. We left before she did.'

'Have we ever had any official dealings with this character Mercier?'

'Good lord, no. He may play for high stakes, but always at the Cercle Démocratique in the Rue Favart; that ought to place him for you.'

'To reserve an entire table for yourself, alone, in a floor-show restaurant, even a four-star one, implies *some* sort of personal relationship with the manager.' Belot glanced at the clock. 'I must get down to the Gare de Lyon. I've got to meet the father of that poor child who committed suicide yesterday.'

'I've just been reading about that,' Vavasseur said.

'Simon will drive him straight round to the hospital, while I—' he broke off. 'Look, what time does this *Seau Grenu* place shut?'

'When the last customers leave, about seven o'clock in the morning. Mercier must stay on quite a bit longer—he's got the accounts to check, and quite a bit of ordering to do. Shouldn't be surprised if he's got a flat on the premises.'

'Bachelor?'

'Yes.'

'I'd have time to pop round there before the meeting with those art-experts in the Rue de la Ferme—'

Vavasseur said: 'I don't follow you.'

'So much the better for you,' Belot told him. 'I'm steering without a compass, through pea-soup fog, across waters that get more crowded every moment!'

4

With one last expiring effort, the locomotive drew to a standstill; it was as though this stopping, far from being dictated by the way the railway had been built, was really the engine's death-agony. Belot, standing at the barrier, was on the look-out for poor Chênelong. But there was a crowd, and Chênelong was not a tall man.

'Look, I can see him,' Belot said to Simon. 'Over there, all in black.' He took a step forward.

'Oh, M Belot!' Chênelong exclaimed, hands outstretched. He might have been some traveller greeting a long-lost friend. 'You came in person! Tell me I haven't got a murderer in the family—that my little girl didn't kill anybody—that she merely succumbed to a gesture of madness—'

People were beginning to stop and stare at them.

'Of *course* you haven't,' Belot said, gritting his teeth in an effort to sound convincing. 'It's a dreadful misfortune, but *nothing worse*.'

Someone behind Chênelong, even smaller than he was, stepped neatly out of his shadow and said : 'Good morning, Chief Inspector.'

'Mme Berger!' exclaimed Belot, in genuine surprise. After that letter to Augusta . . . Let's hope Chênelong doesn't find it among his daughter's papers! No, that was impossible, it had been burnt. Simon must have had the same reaction at the same moment. He ought to introduce Simon. But Grandmother was speaking again, not to explain her presence, but to ask a question.

'Jean-Marc is not here? Are you still keeping him locked up like treasure-trove?'

Bloody aggressive woman. The hell with it, then. 'He's in jail, *madame*. On a charge of uttering forgeries.' Without waiting to see the effect his announcement would have, Belot turned to Chênelong and said: 'This is Inspector Rivière. He will drive you wherever you need to go.' Suddenly he felt—for the first time in his life—a need to drop his official *persona*. He added: 'Simon Rivière is my godson, and like a real son to me. He knew your daughter slightly, and thought a great deal of her.'

Chênelong sighed unhappily, eyes downcast. He took Belot's arm, and they moved off. Grandmother brought up the rear, with Simon. She had weathered the shock of the forgery charge, and saw that this was not a propitious moment for recriminations. Give it five minutes, she told herself. Let the other two take off. Then I'll shake some facts out of this brute. She openly quizzed the man now walking beside her, and then said, in a low enough voice for him to have to bend down; 'You saw Augusta in connection with this—affair?'

'Yes, *madame*.'

'Bearing in mind the delicate manners for which your profession is famous, are you quite sure you were in no way responsible for her final decision?'

Whatever happens, Simon thought, I mustn't blush. She'd assume it was out of shame. He blushed. She took it for anger, and felt herself suitably revenged. But it was, in fact, shame.

When they reached the waiting car, Belot turned and said: 'Are you going with M Chênelong, *madame*?'

'Since he is no longer on his own, no, monsieur.'

Belot said to M Chênelong: 'Forgive me for not accompanying you, but I simply haven't a moment to spare this morning.'

That's for my benefit, Grandmother thought. But he's making a great mistake.

'We can meet this afternoon, though,' Belot went on. 'Where and when you like.'

'No, no,' Chênelong said. 'Where and when *you* like. You must not waste one moment in your hunt for a criminal who has *also* killed my daughter, if in fact she has not killed anyone. But unfortunately I have no information that could be of use to you.'

He got in beside Simon and the car drove off, leaving Belot and Grandmother standing motionless side by side. 'Well, I must be off,' Belot said.

Grandmother said : 'I too, provided—'

He had no option but to meet her eye. 'Provided what, *madame*?'

'There is something I have to tell you,' she said. 'It's the only reason I came up to Paris—Frédéric,' she added, giving him her famous chilling stare.

Belot budged not an inch, but felt he could afford to leave no stone unturned.

'Five minutes, then,' he said.

'That's all we need.'

'Right. The stationmaster will put a room at our disposal.'

They were shown into an empty office and left there. Grandmother took out Jean-Marc's notebook from her bag, and opened it at the key page.

'My grandson's accounts,' she said.

Belot skimmed through the various sums, and checked their total. 'Christ,' he said. 'And who, pray, is Mme B.?'

'That's what I was going to ask you.'

'Obviously someone living in Paris, to whom he could remit each of these sums without intermediary, and without trace. I suppose you don't know anyone here whose name begins with B?'

'No one—except for yourself.'

Belot could not restrain a smile at this, which made Grandmother smile too.

'We'll ask him,' he said. 'He's as slippery as an eel, he lies his head off—but when he sees we know something, he generally comes clean.'

'He'll get a big surprise to see you in possession of this notebook,' Grandmother said. 'Tell him you got it from me, that I came up specially to give it you.'

'He'll feel betrayed?'

'Wait a bit. First put me in the picture about this forgery business.'

Belot said : 'Well, it certainly doesn't seem to have worried you over-much.'

Grandmother made no comment on this remark, but sat and listened to what Belot told her, looking as impeccable as ever. After a night in the train, without a couchette, she still seemed as fresh as she did after her daily shower in the Rue Dumont.

Belot was saying : 'The first sums are all alike. They must represent his monthly salary at Pauguin's. The later ones will be the compensation he received—pretty lavish compensation, too—for those "copies" and their signatures.'

'There's no doubt about it,' Grandmother said, 'he's a very talented boy. Chief Inspector, there's something I'd like you to tell him, if you would. Something I feel rather strongly about. Of course I would have been happier if he'd made all this money from pictures signed Jean-Marc Berger—there can't be many young men who get an opportunity like that. But I'm very glad he didn't get it as the price of—I'm sure you see what I mean.'

'Yes indeed, *madame*,' Belot said, respectfully.

She quizzed him again, in an all-but-insulting manner.

'I detest men who exploit their charm,' she said.

He nodded. 'Don't worry. I'll tell him.'

TWELVE

The surprise of the *Seau Grenu*

I

WITH Simon thus occupied—and if Chênelong took him round to the Rue d'Assas afterwards, so much the better; despite her innocence the girl must have known more than she let on, must have left some clues behind—Belot went off to pick up Blondel in the Rue des Martyrs, a few doors down from the *Seau Grenu*. He spotted him from his taxi, stopped a little before he got there, paid off the cab and joined him on foot.

'Smashing exterior,' Blondel said. 'Looks pretty hot inside, too. Took a look through the open door, there's some sort of a servant cleaning.'

'Let's go,' Belot said.

The lighting—discreet to the point of bare visibility—revealed a vast room all done up with wood panelling; the effect was rather like an armoury in a Scottish castle. All the tables had been pushed into the corners. The central dance-floor gleamed as though fashioned of some magical substance.

'Another diamond,' Blondel said.

The servant, an elderly, scrawny man, was busy using a vacuum-cleaner, which emitted such an ear-splitting din that he never heard them come in. When he saw them, he said: 'Half a sec while I turn this thing off. All right, can I do anything for you?'

Belot said: 'Is M Mercier in?'

'What's your business, then?'

'Personal.'

The cleaner pulled a face which indicated that he'd heard this line before. 'You all say the same thing,' he complained, 'and in the end I'm the one who gets into trouble. He sees travellers—sales representatives, I mean—every day at four o'clock. In the afternoon, that is, obviously.'

'We're not sales representatives, and I give you my word you won't get into trouble. But I'm afraid if you refuse to let us in, we're coming in just the same.'

'H'm,' the old man muttered. 'Maybe you aren't, at that. Otherwise you'd have started by slipping me something. All right, then, if you'll just follow me—M Mercier's office is in the passage behind the orchestra-dais. If he isn't there he'll still be around—he's got a flat upstairs.'

As they walked past the dais, with its ghost-like instruments, Belot said : 'Business good?'

The old man said, with great pride : 'We turn away more than we let in.'

He knocked at the first door in the corridor. A rich baritone voice said : 'Come in.'

'Two gentlemen to see you, M Mercier. On personal business.'

'Oh, really?' He appeared in the doorway. Belot and Blondel both stared at him. 'M Mercier?' Belot repeated, mechanically.

'In person. You are—'

Belot glanced fractionally towards the cleaner.

'That's all right, Jean,' Mercier said. 'You can go now.'

As Jean shuffled off, his conscience allayed, Belot at once said : 'Forgive us for coming round at this hour. I am Chief Inspector Belot, of the Crime Squad, and this is one of my assistants, Inspector Blondel.'

'Do come in and sit down, gentlemen. This hour of the morning is nothing unusual for me—except that as soon as I've finished my accounts I'll be able to go to bed !' He settled himself behind his desk, which was covered with neat piles of papers. 'We don't generally get inspectors from your branch calling on us—I'm very glad to say. How can I be of service to you?'

'You've probably heard about the crime which took place last Saturday out at Neuilly. It was in all Tuesday's papers.'

Mercier's face assumed an appropriately solemn expression. 'Indeed yes. One of my patrons, Mlle Sarrazin. A most dastardly crime—'

Belot produced a small bag, and from it took the musical-box. 'We found this object in the possession of her maid. Mlle Sarrazin brought it back from here late Saturday night—or early Sunday morning.'

Mercier did not need a close scrutiny to recognize it. Belot returned the musical-box to its bag, and the bag to his pocket.

'That's right,' Mercier said. 'Mlle Sarrazin was here for the gala opening on Saturday.'

'Did you know her well?'

'I wouldn't go so far as to say that. She was never a regular at any of my establishments, she just dropped in occasionally. Still, in our line of business we have to possess an infallible memory for names and faces. Names are easy enough—the customer gives his name when he books his table, and we take care to remember it!' After this brief sally, the tone of his voice dropped once more. 'As regards faces, when a woman is as beautiful as poor Mlle Sarrazin was—' He broke off for a second. 'You, I take it, saw her when she was dead, Chief Inspector. You never knew her charm, that radiant personality of hers. And the radiance sprang from intelligence, you see. People maintain that women don't need intelligence. She proved the opposite.'

Belot seemed to appreciate this tribute. 'She must have made a great impression on you,' he said.

'I realized that when the news of the tragedy broke. The

thought of never seeing her again, even if only once every six months—'

'You never had any occasion to visit her at her house?'

'Never. I had her address in my files, but that was all.'

'I suppose you knew the people who accompanied her when she did come?'

The reply was categoric: 'She always came alone.'

'Isn't that a little odd?'

'Chief Inspector, the reputation of my establishments—' Mercier left it at that, as though no further comment were needed.

Belot said: 'I thought she had some interest in your business, that she was, as you might say, on her own home ground, perhaps?'

'Absolutely not. Let's not beat about the bush: to all intents and purposes *I* am the company. My sleeping partners are a bunch of elderly caterers, whose influence remains minimal.'

'Within the limits established by law,' Belot said, politely, 'you are at liberty to make your affairs prosper as seems best to you. Let me turn back for a moment to Mlle Sarrazin, who remained alone, it seems, in places where solitude is scarcely the fashion. She had a fiancé—a young fiancé—'

Mercier's dark eyes glinted.

'So it would seem.'

'You never saw them together?'

'No one ever saw them together! For two nights now some of my patrons who were in her circle have been talking about nothing else. It came as just as big a shock to them as the murder! I think we really ought at least to consider the possibility that this self-styled fiancé may be, to put it politely, a complete fantasist. You talk about her passion for solitude, Chief Inspector—but Mlle Sarrazin never concealed her pleasure at meeting people she knew.'

'Yes,' said Belot, 'she gave evidence of that on Saturday

night. After a while she left her table and joined another party—where, it seems, she became very animated.'

'Some colleagues of yours were among my guests,' Mercier said.

'But we don't know *who* was at this table.'

'Unfortunately, nor do I. My official duties kept me in the office or around my stars' dressing-rooms most of the time—I spent very little time in the restaurant itself. I'll ask my number one *maître-d'hotel*. When I know the number of the table, at least that'll give me the name of the man or woman who reserved it. However, that means waiting till eight o'clock this evening. Ernest, the *maître-d'hotel* in question, lives out at Vaucresson and isn't on the phone. If I may, I'll call you when I get the information.'

'Please don't trouble yourself,' Belot said. 'I'll be back at eight.' He got up, and Blondel did likewise. 'He may have happened to catch a phrase, a remark which might prove useful to us. Could you let us have your Saturday evening invitation lists now?'

'Certainly I could.'

They were there on the desk. Belot pocketed them, and thanked Mercier. 'One last question,' he said. 'Did Mlle Sarrazin strike you as a little preoccupied on Saturday, perhaps even a bit worried?'

'Certainly not, Chief Inspector.'

Mercier insisted on escorting them as far as the entrance to the restaurant. Jean was nearly through putting back the tables, with an easy dexterity which neither his age nor his skeletal figure would have led one to suppose he possessed. Belot and Mercier exchanged an energetic handshake, which lasted as long as it took Mercier to say: '*Anything* I can do to help you, please let me know. It will give me the *most* sincere pleasure to see the person guilty of so dastardly an offence pay for it with his life.'

2

'Don't look back,' Belot said to Blondel, without turning his head. 'He's probably still there in the doorway watching us go.'

'It absolutely took my breath away,' Blondel said. 'Unless we're up against a quite extraordinary coincidence—'

'Oh sure, maybe Jesus had a twin brother, too. Don't look as though you're in a hurry. Just stroll along. You'll have to come back here. But it's true, apart from the absence of a moustache, he's a dead ringer for the Baron, this character who turned up in Springfield and Richmond and heaven knows where else. He's certainly got the necessary blarney.'

'And he's the American, too—'

'According to Jean-Marc he is,' Belot said.

Blondel had his breath taken away again. '*What*, Chief? You always looked as though you believed his story, right from the beginning—'

'And now I'm having doubts. All right, yes. Yesterday evening we provided him with a portrait. There was nothing to stop him latching on to it. I believe in the existence of the character who substituted one case for another. But the fact that this character is said to have an American accent, when we know Mercier's visited America, the fact that he's the same height, looks the same, has the same features—all this might equally well suggest that our young forger wants to get his own back on an accomplice whom he regards as responsible for his *previous* misfortune, by substituting him for the mysterious character who was determined to be revenged on him. He wasn't lying when he swore he didn't know this person; but he would be lying if he said he'd never met Mercier.'

'You mean,' said Blondel, very disconcerted, 'that the fake

Van Gogh trio—the Sarrazin woman, Jean-Marc and Mercier
—might be a quartet?'

'Or else that the American is right outside this sphere of
interest altogether, that he's operating on altogether different
terrain, where, as you say, there's Jean-Marc, and the
Sarrazin woman, but not Mercier.'

'You really think—'

Belot grinned. 'Unless I'm just trying to teach you your
job as a way of not getting bogged down in mine. All right,
back you go now. Keep as close a watch on the building as
you can—main entrance, restaurant, and the service door in
the Rue Condorcet. I'll call up from the nearest *bistrot* and
get someone to relieve you as soon as possible. If he comes
out, you follow him, of course. When your reliefs turn up,
just ferret around the place a bit. Get a look at his car, that's
important. I'll alert the passport and identity-card boys. And
then I must get out to Neuilly—the boss is probably there
by now.'

'Why not arrest him right away? The artist's in jug, and
his distributing agent ought to join him there.'

'I need to know a little more about the lady behind it all
first.'

All the gentlemen assembled in the two *salons* of Mlle
Sarrazin's house could have been taken for close relatives of
the deceased. Their coats were black, their faces gloomy,
and they carefully avoided looking at one another, exactly
like a group of legatees before the reading of the will.
M Malebranche, standing before them, was not unlike the
family lawyer. The actual truth of the matter was rather
more devastating; each of these art-experts was wondering
if this meeting would ring the death-knell on his reputation.
They had all read the morning papers, and learnt of the existence of a number of forged Van Goghs, painted by *Mlle
Sarrazin's fiancé*—that was the really incredible thing—and
already disseminated throughout the world. With certificates
of authenticity? And if so, which of them had been res-

ponsible? When a distinguished lady-collector could stoop to such criminal traffic, why should she have scrupled to exploit them—great innocents that they were, one and all? Each one searched his memory, relaxed when he failed to recall any such transaction, and then began to worry again as it struck him that a man who forged Van Goghs could equally well turn out Monets, Cézannes, Renoirs, or God knows who else, provided the signature was enough recompense for his trouble, and was paid for at the going rate for a genuine canvas. When Belot appeared, this was precisely the question Malebranche was asking. How much, roughly speaking, in the judgment of the experts, would a good Van Gogh fetch, one about *so* big? On this the assembled company was unanimous: two million francs. Twenty million for the ten of them, Belot thought, and maybe more if Jean-Marc got more out of the deal than he's let on. Just what ended up in whose pockets, singular or plural?

'We have invited you here, gentlemen,' Malebranche now said, 'to endorse our belief that the pictures which you see around you are, without exception, genuine. Since yesterday, our opposite numbers in various countries have been gathering further complaints such as those the Press revealed this morning. Clearly, we have to be positive that this famous and quite exceptional collection does not also include any items manufactured *in situ*. I have nothing else to ask of you today.'

Nothing else? In the space of a second the gathering shook itself, like a sparrow after a dust-bath, and became quite relaxed again, ready to believe that a maleficent curse had been put on it for a while. Everyone, with meticulous and authoritative care, now embarked on an examination the outcome of which was never in doubt, since all the works collected by Mlle Sarrazin were familiar to anyone with the least claim to be regarded as a specialist. Belot remembered a remark Jean-Marc had made the previous evening, about her selling forgeries so that she could keep her genuine pictures. Was Mercier so infatuated with her that he was prepared to risk exposure simply to make it possible for her to hang on to them? And without asking anything for himself? Even though he was an inveterate gambler, for the highest stakes? The Cercle Démocratique in the Rue Favart hasn't installed any penny-in-the-slot machines yet as far as *I* know, Belot thought.

As soon as they had pronounced verdict, the experts hurried through the hall towards the exit. In their haste to be gone they did not notice the special 'demolition team', which was only awaiting their departure before it 'took the place apart like a bloody watch', under the direction of Sergeant Malicorne (whose formula this was).

'Can I give you a lift, Belot?' Malebranche asked.

'Thank you, Commissioner. Just as far as Saint-Germain-des-Prés, if you wouldn't mind. That's where I propose to begin my search for Mme B.'

3

'Ah, Chief Inspector!' exclaimed M Bédat, scarlet with excitement. 'Such news we've been having, eh? No doubt about it, every day brings a fresh crop of sensations. I hope you're not still cross with me for feeling I couldn't do anything about that suitcase last night? I'm sure that now—' His arms went out as though to encompass an invisible but manifest image of Truth. One glance at his visitor, however, made him decide to leave it at that.

Belot said: 'I would like to have a word with Mme Bédat, if that's possible.'

M Bédat snickered. 'Possible? I don't know. Wouldn't be for me, and I'd be very surprised if you made it, either. I'll tell you straight out, without mincing matters—my wife isn't a normal woman any more, she's a kind of weeping fountain, a cataract of tears. Right up till this morning she's been bawl-

G*

ing me out for God knows how long on the grounds that I wasn't wholeheartedly behind the boy over this business. "Such a wonderful boy", she'd say. "Ah, the poor innocent child, living through such a nightmare—as if it wasn't bad enough for him to be widowed before his wedding, someone has to chop up his fiancée and present him with the results. And now you're trying to kick him when he's down, you bastard!" I tell you, if I'd stood up to her we'd have both ended up in jail. I prefer to maintain a reasonable silence, though I must say it's an effort. But ever since she read this morning's paper, with the forger's confession in it—'

'You dirty liar, Bédat! Get out of my sight!' The voice came from behind Belot; it had Bédat's Southern accent, but was fresh, almost child-like in tone, which made its violence all the more surprising. 'You're worse than anything I can think of in this world *or* the next, and that's quite something, I'm telling you!'

Belot turned round, taking off his hat as he did so. This young girl's voice belonged to an extremely stout woman in late middle-age. Even the one step forward he saw her take showed what difficulty she had in walking. Her vast bosom was buried beneath an impeccable wool dress. She smelt of lavender, and her eyes were lavender-coloured. She had, quite obviously, been crying, and made no effort to conceal the fact. She was twisting a handkerchief in her fingers, as though she wanted to strangle her husband with it. Belot was wont to describe people whom he found in this state as 'non-functioning criminals'. He preferred them to the other sort.

'And you, monsieur, I take it,' she went on, 'must be a police officer? I don't know what you're after here, but I'll tell you one thing you'll find—a mother. A real mother. I've never had a child of my own, and when you look at the husband I've got it's clear that Divine Providence took a hand in the matter. But if I had had one, I'd have liked him to be like this boy, and I don't care if he is from Lyons! Forger, eh? Why not a murderer while you're at it? We know how you extract these so-called confessions to suit your own book. Only a miserable bastard like Bédat here would dare suggest that I'm crying because I'd "discovered his unworthiness". I'm crying because of the suffering you've inflicted on him in prison. Torturers!'

Bédat had disappeared during this tirade. Belot would not have been in the least surprised to see Grandmother's ghost standing where he had been. The fascination which Jean-Marc exercised, not so much over individual women as over Woman, was really something quite exceptional. Belot drew up one of the two chairs in the little office and said: 'I shan't take up much of your time, *madame*. Whatever unjustified suspicions you may have concerning us—' he sighed heavily, with a sad shake of the head, thinking: Why should we leave criminals with a monopoly over self-dramatization? '—it is *not* our purpose to victimise anyone. I am here to obtain *your* testimony. *You* are the person that young Berger trusted. The possibility of providing him with an *effective* defence lies in *your* hands.'

Mme Bédat, who had listened to all this in complete silence, now lowered her heavy body into one of the chairs, and showed no visible reaction when Belot followed suit.

'How do you know he trusted me?' she asked. 'Has he told you about it? It can't be easy talking to someone like you, you're so scary. The poor boy's naturally nervous, he's a very sensitive, introspective personality. If somebody treats him roughly, he'll say anything, *anything!* Even admit his guilt when he's innocent!'

Belot breathed in a great waft of lavender and murmured: 'He entrusted his money to you.'

'That is correct, monsieur.'

'We know how much.'

'Well, there you have the advantage of me. All I know is the number of envelopes he gave me. Three, there were, and on each of them he wrote, in that beautiful handwriting of his, that looked like a pattern-design, "The property of Jean-Marc Berger".'

'Would you care to let me see them?'

In the same decisive tone she said : 'No, monsieur. And no one in the world can make me. Besides, I'm suffering from amnesia, I no longer recollect where I put them, can you believe it?'

'No, *madame*,' said Belot, tit for tat. 'But since they are in your care, I'm satisfied. You will defend them against all comers, just as you have defended them against me.'

The blue eyes which went so well with that voice of hers showed a certain degree of surprise, perhaps even of perplexity.

'You talk like a lawyer,' she said. 'That's unusual in a policeman.'

'And you talk like a guardian angel, which must be even more unusual in a hotel-keeper's wife. I take it M Bédat doesn't know you have young Berger's fortune in your keeping?'

'I'm on my guard against *all* thieves.'

'You realize it's a very considerable sum?'

'So much the better for the poor boy—at least that'll be there for him when this dreadful business is over. He was so happy, you know—every time we had a moment by ourselves he'd tell me about it all—the house out at Neuilly, his girl-friend and her art-collection—'

'Before he left on Sunday evening—'

'That's right, to fix up about the wedding—'

'—he paid her a visit.'

Mme Bédat nodded in agreement. 'She rang up late that morning. I took the call, because on Sundays Bédat goes off on a pub-crawl with his good-for-nothing friends. And do you know, for the very first time she gave me her name. I always recognized her voice every time she phoned, but she always used to say—' Mme Bédat here imitated the Parisian accent '—"Could I speak to M Jean-Marc Berger, please? This is a friend of his." But on Sunday she said, straight off,

"Mlle Sarrazin here, I'd like to speak to Jean-Marc Berger. I hope he's in?" And I said, in my best voice, "Yes, Mademoiselle, he's in all right, but he may be having his Sunday bath, especially since he's going off on a trip tonight." She said, "Yes, it's because of that, he was supposed to come and see me in the evening before he left—but I'd be glad if he could come earlier, during the afternoon, say." I told her to hold on, and called the chambermaid. In fact he hadn't taken a bath because of his chill. He came down right away, they talked for a bit, and then he said, "All right, fine, that's that, then." '

'He must have come back late that afternoon to pack his bags, surely? Didn't he say anything to you then?'

'No, but the fact is, with all that rain we had on Sunday afternoon my pains kept me pinned to my bed like a proper martyr. He just put his head round the door to say goodbye. "Poor Madame Bédat," he said, "get well soon." And I said, "You too, Jean-Marc—you don't look so good yourself. Take care of yourself and come back soon." '

Two tears rolled down her fat cheeks from under the closed eyelids. Belot thanked her, and withdrew.

4

By that evening the latest results of the enquiry were as follows :—

Mercier's car corresponded exactly to the one which had picked up Jean-Marc that Sunday (and which the pseudo-American claimed to have hired); on this point the descriptions provided by the said Jean-Marc, by the porter (Lucien Girouard), and the policeman (Raoul Larrouy) were in complete agreement.

On the other hand, neither the Préfecture nor the American Consulate had any passport in the name of Luzarche recorded in their files (naturally enough), and Mercier's most recent one was ten years old. If Mercier really was Luzarche, this would tend to confirm one of Picard's hypotheses: that he used *two* false passports during the winter, not only the one in which he figured as 'Luzarche', which he kept for the benefit of American hotels, but another one to enter and leave the country.

M Chênelong and Simon Rivière had found nothing useful in Augusta's papers. M Chênelong had aged visibly in a few hours. He had booked a seat on a coach that was leaving for Lyons the following day, and checked in to the nearest hotel to wait for it. Grandmother had decided to keep him company right to the end. During a second interview with Belot, in his office, she said, by way of explanation: 'It appears that these motor-charabancs have extremely comfortable seats. Personally I have always preferred to travel by road. But can you imagine a car in our family, with the sort of sons I've got?'

Belot did not enlighten her as to the identity of Mme B., and she only asked him one question: 'Do you think this business is likely to be cleared up fairly soon?' She nearly added 'Frédéric', but Simon was there.

'I think so, *madame*,' Belot replied.

She bit her lip, then said: 'It'll be for the best, whatever happens.'

Washington had notified them of two further complaints. Another had come in from Montreal, and yet another from Milan.

Since that morning (though keeping his powers of thought and concentration tuned to maximum efficiency) Belot had been constantly on the alert for any sign from the search-party out at Neuilly. Nightfall only served to accentuate his impatience. He became taciturn, disagreeable almost. Seven o'clock. Eight o'clock.

At twenty past eight Malicorne appeared, dead beat but satisfied, and brandishing an ordinary white envelope, of more than usual thickness. He crackled it in Belot's ear.

'That's not banknotes,' he said. 'Must be papers.'

They had found it in an old edition of Voltaire's novels, between pages 276 and 277, on one of the highest shelves in the library. Belot took it, turned it over and over in his hand. 'No,' Malicorne said. 'There's nothing on it.'

THIRTEEN

'No need for introductions'

I

AT midnight, Belot and Simon were standing in Picard's office, wearing coats and hats. Belot said : 'Right. We're off. Blondel and Toussaint are already on watch there.'

'That makes no odds,' Picard said peevishly, from behind his desk. 'I'd have been much happier if you could have done it somewhere else.'

'Why? Nothing like a bit of music to brighten up an arrest.'

'Especially with stray shots by way of accompaniment. Thanks a lot.'

Belot shook his head.

'The only stray shots at the *Seau Grenu* tonight will be those that the customers have already paid for through the nose.'

'*Inshallah!*' Picard said. 'We shall eat a sandwich to your good health to fortify ourselves while we wait. Truflot?'

'Yes indeed, sir. He who dines sleeps.'

This was another axiom of Chicambaut's : hence his reputation of not sleeping otherwise.

Belot and Simon had got Lacroix as their driver. On the way Simon asked Belot : 'Are you superstitious?'

'Yes, like everybody. Why?'

'I just thought : It's not raining, everything will be all right.'

'If it had been raining, would you have said : It's going to go badly?'

Simon thought for a moment. 'I suppose not. I'd have found something else to cling to.'

'That's all very convenient,' Lacroix said, 'but—'

'There's no but about it,' said Belot. 'He's right. Superstitions are there to support us, not to discourage us.'

Lacroix said: 'I am a Protestant.'

This remark proved a conversation-stopper.

When they reached the Grands Boulevards, Belot said: 'Go down the Rue des Martyrs, and drop us off a bit before the Rue de La Tour-d'Auvergne. After that, continue as far as the Rue Condorcet. You only need to go a few yards down it: the first door on the left is the service entrance. Park as near to it as you can—that's the way we'll be coming out. You'll find Blondel or Beauchamp or the two of them there.'

When they got out, even from a distance they could see a long queue of cars outside the restaurant, proof of its newly-established fashionable popularity. Two beggars were hanging about on the sidewalk—one was Toussaint, the other the genuine article—at a discreet distance from the gold-braided commissionaire, a giant of a man. When Belot and Simon passed Toussaint, he made no sign. Nothing to report: perfect. Any trouble at this stage would be undesirable: the commissionaire obviously had a bell-push hidden away in some corner of the wall to warn people inside.

'To judge from his medals,' Simon whispered, 'he's not averse to a good dust-up.'

'Nor the tips they earn him,' Belot said.

The hero under discussion now addressed them in person, one eyebrow a trifle raised because they were not wearing evening dress, and had come on foot. 'Good evening, gentlemen,' he said. 'May I enquire if you have booked a table? We're full up.'

Belot said: 'Some friends are expecting us.'

The eyebrow, reassured, fell back into its natural position. Nevertheless the giant followed these newcomers, without being exactly certain why. Between the massive door and a heavily curtained portière—which did not however keep out the sound of music—was a rather stuffy little cloakroom. The girl-attendant reached out bare arms, as pretty as she was, to take the new arrivals' hats and coats.

'No thank you,' Belot said.

'But—' Her surprise was unfeigned, and considerable.

'These gentlemen will take their hats and coats off at their table,' said the giant, who was clearly on the point of developing eyebrow trouble again.

'Ah, I see,' she said. 'I'll show you in, then.'

He lifted the curtain. There was an immediate, battering assault on eyes and ears alike; blasts of jazz behind a babble of conversations, dazzling lights, the movements of couples on the crowded central dance-floor. Superimposed on that morning's dim emptiness, the scene reminded Belot of an evening *from the past*, the sort of thing one sees in films about dead houses that some memory brings to life again. Why not that Saturday evening—even without Huguette? But reconstructing the past did not form part of his immediate programme—we can do that later if there's time, he told himself. Someone was threading his way quickly towards them between the tables (though the pretty cloakroom attendant was still with them, the giant commissionaire had not ventured further than the doorway). This person wore a dinner-jacket, whereas the waiters were either in tails or else sporting white mess-jackets with gold-braided epaulettes. His features and bearing proclaimed a motto by no means within everyone's reach : Willingness with Dignity.

'You are M Ernest?' Belot asked.

A motto which might also embrace two further qualities : Clairvoyance and Judgment. Ernest did not conceal his embarrassment.

'You are the gentlemen who were here this morning? Too bad, I was expecting you at eight o'clock this evening. Now, I—'

A violent clash of cymbals cut off his sentence and the music at one and the same time. The noise of conversation faded away, the lights were dimmed, the dancers returned to their tables (practically groping their way in the dark), and someone carrying a small microphone now sprang on to the dais, which had become a bright glittering focal point beneath the floodlights.

'Ladies and gentlemen,' he announced, 'though I have interrupted your dancing and your conversation, I am confident this will neither displease nor disappoint you—'

'Yes, yes, I know you're very busy,' Belot whispered, 'but—'

Someone at a nearby table went *sssh!* and the voice from the microphone proceeded.

'The second part of our show tonight will in fact begin with its high-spot! You have already had a chance to appreciate various dazzling attractions (clash of cymbals) assembled from the four corners of the world (*clash!*), from the centre of those four corners, Paris (*clash!*), and from the very centre of this centre, Montmartre (*clash! clash!*), to obtain, from you, their ultimate stamp of approval—for though the world, and Paris, and Montmartre, may propose such honours, it is the clientèle of the *Seau Grenu* which ratifies them (*clash! clash!*)'

Belot tried again: 'It's of no importance, what we want now is a word with Monsieur—'

'*Quiet!*'—from several tables this time.

Ernest just managed to make out the last word of Belot's sentence, 'Mercier', as a kind of visual grimace. He responded with a hopeless shrug, as though to say: Who could get through that lot?

'But,' the microphone continued, 'the lady you are about to hear now, and on several other occasions during the evening, is one to whom you long ago granted your accolade! I give you the beautiful, the divine, the incomparable Gina—Hermann!'

There followed a burst of applause, a roll on the drums, and another final clash of cymbals. Normally Gina Hermann materialized, in all her bewitching magnificence, as soon as her name was uttered. But now, as though by some telepathic link between Ernest and the announcer, she failed to appear. This unforeseen hitch, which did not in the least disturb her prospective audience, gave the *maître-d'hôtel* and his ill-omened visitors time to cross the restaurant, skirt the corner of the bandstand, and vanish through the swing-door into the corridor. Only then did the microphone pronounce Gina Hermann's name a second time—now, clearly, with the desired result, since the orchestra struck up, and the volume of applause increased tenfold.

Ernest said : 'I can give you the information you wanted, gentlemen, if you like—'

'Later, later,' Belot said. 'You were waiting for us at eight o'clock. And since we know our way to M Mercier's office, you needn't stay any longer.'

Ernest felt Simon's hand on his arm, gently but firmly turning him round the way he had come. Belot marched up to the door, knocked, and went in without waiting for a reply.

2

'Hullo!' said Mercier, who was on the point of coming out, 'what's the meaning of this?' He was wearing a white tuxedo, and looked a model of elegance in the middleweight bracket.

'Nothing, M Mercier, nothing at all,' Belot said, tossing his hat on to the nearest chair. Simon, who had followed him in, now shut the door and took up a position immediately in front of it.

Mercier stared at him, furious. 'They're waiting for me in the restaurant!' he snapped.

'Gina Hermann hasn't begun her first number yet,' Belot

told him, noting at the same time, with satisfaction, that the office was completely sound-proof.

Mercier controlled himself with an effort. 'What do you want with me? I told you everything I could this morning.'

'Tonight I'd rather hear what you *couldn't* tell us. Anyway, this is about something different. Have you ever visited the United States?'

Mercier seemed slightly taken aback. 'The United States? Yes, often.'

'When was the last occasion?'

'Oh, at least ten years ago. Before the opening of my first nightclub, the Four-leafed Clover. I went to see all the main show-business agents—just as I did in other countries.'

'Very interesting. You're quite sure you haven't been back within the last ten years?'

'You can check my movements in your own records,' Mercier said. Belot made no comment on this. 'Look, Chief Inspector: I know my duty as a citizen towards the police. But I also know my rights. It's going too far to take advantage of my good will by turning up here in the middle of the night and asking me a lot of damn-fool questions—'

Belot remained quite unruffled. 'You work at night,' he observed. 'It's the equivalent of day as far as you're concerned. I can't claim as much for my colleague and myself. Do you like painting?'

Mercier narrowed his eyes, and seemed to be smiling; but he was very much on the alert for Belot's follow-up, which came without a second's pause.

'The painting of Van Gogh, in particular.'

The smile vanished; the air of self-assurance did not. 'Van Gogh? Why Van Gogh? Ah, that reminds me of something —but not, I think, something different. We're back to Mlle Sarrazin's murder, aren't we? Yes, that's right, the papers made great play with her remarkable collection—'

'We have every reason to believe,' Belot said, 'that she had assembled a second collection, also of Van Goghs—except that these happened to be forgeries; and that you were kind enough to dispose of them on her behalf in the U.S.A., travelling under an identity as false as the goods you were selling.'

Mercier seemed genuinely interested in this suggestion. 'Would it be tactless to ask just what identity?' he enquired. 'Or would you rather search the premises first? Either here or upstairs in my flat, take your choice. Presumably you need some evidence—a fake or two, incriminating documents, that kind of thing?'

'After last Sunday's drama,' Belot said, 'I'd be very surprised if you hadn't taken the trouble to dispose of all such tell-tale material. No, I think we can do better than that.'

This time Mercier laughed heartily, though his eye was as sharp and watchful as ever.

'Witnesses, eh? You've brought witnesses from America to confound me! Send them in, Chief Inspector—to console them for their useless journey, and you for your disappointment, the *Seau Grenu* offers you champagne on the house—'

'Keep it well chilled,' Belot said, picking up his hat. 'The meeting will not take place here.'

Mercier's laughter abruptly died away. In a flash he was transformed into something very like one of those screen heroes—some remarkable lone wolf or guerilla leader—who is on the point of escaping from his closely guarded cell, knocking out ten adversaries single-handed in the process. And there are only two of us, Belot reflected, though without any real qualms, this not being the cinema.

'Do you want to provoke a scandal that will force me to close? Do you mean to ruin me?'

'If you want to avoid a scandal, it's entirely up to you. We shall go out by the Rue Condorcet service entrance. A car is waiting for us there.'

Mercier took a deep breath.

'Will you at least let me warn my *maître-d'hôtel*?'

'One of my colleagues will do that for you.'

'Looks as though you've turned out in force,' Mercier

remarked. 'And how long is this, ah, confrontation liable to last?'

'As short a time as possible, I assure you.'

Simon opened the door. A wave of applause came surging down the corridor, bearing with it, like some Venus Anadyomene, the gorgeous Gina Hermann, as resplendent as ever, despite the absence of floodlights to enhance her appeal. She descended on them from their right just as they were on the point of turning left.

'Well, well, Mercier, *mon petit!*' she said, in a professionally sultry voice. All three of them stopped dead. 'You didn't come and listen to my number—don't you love me any more? And what do you mean by going out when I'm due back on-stage again?'

'Address your complaints to these gentlemen, Gina. They're taking me away with them.'

She laughed. My God, what a laugh, Belot thought. The *Society of Legitimate Wives* should offer her every possible inducement not to laugh, ever. Her gaze, meanwhile, had come to rest on Simon. She inspected him as though she had just received his homage.

'Well, well!' she said again, with a flutter of eyelashes that was rather overdone for so narrow a corridor. 'What have we here? Gangsters?'

'Worse than that, Gina.'

'I'm sorry, *madame*,' Belot said, in his most paternal voice. 'M Mercier will have his little joke. We're just friends of his. Come on, monsieur, let's go.'

3

The American. For twenty-four hours now Jean-Marc had been sitting on the edge of his bunk—he had not slept all the previous night—waiting, waiting until someone should deign to send for him. His whole body was still tingling, to the very roots of his hair, from the excitement provoked by this revelation. The American, the false American, the monster who had cut off Huguette's hand, who had killed her, and afterwards had tried by every means at his disposal to put the blame for *everything* on him, Jean-Marc—this was the man who had been selling his Van Goghs in America! When the Superintendent read out that extract from the cable, and he'd recognized the description, and cried out 'The American!', why hadn't they gone on? How could they treat so vital a development as a mere detail? They had stupefied him with their savage interrogations, well, of course they had their own reasons for acting that way, he ought to have come clean about the forgeries much earlier, but after all, it was the murder that was the really important issue. When he furnished them with this key link between the two affairs, why had they treated it so lightly? He had merely had to say 'The American!' and that was it—fine, good night, guard, take him back to his cell! What was more, up till now, whether at Lyons or in Paris, they'd gone on at him till he was ready to drop. But from then on, except for his morning coffee and two meals a day, he had been left in complete isolation. Stillness and silence enfolded him, cocoon-like. He had not even been let out into the courtyard for fresh air and exercise. Maybe they were trying to break him down slowly, having failed by other means. 'What have I done?' he asked himself. 'What have I done? Huguette.' He could still see her as she had been when he left that last time, standing there, a look of surprise on her face, just staring at him without saying a word —he should never have gone off like that, but surely Fate should have done *something* to prevent their never seeing one another again, to stop the appalling course events took? How desperately he'd wanted to send her a telegram from Lyons— yet her hand was already there in the case, and had been since the night before . . . But she didn't really love him, no, she had simply decided to change her approach a little, she was trying to possess him in a subtler, more deceitful fashion

—when he met her he'd thought he might escape the fate of the Bergers, *Berger*, shepherd, what a revealingly symbolic name, you virtually had to spit the first syllable when you pronounced it, Berger, shepherd, sheep-dogs, *chiens de Berger*, dogs that turned into Bergers, a family of dogs, couchant or rampant, grandfather, father, mother, uncle and all! After all, they'd got no more than they deserved since they deserved *nothing*. But he was an artist, a true artist—he deserved to be recognized, surrounded by adoring fans, made much of, with an exhibition in one of those modern galleries that could give you a reputation—and an assured market value—overnight, where beautiful ladies like Huguette would swoon with pleasure at his pictures, things like 'The Banks of the Saône' and the 'Pont des Arts' or 'The Luxembourg Gardens', with all the little details he did so well, or his imaginary oceans with their tropical light, but only his bloody old fool of a grandmother took them seriousy and what earthly good was *that*? The only result had been to make him turn out fakes, forgeries, imitations, what you will—perfectly legitimate when he did it at Pauguin's, criminal forgeries when he turned out stuff for Huguette. And there was another inexplicable thing. Since the Superintendent had decided to bring this charge against him, why hadn't he been given the opportunity, at the same time, to select a defence lawyer? As he stared at the door this was something else he half expected to see: a begowned advocate, saying 'I have been officially appointed to act as counsel on your behalf'. But that he didn't want. People 'officially appointed', in whatever profession, never really put their heart into what they were doing, it was just another job for money, grabbing a bit more cash. Grandmother would find him a lawyer, she could afford to pay top fees with all that money she had tucked away. There was no question of his dipping into the savings old Ma Bédat was looking after for him, nobody knew about them and she'd let herself be cut into little pieces rather than betray him. Cut into—The severed hand, Huguette's hand that this American had chopped off—what was there between them? Just about everything, obviously, it wasn't Augusta who had been his mistress, it was *she*! And now this despicable person had been found, was perhaps even under arrest, couldn't they give him, Jean-Marc, at least that much reassurance, admit the truth of his testimony on this vital point? The whole pattern of his life had turned him into a habitual liar. Now, for once, he had been able to speak the truth, the whole truth, without premeditation. He was sweating with fright, and found himself clenching his teeth as hard as he could, otherwise he'd start that mad laughter again, he couldn't stand much more of it, like a skeleton in this tomb of a cell—

Footsteps. A pause. The key turned in the lock, the door swinging open to reveal a sleepy-looking guard holding a pair of handcuffs. Jean-Marc stood up, unable to find words. Finally he asked what time it was.

The guard interpreted this as a complaint, since the alarm-clock in the orderly-room had shown the time to be one o'clock when the call came through. 'This is something special,' he said.

Jean-Marc held out his right hand, and one of the hand-cuffs clicked shut round his wrist; after a period of blankness such as he had just been through any noise was welcome. The other, with the chain, served as a kind of leash, a dog-leash for a *chien Berger*. This guard was undoubtedly a neurotic character. As they emerged into the empty corridor he remarked: 'All this emptiness, enough to make anyone run for it.'

Jean-Marc scarcely heard him. He was ruminating over his previous remark: 'This is something special.' And also, though this he had not given a thought to since the previous evening, 'Forgive me for everything.' The sheer joy he had felt on first hearing these words! Little of it remained now. But they wouldn't send for a common-or-garden forger in the middle of the night. Something else, some fresh development must have taken place. The sweat trickled down from his armpits to his waistband.

When they reached the senior officers' corridor, the guard asked the orderly: 'Where am I to take him, then?'

The orderly pointed to Picard's padded door. Some new development, Jean-Marc repeated to himself. Since it's in a setting I know already, it's bound to catch my eye right away. The guard tapped gently on the inner door, and a voice—that of the Superintendent, undoubtedly—gave a brief mono-syllabic grunt by way of reply. If such a sound was audible, there couldn't be many people in there, which meant nothing out of the ordinary. The guard opened the door as cautiously as a burglar.

4

Jean-Marc was wrong; the room was crowded. Apart from the Superintendent himself, and that bald character who was always scribbling away in the corner, he saw Belot, wearing a raincoat, sitting beside Picard—not to mention two younger men, also with raincoats, who had stationed themselves on the far side of the room. He had never seen either of them before, but they were pretty obviously part of the set-up. (They were in fact Simon and Blondel.) No one either spoke or moved. The air was thick with tobacco smoke, which stung the eyes and nostrils. The guard unlocked the handcuffs, saluted, and withdrew.

'Sit down,' Picard said, brusquely. He nodded to one of the two chairs facing him, with as much space between them as possible. Simon came and stood behind him; so did Blondel. Jean-Marc could feel their presence, as though they were physically pressing down on his shoulders. The empty chair appeared to have been left free.

'Truflot!' Picard called.

'Right, sir.'

He opened another door, not the one through which Jean-Marc had just come. It was the way he had entered the office the night before, after being kept waiting for hours in the little room that lay beyond it. Three more men now appeared. He saw only one of them, the tallest; and this time it was all Simon and Blondel could do, really bearing down on his shoulders with their full strength, to keep him in his chair.

'That's him!' he shouted. 'That's the murderer!'

Almost at the same instant Mercier roared out: 'There he is, the little shit—!' His always full voice had become an ear-splitting bellow, and the violence of his reaction eclipsed Jean-Marc's.

Toussaint and Beauchamp held him fast by the elbows. Despite this, and the handcuffs which they had taken the precaution of slipping on to his wrists before entering the room, it seemed as though nothing could control his vehemence.

'Perfect,' Picard said. 'You sit over there, Mercier. And unless you quieten down this minute, we'll take steps to make you.'

By a kind of self-contradictory movement, Toussaint and Beauchamp had to get the wild beast into the arena while at the same time preventing it charging. Mercier panted and roared, his chest heaving under the white dress-shirt which—taken in conjunction with the handcuffs—looked more like a de luxe straitjacket. 'You're holding this bastard just to protect him from me—the despicable coward, the filthy little shit—'

Almost in a whisper, Jean-Marc kept repeating: 'It's the murderer—it's the murderer—'

If Mercier looked like a madman, Jean-Marc felt he was going mad. In this crammed, brightly-lit, smoke-laden room, face to face with the raging monster that was Mercier, what Jean-Marc saw was Notre-Dame, the rain and the darkness, what he heard was that odd accent, that laugh, the *affability* of the man. His fear had grown to quite immeasurable proportions, there was no need for anyone to hold him down now. Only Simon was standing behind him. Blondel had gone over to help Toussaint and Beauchamp. Gripping Mercier by the neck and elbows, they forcibly dumped him on the chair.

'Just as I thought,' Picard said, when order had been restored. 'No need for introductions. And in fact you've given us rather more than we bargained for, accusing each other of the crime we're investigating—at least, that's true of you, Berger; Mercier, you seem to be satisfied with rather vaguer insults, though they're certainly violent enough.'

He provoked just the reaction he had hoped for. Mercier, whose panting had quietened a little, as though to let him hear what was said more easily, now burst forth in another furious tirade.

'That's the limit! Vague insults? I could lay my tongue round some far more terrible and crushing ones, and still fall far short of the truth! Murderer? Yes, of course he's a murderer, *the* murderer! But for me it was something *far worse* than murder, can you understand that? I'd loved this woman as no one ever loved before, loved her since she was a young girl—in the background, always in the background, but it was something, at least, that she regarded me as her friend, that sometimes she had need of me! And finding her dead, killed by this, this contemptible little guttersnipe, who'd used every trick in the book to squeeze the last drop of love and devotion out of her—and more tangible benefits, oh yes—'

He sounded as though he were on the brink of tears. Through chattering teeth Jean-Marc whispered: 'It's not true —it's not true—'

'You'll talk when I'm ready to question you,' Picard said, without taking his eyes off Mercier. 'I gather, then,' he continued, 'that contrary to what you told us a little while ago in your office, Mercier, you now admit that you had a close personal relationship with Mlle Sarrazin—we'll come back to that in a moment—and that you were present at the scene of the crime. Correct?'

Mercier by now had regained control of himself. He really

looked for all the world like some legendary Neapolitan tenor. He spoke to himself, thus sidestepping the question.

'When I found the body of this person I had cherished so dearly, and who had been so appallingly punished for her illusions, the first and foremost thought that exploded in my brain was to strike at the murderer in such a way, to put him in such a position, that he could not escape the justice of men while awaiting that of God—'

'Are you a religious man, Mercier?' Picard interjected, sceptically.

Mercier put into his voice all the persuasiveness of gesture which the handcuffs prevented him from making.

'I knew I was then, monsieur—it was my moment of truth. I had been sent there for this purpose. The spirit of vengeance dwelt in me—'

Picard made a sign for the handcuffs to be taken off him. Belot took advantage of this momentary pause to remove his raincoat, fold it carefully, and slip it under his chair. Even this movement on his part was enough to make Jean-Marc's eyes at once turn in his direction, as always. He refused to take any notice.

Mercier, chafing his wrists, went on : 'I went round because of a presentiment I had. The night before, at the gala opening of the *Seau Grenu*, before going home, Mlle Sarrazin came up to my flat for a talk with me. She had finally decided to stop her illicit trading in Van Gogh forgeries. I'd been begging her to do just this for a long time already—oh, I know I dirtied my hands in the racket myself, but then I could never refuse her anything. It was that infamous little blackguard over there who persuaded her to go in for it in the first place, just because *she* could never refuse *him* anything, either—'

Behind this flow of crisply articulated words, which aroused something more than mere professional curiosity in those listening to them, Jean-Marc's leitmotif continued to provide a thin, miserable counterpoint : 'It's not true . . . Liar, liar, filthy liar . . . It's not true . . .'

Mercier went on: 'She had told him of her decision, and he came out dead against it. He just couldn't bear the idea of never again laying those dirty paws of his on the big lump sums he'd been collecting for his forgeries. If she told me once, she told me a hundred times, he loves money like some mean, grasping miser, while people like she and I have only acquired the stuff to spend it—she on her collection, I on women. But he hoarded it.' Mercier turned to Jean-Marc, fairly spitting the words at him. 'Your "pile"! You were always on at her about wanting to make your "pile"! Oh, I know you've got it stashed away somewhere, but it'll be found in the end!'

'It already has been,' Belot informed him.

A startled exclamation escaped from Jean-Marc's lips, but no one took any notice.

'Excellent, oh excellent!' Mercier said. 'The worst punishment he could have! Well, he flew into a rage, and threatened her in the only way a coward knows: he said he'd denounce her to the police. If she hadn't revoked her decision before he left the following day, Sunday, and guaranteed him another big hand-out, he'd turn her in on the spot.'

Jean-Marc had closed his eyes. His lips still formed the words: 'It's not true—it's not true', but they were no longer audible.

'I reassured her,' Mercier continued. 'Knowing what a contemptible little rat this creature was, I advised her to threaten him for a change. I told her, "Make him think this is a big gang, and that if you tell us what he's up to, his life won't be worth tuppence." How could I have known he'd have so appalling a reaction? And yet I must have feared something of the sort in my subconscious mind, because on Sunday afternoon, about five o'clock, I suddenly decided to go and see her.' His voice dropped to a whisper. 'It was all over by the time I got there.'

'Who let you in?' Picard asked.

'The front door was ajar.'

'What about the outer door?'

'I had a key to it.'

'But not to the other one?'

'Yes.'

'Well, well,' said Picard. But he did not dwell on the point. 'And where did you find the victim?'

'On the yellow divan in the main drawing-room. Stretched out full length on her back, eyes open, an expression of amazement on her face. I didn't see any wound, but the patch of blood at neck-level was quite explicit enough.'

'You didn't make any effort to see if she might be alive? You decided there was nothing to be done, just like that?'

'Yes indeed. I fought in the war. If it taught me nothing else, it certainly taught me that.'

'Did you consider it normal behaviour not to tell anyone about your discovery?'

'I told you before and I tell you again, all I could think of was *him*! Her left arm was dangling down beside the divan, with the hand actually resting on that chequered carpet—and I saw it pointing towards the murderer!'

'Explain yourself.'

'There was this trumpery ring he'd given her as a New Year's present—she liked to wear it, as a sort of rich woman's whim. Well, this ring, a cat's-eye, was no longer on her finger. I thought: It's impossible, he can't be stupid enough to suppose that he'd divert suspicion from himself by removing it. It must be around somewhere. I found myself filled with an absolute certainty that it was this hand itself which must point the finger of accusation at him. No, please don't ask me for details, not now! I *had* to find that ring again, and put it back on her hand—the rest would come to me naturally. I behaved like a sleepwalker. Up I went to the first floor . . .'

Jean-Marc's eyes had opened again, and were full of attention. He had resumed the pose which Belot knew so well, that of a hypnotized animal. His lips were no longer moving.

'. . . I turned out every drawer in her bedroom,' Mercier

went on. 'In the end I found it—not with the rest of her jewellery, in a casket, no, it had rolled under some material and lodged in the folds of a Chinese wrapper. It was at this moment that the idea for my plan came to me. I had to stop the murderer from going off and spinning some yarn or other to his family, from enlisting them as his accomplices—I was damn sure they'd be no better than he was. I went up to the attics, and picked out a small case from my poor dead friend's luggage. The door to the studio where the fakes had been turned out was open, and I went in. I saw all the stuff at the back of the room that he'd wrecked and trampled on. The motive for the crime was staring me in the face. All the same, I shut the door and put the boxes and trunks back in place, so as not to distract the police from the essentials when they arrived.'

'Very thoughtful of you,' Picard said.

'As I went downstairs, I took the Chinese wrapper from her bedroom, and two towels from the bathroom—something to fold *it* in. When I reached the drawing-room, I got down on my knees and slipped the cat's-eye ring back on the finger which had rejected it, as a symbol of betrayal. Then I fetched a chopper from the kitchen, and—and, yes, with a single blow, with one sharp stroke, I did the deed.'

'Leaving no fingerprints anywhere.'

'I must have still been wearing my driving-gloves, I can't remember. Then I took myself off.'

'Where?'

'To find him. It was crazy, but in fact it worked. I hung around near his hotel in the Rue Bonaparte. I saw him come back about six o'clock, looking the way I hope he'll look when they guillotine him. And that was proof of his crime, too—'

'Oh no, no!' Jean-Marc breathed. 'He's lying, he's lying, he's lying!'

Picard said to Mercier: 'You recognized him. Are we to infer that you knew him without his knowing you?'

H

'Mlle Sarrazin pointed him out to me from a window one day, after he had just left her.'

'Right. Go on.'

'I parked down the end of the street, and waited, till quarter past ten. With a downpour like that, and on a Sunday, nobody took any notice of me. When I saw him come out and stand there under the porch of his hotel, first with some man or other, then alone, a kind of intoxication came over me. I would play with him as one might play with some deadly snake before crushing it. I assumed an American accent—'

'Which you had had the opportunity to study *in situ*,' Picard said. Mercier ignored this interruption. 'I faked a breakdown for the necessary amount of time. When we reached the Gare de Lyon, I left him with the cases—with *the* case. I had the courage, the heroic self-restraint, not to strangle him with my bare hands. That would have been too easy an end for him.'

'And supposing he'd left Paris without your managing to make contact?'

'I don't know what I would have done—but I'd have found him somehow! The one crucial problem was that of making him open the case *in public*. The way things went, he could have done so either in the train, or on Lyons station, or in a taxi, or before some member of his family. Wherever the thing happened, he was bound to experience, in public, the kind of shock that a nature like his would be quite incapable of coping with.'

Picard had not once glanced at Jean-Marc during this indictment. Now he turned his chair a few inches, and at once it was as though the two of them were alone in the room. He said not a word; the gesture was enough. From the depths of his nightmare, from behind the drivel of repetitive protest he had been muttering, this was all Jean-Marc had been waiting for.

'It's not true—none of it's true. He's the one who killed

her. Killed her before he cut her hand off. We had an argument, that's true, we were quarrelling, we almost came to blows—then I flung out of the house, I was tired of being treated so badly, but that was all, nothing else happened, nothing at all, I swear it didn't, Superintendent, by everything I hold holy I swear it! When I left, Mlle Sarrazin—Huguette —was still standing there, not lying down, standing! Near the divan. She'd just got up, she was going to hit me, to box my ears as though I was a naughty child, that's why I left, there and then, and she was so astonished to see me go that she never said a word. I turned round for a second at the door, and she was just standing there, staring at me. Staring at me—'

FOURTEEN

A question of choice

I

'You say you "almost came to blows"?' Picard enquired, with some interest.

Jean-Marc attempted to smile, by way of reassuring him, or reassuring himself (though in this place, and under such conditions, what hope had he of doing so?).

'Oh no, Superintendent, I don't know why I said that! Quite the contrary, in fact—it was to avoid any such thing that I got out of the place, took myself off! There are days when everything goes wrong with the people you love, and this was one of them, from the first words we spoke to each other. Besides, I was feeling unwell—'

Mercier was breathing deeply, as though once again he could barely control his anger.

'You "almost came to blows",' Picard repeated. This was the only point that interested him. 'Explain yourself, please. Up till now you have always maintained—at Lyons, here, everywhere—that your final meeting went off marvellously, that you'd just gone round to say goodbye before travelling down to Lyons and telling your family you were definitely getting married.'

'That's what I intended to do, Superintendent—and that's how it should have been, and it's my fault that things turned out differently. It's because I didn't understand, because I didn't want to see the truth! Even till a few moments ago, in my cell. It's only now that I'm beginning to understand—after all these accusations, all these lies!'

Simon and Blondel each placed a hand on Mercier's shoulders.

'You're beginning to understand what?' Picard asked. 'That she *genuinely* wanted you to drop turning out fakes, *for your sake*, out of love for you?'

'But Superintendent—!' Mercier exploded.

'Shut up, Mercier, or I'll have you taken down to the cells.'

Jean-Marc began to sob. 'Yes, that's it. Oh God, yes—'

Belot placed two fingers on the corner of the desk. Picard nodded to him. 'Please go ahead, Chief Inspector.'

Belot turned to Jean-Marc and said: 'What about the conversation you described for us yesterday, when she begged you to forgive her, and said there was to be no more copying, and talked of marrying you right away, and going off to Holland for the honeymoon? Am I right in supposing that she did not in fact say all this a week earlier, but that it was last Sunday, during your final meeting?'

Jean-Marc stared at him in amazement, as though he were some kind of magician.

'Yes, that's right,' he gasped. 'But how did you know?'

Belot made no reply. He merely said to Picard: 'That's all.'

'And why,' Picard asked Jean-Marc, 'did you tell yet another lie—this idiotic change of date, I mean?'

'That's how I remembered it—it was marvellous that other Sunday, the time I sent the telegram to Lyons, I suppose I wanted to keep it separate from that awful last day—'

'When you "almost came to blows",' Picard broke in, with sudden exasperation. 'If you go on stalling for one second longer—'

'No, Superintendent, I won't, I promise! She'd rung up that morning, asking me to go round in the afternoon rather than the evening. The outer door was open, and I closed it behind me. She opened the front door herself. She was wearing one of those pretty wrappers she had. She took me by the

H*

hand and said, "Come with me." At the bottom of the stairs, on the second tread, she turned round. She often did that, it brought her up to my height, so she could look me straight in the eyes. That's when she said the things I told you about, holding on to the lapels of my coat all the time she was talking. She didn't wait for me to make any response, she just said, "Let's go up there now." As I followed her, I couldn't believe what she'd said, I kept asking myself : What's she keeping up her sleeve? What don't I know? When we reached the first-floor landing, she said, "Not here, upstairs." And when we got there, she cheerfully opened the stove and showed me my latest copy, burning! She'd done it, of course. I tried to save it, but Huguette slammed the trap down, came within an ace of crushing my fingers, too. This made me absolutely furious. "All right!" I shouted, "if you want to destroy the lot, here goes!" I hurled myself across the room, flung my palette and tubes on the floor, smashed them up, trampled on them. I kicked holes through my canvases, I was crying with sheer rage. "You don't want us to work together any more, do you?" I shouted at her. "All you want is a fancy man, a tame gigolo—" And she said : "Are you crazy? Don't you understand? You're all I've got! You're all I've got! If I lose you, I'll have nothing left—" '

The two men had exchanged roles : it was now Mercier who cried : 'Liar! Liar! Make him stop—'

But nothing could stop Jean-Marc now, even if Picard had wanted to, which was by no means the case. Too bad if almost every phrase he uttered revealed some earlier lie; he had to make his stand.

'I couldn't believe her,' he went on, 'I just couldn't believe her. I walked down to her bedroom, and she followed me. "That's right, darling," she said, "let's make love." But I didn't want to, by now I didn't know what I was doing. There was this photograph of her in a swimsuit I had—I took it out of my wallet, and stuck it on the mantelpiece, and told her the only person she really loved was herself. Then she

tore the cat's-eye ring I'd given her off her finger, and flung
it into a drawer of her dressing-table, and screamed at me to
get out, *get out!* I did. But she came after me again, down
to the drawing-room. "No, you can't go," she said. "I forbid
you to!" And I replied, "After what you've done to me,
why should I care?" She put on that nasty glacial expression
she had, she could be really terrifying sometimes, and she
said, through clenched teeth, "You bloody little fool." I
got the impression she felt like clawing my eyes out, and
I said, "Don't you dare touch me! Or else—" And then
I grabbed a paperknife off the pedestal table, just to scare
her—'

Mercier suddenly exploded again. 'That paperknife, you
little bastard, was a souvenir I made for her myself, in 1918,
from a German shell-case! She was my favourite god-
daughter then, and I sent it her as a keepsake, from the
front—'

'Maybe, maybe,' Jean-Marc said. It was a reply, yet it
was not addressed to Mercier. 'But that's of no importance.
Obviously I couldn't *use* it. When she made as though to hit
me, I raised my arm to ward off hers, and she turned her
head away, that's all. I'll swear I never even touched her.
It just surprised her, that was all, and she stared at me, and
at that moment I felt so ashamed that I just turned and fled,
right out into the street.'

He gave a little groan. Picard remained silent for a few
seconds. Everyone was tensed up for another outburst from
Mercier, but the silence took him by surprise. He was watching Picard, who said: 'She was dead.'

'She was not,' said Jean-Marc, with the conviction of one
stating the obvious. 'While I was walking—I walked all the
way back to my hotel—I went into some café, I can't
remember where now, to ring her up and say I was sorry
for taking off like that, and tell her I was going to Lyons
anyway, and that we'd get married, of course we'd get
married! She picked up the receiver—'

'Impossible!' said Picard.

'Yes, Superintendent, she did. But she wouldn't answer me a word, though I begged and pleaded with her, she just wouldn't answer—'

Picard glanced at Mercier, who shrugged his shoulders to indicate that it had been him. Jean-Marc saw both the look and the reaction it produced.

'You mean it was him who stopped her speaking? Just as I thought—'

'No,' Picard said, opening a file, 'she was dead.'

'You mean he'd already killed her?'

'No. You had.'

'But how? Even if the point of that paperknife had just brushed her skin, let's assume that for a moment, yes, all right, let's assume it, I couldn't have done her any real harm, I'd have felt it. Surely you *feel* it when you stab someone? Besides, she'd have screamed, or groaned, or—'

'She was dead. I have here the report of the medical expert who examined her. It is very specific. Your instrument touched her at a particular spot which causes instantaneous death.'

Jean-Marc refused to give up. 'But there'd have been blood, a gush of blood—'

'Not necessarily. Just as it's quite possible that she didn't collapse right away, and might indeed have appeared alive still when you left.'

Jean-Marc clasped his hands together in supplication. His grandmother could not have resisted the picture of distress he presented—distress in which fear was not the sole element. 'Look, Superintendent,' he sobbed, 'supposing I'd only wounded her, nothing more? Couldn't it have been Mercier who finished the job? After all, he had the nerve to cut off her hand—'

Mercier never budged. Picard shook his head. 'No,' he said. 'You did it alone.'

The boy swayed on his chair. As though from a great

distance he heard a voice say: 'What did you do with the
paperknife?'

He just managed to find the strength to say: '. . . the first
drain . . .' and then, exactly as he had done in the dining-
room of his family home when the case was opened, he
slumped to the floor in a dead faint.

Picard told Toussaint and Beauchamp to take him down to
the infirmary. 'And after that,' he added, 'have him put back
in his cell. I'm through with him.'

2

Jean-Marc's removal was conducted in silence. After he
was gone, the room seemed empty, though there were in fact
still six people present. Despite the light and smoke and heat,
that electric tension had gone out of the atmosphere. This,
to judge by his behaviour, was certainly what Mercier felt.
He leaned back in his chair and crossed his legs. He looked
positively dandified: no foaming at the mouth now, and his
evening dress conveyed no hint of a straightjacket. When he
spoke, the same relaxation was apparent.

'I am most grateful to you for having let me hear that
appalling confession, Superintendent. It cleared up a great
deal for me.'

Picard made no reply. He had closed the autopsy file again,
and now just sat there, silent and abstracted. Belot's reactions
were very similar. Blondel and Rivière were now down at the
far end of the room, with Truflot, who had put down his pen
and huddled over his desk, chin on hand. The overall effect
had the curious unreality of a waxwork tableau at Madame
Tussaud's. Mercier now sat up, uncrossed his legs, and
assumed an expression of willing attentiveness. This meant
that he, if no one else, had to drop the waxwork pose.

'Oh well,' he said. 'I suppose it would be naïve to suppose

you'd let me go free after nailing me as an accessory in a
forgery case, right?'

Picard lifted two fingers and dropped them again, as
though to say : Are you kidding?

'Even if I could prove that I acted in good faith?'

Picard could not keep back a smile at this. He added,
briskly : 'There's also the matter of that severed hand. Abusing
a corpse in such a fashion is an indictable offence.'

Mercier flared up again at this. 'When I acted solely out
of love?' He breathed deeply to calm himself, and made as
though to stand up.

'Just so,' Picard said. 'Sit down, we haven't finished with
you yet. Chief Inspector Belot has something to show you.'

Without moving from his chair, Belot reached into his wallet
and took out the thick envelope that Malicorne had turned
over to him the previous evening.

'Though it does not actually bear the name of any
addressee,' he said, 'this letter is clearly meant for us—if you
can call it a letter, that is. Your connection with the person
who wrote it is close enough, I think, for you to recognize her
handwriting, even from a distance.'

Rivière and Blondel had moved back behind Mercier. He
watched as a number of sheets were removed from the envelope, unfolded, and held out for his scrutiny. He said not a
word. 'The date is specified,' Belot observed. '*Palm Sunday,
1930*. Last Sunday, in fact. The day of the murder.'

Having thus concluded his preliminary remarks, he proceeded to read the text, very carefully, and in a flat, impersonal
voice :—

'Since waking today I have been assailed by unpleasant
presentiments, and feel that I should spend some part of this
morning setting down what follows. If the future should justify
my forebodings, I cannot imagine that *anyone*, other than
the police, will have the time or opportunity to search this
house, particularly the bookshelves. So this note will be placed
in one of the books, chosen at random.

'Last night I went to the gala opening of Paul's new night-club, the *Seau Grenu*, in the Rue des Martyrs. I felt obliged to attend. I have always been completely frank and honest with him; he has always insisted on this, and for me it has always seemed natural. How else could I have envisaged our relationship? The more secrets there are in two people's lives, the fewer they should have from each other. Life itself may change, but that factor should remain constant. This fundamental element in our relationship was inculcated by him from the time of our first meetings, twenty years ago now. Yet today I see that only I adopted it without reservations, perhaps because it, like my habit of careful reflection, was temperamentally congenial to me.

'I love Jean-Marc. I can write that this morning as a self-evident fact, an absolute truth, examined from every angle during the past few weeks, and felt for months before that, though I would not, then, admit it, even to myself. I love him in every way. Clearly he is the opposite of all I had known before I met him. I told him I wanted to marry him. He didn't believe me. But he will surely believe me tonight, when I tell him I don't want him to make any more copies. I feel ashamed of having dragged him into such activities. I feel ashamed of having kept him apart from my normal life. I shall ask his forgiveness. We'll get married right away, and go away from here. We'll go and seek a blessing from the skies that Van Gogh knew. I shall let him paint anything he wants, just as he pleases. After all, he's still so young—surely *something* might come of a complete change of surroundings? I shall compensate all those who purchased his copies, as soon as possible. They're so marvellous that no one is ever likely to spot them, but what worries me is the thought of him being given away. By Paul, obviously. Only the three of us are in the know.

'Here is what I told Paul last night (always excepting my ultimate fear). We were up in his flat on the first floor. I went out of the restaurant as though leaving; I'd asked him to spare

me a few minutes upstairs. He had guessed what was coming.
Our relationship has deteriorated badly since the beginning
of the year. He had never had the occasion to see me enam-
oured of anyone, except him. To tell the truth, I ceased to
love him long ago; he could pick up all the women he liked
without my attaching the slightest importance to it. He knew
that, but he didn't mind, because I had no one else in view.
At first, Jean-Marc struck him as Providence personified! *His*
providence. It was he who thought up the idea of making
copies. One pleasant habit he'd got into—I have to state that
I went along with it—was that of regularly touching me for
large sums. He couldn't bear the thought of my resources
dwindling, and he was casting around for ways to boost them
again. This was his solution. He promised me that neither
Jean-Marc nor I would run any risks, since he intended to
deal with all external contacts. I accepted this, like everything
else, with my usual feeling of relief. After our relationship
began to get strained, I began to wonder if he might not put
pressure on me to sell my pictures. I would have done it—not
those of my favourite, of course, but there are the others,
though I'm deeply attached to them too. His idea was one I
found very seductive. Most collectors are fakes themselves,
anyway. They don't give a damn where the signature is, on
a picture or a bill of sale, provided it adds to their wealth
or their self-esteem. To exploit this contemptible attitude has
never struck me as in the slightest degree reprehensible. But
first and foremost, with the very first experiment I realized
I was on to a new and sensational game, which obsessed me
in the same way that Paul was obsessed by roulette. I had
witnessed the creation of a Van Gogh! Jean-Marc's virtuosity
is such that he painted to my specifications exactly in the
manner that an original creative artist will develop his own
ideas. However, I am not setting down this testimony in order
to analyse my feelings. Paul's reaction was terrifying. On
several occasions during our first years together I experienced
his violent outbursts, and feared the worst. But then I was

involved with him, and yielded instantly. Everything was different. In the last resort what I did came as no surprise to him, though. He had guessed what I felt for Jean-Marc before I was even prepared to admit it myself. He knows me too well. But such a decision! I thought he was going to kill me. That was silly of me, roulette isn't a drug, it doesn't destroy one's basic self-control. Paul couldn't kill me *on his own premises*, anyway. But here, in this house, to which he alone has the key?

'Since waking up, I have become convinced that he is planning to liquidate both of us, in such a way that my death will be blamed on Jean-Marc. He gave away his intentions last night, just as I was leaving him. He said—and these are his exact words—"Take care! If you persist in this plan, if you betray me, if you rob me of my due, you'll pay for it, both of you!" I'm impatient to see and talk to Jean-Marc again. I don't want to be alone any more—strange, when I always had such a passion for solitude! But is it all too late? Very well; I am following Paul's advice. I am taking care, taking precautions. I long ago made arrangements to bequeath my pictures and other possessions to various national museums. All I have left to dispose of is my life. To anyone who finds and reads these pages, I hereby declare and affirm that if I die a violent death, whatever the apparent circumstances, my murderer will be Paul Mercier.'

3

Belot added the final sheet to the rest, folded them, and replaced them in the envelope. This operation claimed his entire attention. Picard alone was watching Mercier. His face had flushed a heavy red, and his upper teeth were gnawing at his lower lip. Picard left him plenty of time to come up with some spontaneous reaction. Nothing happened. At last he said: 'Well, Paul Mercier, what have you got to say for yourself?'

Mercier's teeth released his lip, and his eyelids flickered. Picard asked himself whether they had flickered at all during the reading of this document. He rather thought not. But one thing he *was* sure of, and that was that Mercier's eyes had never once shifted away from those sheets of paper.

Mercier sniggered and said : 'Well, Superintendent, if you hadn't elicited so irrefutable a confession just now, *with me there as an eyewitness*, I'd be in real trouble, wouldn't I ?'

Picard picked up his ruler. 'Your presence was not merely accidental, M Mercier. It will now enable us, shall we say, to confront you with yourself. And I'd say you *were* in pretty real trouble.'

Belot had put the envelope down on the corner of the desk. He now said, in a quiet, unemphatic voice : 'You went there with the intention of killing her, didn't you ? Oh, spare us your fine frenzies, please; there's no one left here for you to terrorize. If you feel a mild dust-up would help you into better spirits, that's another matter. Not that you were ever in particularly low spirits, were you ? In fact your cheerfulness kept pretty constant—*except* on that Saturday night, after Mlle Sarrazin had told you she was seeing young Berger on Sunday evening. You visited her to do just what she had predicted you would—she was an extremely intelligent woman, no doubt about it. Which was, kill her. Then you intended to wait in the Rue de la Ferme until the boy arrived, exactly as you afterwards hung about in the Rue Bonaparte waiting for him to leave. You meant to follow him into the house, and catch him "in the act". And then you would have brought us in.'

Mercier, it was clear, had finally opted for a non-violent discussion. He said : 'You'd still have found this letter; and what makes you think that little bastard would have confessed in such circumstances ? He'd have protested his innocence to the last. I'd have been crazy to try a trick like that—'

'You *were* crazy,' Belot told him. 'The idea of such a letter had never even crossed your mind. Unless—the real reason why you turned the place upside-down in the way you did was not so much to find the ring as because you guessed an incriminating document might be hidden somewhere? Oh yes, you were crazy, right enough, and with good reason! The crime you had come to commit, and then blame on someone else, had already been committed by that person, and blamed on you. He had even used a weapon that was your present.'

'Look, *copper*,' Mercier said, 'you'll never get a charge like that to stick in court. You've only got one witness, and that's this besotted woman who was hell-bent on destroying me. Where you're right, though, is in thinking I wanted to steam the fuse out of this bomb I'd had planted on me. Would you deny innocent people the right to protect themselves against the guilty—especially when the latter walk right into their hands? Without that hand in the case—I should really have cut off the other one, the hand that wrote all these appalling slanders against me—are you so sure that you would have brought the murderer to book in less than a week, and finally broken him down in less than one day?'

'We shall notify the Chief Commissioner of your outstanding assistance in this case,' Picard said. 'He can send you a letter of thanks at the Santé.'

'Both of you are hopping mad because you can't pin a murder charge on me,' Mercier retorted. 'But, thank God, that's something you'll *never* be able to do!'

'Oh yes,' Picard said, 'when you get down to it you've got some pretty solid reasons for thanking God. Truflot! Two guards to escort M Mercier to his new night club, please. We'll fill in his papers tomorrow morning—*this* morning, rather.'

'I had no chance to bring anything with me,' Mercier said. 'No pyjamas, no town suit—'

'Oh, evening dress forms part of your professional equipment. As for pyjamas, an innocent person needs nothing but a clear conscience to protect him from nightmares.'

The door opened. As Mercier stood up, he stared at Picard with a hatred he no longer bothered to dissimulate, so confident was he of having the last word in the end. Even as he dropped his bombshell, he was anticipating, with relish, the effect it would produce.

'You won't keep me here for long, gentlemen. That valuable document in your possesssion, which you naturally intend to rely on as evidence, speaks of compensating those who acquired forgeries. Tomorrow my lawyer will ask Maître Bravais, the victim's solicitor, to ensure that this admirable last wish is carried out as soon as possible. In such conditions, why should they not drop all charges?'

By way of reply Picard said to the guards: 'Take care of this gentleman, please.'

'Right, Superintendent,' said the older of the two, raising his hand to his kepi, and produced a pair of handcuffs from one of his pockets, as requested.

4

A few minutes later Picard was saying to Blondel and Simon: 'Time you were in bed, *mes enfants*. It's nearly four o'clock. Both of you can have half tomorrow morning off. That's official.'

'Thanks, boss,' Blondel said. 'What a bastard, eh?'

'Maybe,' said Simon, who was still haunted by the thought of Augusta's death. 'But that doesn't make Berger any more likeable.'

Blondel said, reflectively: 'Berger—a boy from a respectable family, with all that talent—'

Picard gave a derisive snort.

'—don't you think the woman probably corrupted him?'

'If you're talking of influences,' Belot said, 'there was

another woman in his life who ought to have made a really remarkable character out of him. And you see—'

'Who might that be?'

'His grandmother.'

'For God's sake, Chief,' Blondel said. 'A grandmother!'

They all laughed and shook hands, to indicate, by this somewhat uncommon gesture, that the case was closed. For the same reason Picard and Belot still lingered on a little, despite their now overwhelming tiredness. Truflot was correcting his notes. Picard said: 'Hey, Truflot, there isn't a bottle of beer around anywhere, is there? This heat's killing me.'

'No, sir,' Truflot said. 'What about opening the window?'

'Why not?'

Belot was meditating aloud. 'Some people thought he was innocent *because* he had his mistress's hand in his suitcase. Others thought he was guilty *because* he had his mistress's hand in his suitcase. He thought Mercier was guilty *because* he'd put the hand in the case. What we get, in the last resort, is one crime committed without premeditation, and one premeditated crime that was never committed at all . . .'

Truflot was doing deep-breathing exercises at the open window. Without stopping he said: 'Don't you think there's a chance of Mercier getting off scot-free?'

Belot said: 'His gambling and nightclubs won't do him any good. Most jurors aren't men-about-town with money to burn.'

'If I were a judge,' Picard said, 'which God forbid—'

'You talk like God,' Belot said.

'Thanks a lot.'

'But I agree with you! To be the judge in such a case as this—'

Picard said: 'I'd come down heaviest on the perjury—and that would mean handing out identical sentences to both of them.'

This time Truflot turned round. 'If you'll allow me

to express my personal opinion,' he said. 'There's perjury and perjury. Young Berger wasn't always lying, he was having fantasies. Retrospective fantasies. He was rewriting his past.'

'Coming from you, Truflot,' said Picard, severely, 'such indulgence astonishes me. And all that fresh air coming in through your window is going to wake me up again if I'm not careful, which would be a pity. It's time we all went to bed.'

Belot said : 'Before we do, I'd like to show a little disrespect to one of my superior officers.'

'What have I done *now*?' Picard enquired, uneasily.

'It's not you,' Belot said, 'it's Superintendent Thévenet. On Tuesday night—'

Picard was suddenly all smiles. 'All right, all right!' he said. 'I'd forgotten, he asked me to ring him up when we'd cracked this case, any hour of the day or night, he said. Just one last little job, Truflot—put a call through to his home. You can take it when it comes through, Belot. I hope you'll let me listen in? Thévenet's always expressed the greatest admiration for you. With any luck you may damp down his enthusiasm a little.'

Truflot got busy. For a personal priority call any other line can be cleared. After a little he said : 'They're ringing M Thévenet now.'

Picard and Belot both picked up their receivers simultaneously. The ringing tone went on and on.

'Hullo,' Thévenet said at last. He had clearly been roused from deep sleep; his voice was slurred like a drunk's. 'Thévenet here. Who's that?'

'Frédéric Belot, Superintendent. I must apologize for disturbing you at such an hour. It was Superintendent Picard's idea. He's on the line too.'

'I'll get you for that,' Picard muttered.

Thévenet was suddenly very wide awake indeed. 'What news?' he asked.

Belot said, absolutely deadpan: 'I'm afraid you'll have to ask to be retired, Superintendent.'

'*What?*'

'You said you would, after that excellent dinner we had together on Tuesday evening.'

'I said that?'

' "If the American exists", you said.'

With growing amazement Thévenet said: 'And he *does* exist?'

'Without being American. He exists. We've got him?'

'That's incredible! Look, though, young Berger *is* the murderer, isn't he?'

'Yes,' Belot said, with a glint of amusement in his voice. 'Yes, he is.'

Thévenet said: 'That's fine. You had me worried for a moment.'

POSTSCRIPT

The Cat's-Eye will probably be my last detective novel, and possibly my last novel of any sort. I had never before written one entirely in the historic present*, and was determined to risk the venture at least once. It is a difficult tense, which will have no truck with grammatical complacency or self-important phrase-making—an austere tense, my friend and teacher Professor Lembourig would call it. However, a whodunit may win it more appreciation than most, since the reader always knows as much as the text at any given point.

Some devotees of sound radio—from an age-group which even in those days could be described as respectable, and possessed of long memories which they enjoy exercising on totally unimportant matters—may recall that about twenty years ago a detective mystery of mine entitled *The Cat's-Eye* was, as they say, put out over the air as a serial play. I would like to hope that they also remember its closing words, Belot's remark to Picard: 'Too simple a story to make a novel out of.' *And that was the truth.* When, despite this, I contemplated doing so, none of my three protagonists—neither Jean-Marc nor Mercier nor the engaging ghost of Huguette Sarrazin —would consent to figure in it as I had originally drawn them for radio. They had been over-simplified, each of them cast in too straightforward a mould. Now they forced me to make their better acquaintance, to *explore* them: and for that I am grateful.

The final order of my detective novels—as determined by the chronological relationship of the five volumes which make up the sequence, rather than by actual date of publication—

*See Translator's Note below.

is now as follows:

The Passenger on the U
Carriage 7 Seat 15
The Fountain at Marlieux
The Cat's-Eye
The Double Death of Frédéric Belot

Twenty years ago—a reaction, I suppose, against those countless horrors with which the world had lately been glutted—the severed hand in the case earned me a certain amount of disapproval, which had not befallen me when I produced a severed head ten years before. I would thus present myself today as the forerunner of a literary movement which no longer baulks at any atrocity. I prefer, however, to claim the status of follower or pupil—considering the nature of the example and the beauty of its circumstances—after having read these final lines of M. Christian Murciaux's article entitled 'Un disciple inconstant de sainte Thérèse d'Avila' (*Revue de Paris*, September 1967). The person in question is Jérôme Gracian.

'Nine months after the Saint's death, Jérôme Gracian went to Alba de Tormes. At the nuns' request he opened the coffin, and found Teresa's body "as whole and undecayed as if it had been buried the previous day". From this perfectly preserved corpse there emanated "a strong and marvellous odour". Gracian yielded to the sacrilegious urge for a relic, and cut off Teresa's left hand, which he deposited in a casket and thenceforth always carried it on his person. During the course of his adventurous life, Gracian at one point was captured by the Turks. They took possession of the relic, and guarded it with great care, as a priceless object. Jérôme Gracian had to pay twenty reals and two gold rings to ransom the Saint's little finger.'

Paris, 1970

Translator's Note

In the French language the historic present has a long and respectable history, merging imperceptibly into such

Latin exemplars as that superb historical rhetorician Tacitus. For some reason, however, it has obstinately refused to acclimatize itself on English soil. Any writer, whether English or American, who attempts it is bound to sound either portentous, artificial, or unintentionally comic, and more often than not all three at once: the one wholly successful exponent of the device, Damon Runyon, got away with it by aiming straight for laughs *ab initio,* thus tacitly conceding the point at issue. In the circumstances, and bearing in mind the very different potentialities of French and English, I have transposed M. Aveline's text, for English-speaking readers, from present to past historic.